IN THE COMPANY OF WILD THINGS

a novel

HOLLY BLAIKIE

This book is a work of fiction. Names, characters, places and incidents either are products of the author's imagination or are used fictitiously. Any resemblance to actual events or localities or persons, living or dead, is entirely coincidental.

Copyright ©2024 Holly Blaikie

All rights reserved, including the right to reproduce this book or portions thereof in any form whatsoever. The use of any part of this publication, reproduced, stored in a retrieval system, or transmitted in any form or by any means, electronic, mechanical, photocopying, recording, or otherwise, without the written permission of the publisher, is an infringement of the copyright law. For information regarding permission contact Cannonball Publishers 225 High Street Ladysmith, Box 1499, B9G 1B1

ISBN 978-1-7770386-2-5

To Jeffrey and the summer of '88

Table of Contents

PROLOGUE	1
FERRY GIRL	3
HOUSE GUEST	6
NEW DIGS	8
LOVE POTION NUMBER NINE	10
ADVANCE GUARD	13
WELCOME COMMITTEE	16
FLOWER TEA	20
REVEALING	24
PARISH PÈRE	27
CHURCH HALL BINGO	31
MINT	35
CHINK IN ONE'S STONE	40
CONNECTED	43
KI	49
BLOOMING	53
CHO KU REI	56
SKINNY SPLASHING	60
GUIDE TO SELFCARE	63
ARE YOU MY . . . ?	66
THE RESISTANCE	68
KINDLY INVITATION	70
MOSQUITO FARMER	73

BLACK AND WHITES	76
WOOLLY BITS	81
SLUGS	84
A THOUSAND CUTS	88
CANDLELIGHT DINNER	94
ENERGETIC EMBRASE	97
IN THE FLESH	101
THE DEVIL YOU DON'T	104
PAPER OR PLASTIC?	108
GO WILD	111
SECRET SHOPPER	115
PARTY PLANNING	118
NEO WHAT?	121
INVASION OF THE BODY SNATCHERS	123
HOOKEY	127
GOOD VIBRATIONS	136
FLIGHT RISK	139
PARTY FAVOURS	143
FORAGERS	148
BETWEEN FRIENDS	154
BEESERK	157
SKELETONS IN THE BASEMENT	159
MENDING	163
BITTER SWEET	168
PEN TO PAPER	174
PARADISE LOST	176
FORGIVENESS	180

SABOTEUR	*184*
POTLUCK	*186*
BEACH DAY	*190*
MIDNIGHT CALL	*194*
KEEP AWAY	*195*
A PRETTY COUNTRY	*198*
SLIP SLIDING AWAY	*201*
YIELDING	*202*
WORK FER YER SUPPER	*205*
INTERNAL BRUISING	*208*
GUILTY CONSCIENCE	*212*
HEARTFIRE AND DAMNATION	*216*
THE SHOW MUST GO ON	*221*
SECURITY	*225*
HOMECOMING	*228*
FAMILY ADVICE	*231*
LIE OF THE LAND	*236*
FOOTSIES	*238*
FAIRY LAND	*240*
WILDLING	*242*

Acknowledgements

Author's Note

PROLOGUE

Ireland, April 15, 1988

MARY NIPS OFF A CORNER of toast then quickly chases it down with a dose of Bewley's tea. "Look, Martin," she says, holding up the morning paper. "Someone wants t' come t' Ballycanew and explore his Irish roots."

The kitchen clock whisks the silence, like dust, around its inner rim — swish — swish — waiting, while Martin, absorbed in *Horticultural Monthly*, swirls a forkful of sausage through his yoke.

"Huh? Is there more sausage? These are better than the ones ye usually get."

There have been times in her ten-year marriage that the clock has kept her company, chop, chop, chopping in time to her supper preparations; times when it has struck off the seconds with the thud of an axe.

She slides the paper across the table and, still smiling, taps her finger on the tiny block of print. "He's offerin' his house on Hornby Island, the west coast o' Canada, if he can stay in someone's house here."

Martin stuffs sausage in his mouth, drags a highlighter through the centre of an article, then circles two seed varieties in each of the top corners of his magazine. A fluorescent frowny face reflects back at him as his free hand gropes for toast. "Can ye imagine the trouble some fool'll have t' go to securin' his valuables? Ye can't just let a stranger into yer house. Good luck to 'im."

Mary nudges Martin's plate and his hand comes down on a piece of bacon.

"Can ye look at me? *I* want to be that fool. The description of his place sounds grand. And when do we ever do anythin' interestin'? Ye still owe me a honeymoon."

Hornby Island, May 1, 1988

BRUCE UNFOLDS THE SMALL SHEET of flowered writing paper and presses it open on the kitchen counter. He rifles through the drawer for a pen and notepad and switches the telephone receiver to his other ear. While the line on the other end buzzes he re-reads the letter.

Dear Bruce,

Our names are Martin and Mary Hughes. We are in our early-thirties and early-forties. Martin is the principal at the local primary and I'm a full-time homemaker. We read your advertisement in the Ballycanew chronicle and would be thrilled to switch houses with you for the month of July. Our mid-century row-house was recently renovated in '86, is well maintained, and close to the village centre. You may be encouraged to know that we spoke with our local priest, keeper of the parish records, and he is happy to help you with your research.

We look forward to hearing from you.
+353 53 555 7488

Kind regards,
Martin and Mary Hughes

FERRY GIRL

THE DENMAN ISLAND FERRY judders with the impact of another wave. White foam purls down the length of the open deck and disappears beneath the car.

"If this was my own car, I'd be right unhappy t' be gettin' all this salt on my engine," says Martin, looking up at the black clouds scuttling overhead.

A summer squall, the ferry man said. Twenty minutes ago, waiting at the Buckley Bay ferry terminal, they were sunning themselves, swilling Koala Springs fizzy drinks, the car doors open, legs baking in the summer heat.

"It isn't yer car, though," says Mary. The ferry bucks up and down again and she braces herself against the dashboard. "Think of it as an adventure. We were havin' such a good time. Don't spoil the mood, so."

"Why would anyone live on an island? Imagine doin' this every day. And now ye tell me we have t' take another ferry after this? What a stupid idea it was, coming all this way. We could've holidayed fine enough in Ireland."

"Ye've been promisin' me a honeymoon for an age now. This seems pretty perfect. It's not costing ye anythin' for hotels, and the school doesn't need ye for another six week at least."

Martin honks the horn of their cheap rental, an early 70's Toyota. It sounds like the buzzer of an aging walk-up. He tries it again with more force and it emits the same feeble sound. "What are we doin' crossin' in these swells? We could sink. Would that make ye happy, Mary?"

Mary cranks the window down and lets the breeze chase through her hair. The water of the straight is a steely grey studded with sharp whitecaps. The matching vortex of cloud above whisks south at speed.

"What are ye imaginin' the tourists think when they take the boat out to Saltee Islands back home? That crossin's rougher than this, and plenty o' people still do it. Besides, you *do* live on an island," says Mary.

"Hardly. Compared t' this, Ireland is no more an island than Australia. Get yer head on straight, Mary."

She pulls her coat from the back seat, opens the car door, and climbs out. Giving him a sharp stare, she slams it shut.

He leans over and looks up at her retreating figure through the lowered passenger window. "Did *ye* know we were goin' t' be stuck on an island it takes two ferries t' get to? Two — Mary." His voice scuttles past her as another gust rattles the deck.

Mary joins other passengers looking over the edge at the waves and the view beyond. She says hello to a woman beside her dressed in an ankle-length pleated-cotton skirt, tube-top and jean jacket. The woman's feet are bare and dirty. Her braided hair unwinds in the wind. There is something familiar about her, and Mary realizes the woman resembles the singer Stevie Nicks, as she looked in the poster of Stevie and her partner that hung on her wall as a teen.

"Ye must be fair cold," says Mary.

"I am, a bit. Is that your car?" she asks.

"It's a rental," says Mary, turning to look at the faded blue Corolla, and the dour occupant drumming his hands on the steering wheel. "But the driver, he's mine. And it's too late t' return him."

The woman laughs, turning her face into the wind to stop the free strands of hair blowing in her eyes. "Are you going to Hornby, or stopping on Denman?" she asks.

"Hornby. Yerself?"

"Hornby. Could you give me a lift to the next ferry? I usually hitch a ride while the cars are in line at Buckley Bay. I got here late today."

Mary pauses. Looks at Martin. He is studiously ignoring her.

"Sure. I wouldn't want ye t' have t' swim. How were ye gettin' there if I said no?"

Another laugh, that to Mary sounds like sunlight sparkling on water. "I always find a way. Just like hitching from Courtenay to Buckley. Sometimes I get lucky, and my ride from Courtenay is also going all the way to Hornby. I suppose I have good karma."

"Courtenay? Is that near here?"

"About half an hour up the road. My dentist is there and when I go I do a bit of shopping. That's my pile over there. Most of it. I pick up things for neighbours, when I can."

The loudspeaker announces they're nearing the terminal and it's time to get into their vehicles.

"I'm Mary."

"Flower. Nice to meet you."

Mary opens the rear door of the Corolla and puts Flower's large rucksack and knit shopping bag on the seat. Flower squeezes in and unrolls the back window.

Martin's mouth drops open and his brows disappear beneath his bangs. He beats faster on the steering wheel, but says nothing.

"We're givin' her a ride t' the next ferry," Mary says, in response to his pointed stare. "This is Flower. Flower, this is my husband, Martin."

Flower brings her hands together in prayer position and nods to Martin.

Before he has a chance to reply, Flower thrusts her head out the open window and whistles to someone standing in front of the car.

"That's Nick. Can we give him a ride too?" She is already opening her door and beckoning him over. "He's a friend that works at the Co-op."

HOUSE GUEST

BRUCE CLOSES THE DOOR of Number 8 Village Gate behind him, sets down his case and flips the light switch. The front room is a shock of orange and hot-pink flower wallpaper. A pea-green carpet is visible in the narrow spaces not occupied by a set of overstuffed white leather furniture. To the left of a peat-burning fireplace, a brass drinks trolley stands pride of place. To the right, a large palm almost touches the ceiling. Above the mantle hangs a brightly painted jungle scene complete with a hissing tiger intent on menacing him.

After thirty hours of sleepless travel, his eyes involuntarily squeeze shut. He cracks them again to peer down the hall. The kitchen, from what he can see, is a calm pastel and he gravitates toward it.

The doorknob rattles behind him and, as he turns, a flimsy metal shopping dolly muscles its way through an expanding wedge of doorway. Enormous bespeckled eyes blink up at him. Before he can open his mouth, the dolly arcs upward and Bruce feels the sharp impact of a wheel on his forearm. Loose fruit hurls from the cloth opening in the contraption; the bright smell of oranges fills the room as they smack walls and spin across the floor.

"Thief! Thief!" the old man squeals.

Bruce, slow to react at first, presses against the wall, crushing the oversized wallpaper blooms. The little man is a lion tamer, his dolly a stool, forcing Bruce to submit.

"I'm sorry. I'm sorry. I'm in the wrong house!" says Bruce as he leaps to the side and dashes out the open door.

Heart hammering, he retreats to a safe distance and pulls the address slip from his pocket. He stares down at the number. He checks it against the number written above the door. They match. He checks it again.

Through the open doorway, Bruce can see the old man in the kitchen at the end of the hall. He's placing cans one at a time into the fridge. He pulls out a drawer beside the sink and forces a bag of carrots inside.

Bruce glances up and down the row of connected houses. As the Hughes advertised over the phone, the garden of Number 8 is immaculate, the tiny square of lawn shaved to within an inch of its life. Not so next door, where cracked pavement replaces grass, and dandelions sprout in the narrow dirt border. On the opposite side, Number 6's garden is even more unkempt. The entire garden is one big Butterfly Bush, with only a narrow tunnel to the door. The lights aren't on at either. This *is* where he's supposed to be.

A woman, mid-thirties, clad in a striped terrycloth robe, brushes past him.

"Ye must be Bruce, now. I'm terribly sorry 'bout this, lad," she calls over her shoulder as she strides into the house and down the hall. "I saw the whole thing, so I did, through the front window, but couldn't stop him in time."

She puts her arm around the old man and murmurs something. She collects his bruised oranges, retrieves the cans and reloads the shopping dolly. Bruce steps back as the man emerges from Number 8 and shuffles, without apology, down the lane in the direction indicated by the woman in curlers.

"That's old Desmond, aye? He used to live at Number 8. Now, so, he lives at Number 12. Long story." She touches her curlers self-consciously and pulls her robe tighter over her narrow frame. Ye'll be wantin' t' get settled."

"Ahh, thank you. I wasn't sure —," begins Bruce, looking in bafflement between the door and the retreating sprite in robe and slippers.

She calls over her shoulder as she ascends her own front steps, "By the bye, we don't lock our doors round here, so, but ye'll do. Goodnight, love."

NEW DIGS

MARY TUCKS THE LAST of her clothes into one of the dresser drawers Bruce cleared for them. He left a satchel of lavender in each, and finding it instantly enamored her to him. She wishes she'd thought to do the same. All she did was leave a note telling him where to find fresh towels and extra quilts. The least she could have done was leave a welcome basket of tea and biscuits.

Martin hauls his suitcase onto the bed, twisting the blue and green tie-dye bed cover as he turns the case in circles and clicks it open. The lid of the suitcase jingles as it hits the mattress. Canadian coins with beavers and caribou slither to the mesh corner of the maroon pocket.

"Why did ye bring coins?" says Mary. "Ye said ye didn't have room in yer case. I left things behind to make room for yer stuff so mine wouldn't be over the weight."

"Séamus next door had the coins from his trip t' the Montreal World Fair. I got a good exchange rate."

"What, are those?" Mary says in a strangled voice, her arms lifting in a gesture of helplessness.

"I wasn't leavin' these behind. What am I goin' to do with myself for a month if I can't garden? Besides, Bruce probably has some shrubs he'd appreciate me tendin'. I need my own shears for that."

"I thought we were goin' t' have a holiday together. This could be very romantic," says Mary.

Martin shifts his case to make more room on the bed.

"Ye aren't expectin' Bruce to do any gardenin' at ours, are ye?"

"No. Not much at all. I left some instructions, ye know, just enough so he's keepin' things tidy. The giraffe and deer'll need their beards trimmed. Easy stuff. Why did ye have t' agree t' a whole month, anyway?"

"I'm goin' to see what groceries we need."

The kitchen cabinets glow with late afternoon sun. Mary's eyes linger on their rosy warmth and she pauses to let the tension in her shoulders unwind.

A hoop, criss-crossed with crocheted threads, dangles feathers in the bay window above the sink. She leans over to examine it. There is a lovely view of the back garden. The corners of her mouth turn up and her eyes slide briefly toward the bedroom at the end of the hall.

A fresh ruckus spoils her revery.

"What's that, Martin?" she calls, still gazing through the window at the garden.

"I said, I need ye to move yer case so that I can have more room."

"Go ahead and move it for me," she says, leaning back to see what he's doing.

Martin is neatly lining up pruning shears of various sizes on top of the coverlet. He lifts his garden gloves from the suitcase and starts a new row with a bag of — "Fertilizer? Jesus!" she crosses herself. "How were we allowed t' get on the plane?? Don't they make bombs out o' fertilizer? What were ye thinkin'?" she says. "You know, they have fertilizer in Canada."

"They might not have my favourite," he barks back. "And it's also a pesticide."

Returning to the sink, she takes in the panorama of overgrown grass sprinkled with daisy, buttercup, dandelion, bleeding heart and aster. Clumps of bramble, spotted with red berries, and pink wild rose, sprout randomly between the seven or eight shrubs abandoned along the edge of the meadow. Saplings of fir, spruce and wild cherry thrown out by the tall dense forest beyond dot the landscape, threatening to reclaim its borders. Her eyes flit from flower to flower, like the bees and butterflies hard at work across the colourful stretch of garden. The disorder is a beautiful, tangled, cheerful mess.

She decides to leave for shopping without making a list — before Martin looks out the back window and has a fit.

LOVE POTION NUMBER NINE

MARY LOCKS THE DOOR of the Corolla and glances around the sunny Co-op parking lot. It was silly to drive here. It took two minutes.

Bordering the parking are numerous shacks sided with roughly hewn timber. One is a gallery, another a coffee shop. The rest look like permanent craft stalls tied together by criss-crossing overhead wires festooned with patio lanterns and prayer flags. Across the street is a filling station she mistook for a farm when they passed through town earlier.

She decides to explore before her arms are full of groceries.

Mary peruses table after table of pottery mugs, plates and vases. There are racks of tie-dye t-shirts and brightly coloured flowing skirts; bleached-driftwood shelves support hand-made hats juxtaposed with jams and fresh honey. Deeper inside the maze of stalls, billowing sheets and errant bedcovers ruffle overhead in the breeze like Monday washing. Clay windchimes chatter, and shell bird houses catch and release pearlescent light. One of the tie-dye bedcovers resembles the one on Bruce's bed.

She stops in front of a refreshment stand and looks at the complex menu of juices. A hand grabs her elbow and she startles.

"Hi, you!" Flower from the ferry is holding her arm and beaming at her. "Have the banana-mango-ginger press. That's my favourite."

"Ye gave me a jump," says Mary, delighted to see the young nomad again. She orders, and carries her drink to a table made from the disc of a huge tree trunk.

"Where are you staying?" asks Flower.

"We've changed houses with Bruce Connors for a month. Do ye know him?"

"Of course I know Bruce! He's one of my closest friends. We were all so glad he found a way to visit Ireland. He's been feeling so alone in the world since his father passed, not to mention the shock of finding out what happened to his dad as a little boy. Those people don't deserve to live."

"Oh, I don't know anythin' about that," says Mary.

"Well, it's not my story to tell. I shouldn't have mentioned it, really. We do hope though, that he finds some family while he's away. For most of his life it's only been him and his dad."

"I hope he does. There are a few Connors in the village, though whether they'd be related I don't know."

Flower's gaze softens, a beguiling smile of straight white teeth lighting up her face. "It's fate that we met on your first day isn't it? Here you are, the couple that's helping him."

"The switch was good for us too. My husband has summers off with his job, but if ye can believe it, this is the first time we've been away together since we were married."

"How long have you been married?"

"Almost ten year."

"And what are you planning to do while here? A month's a nice long time."

"Some explorin', I hope. Martin likes to visit garden shops. I'm not sure for myself. Just . . . anythin' different. I'd love to do somethin' I've never done before."

"Listen, I can't stay," says Flower. "I have a shop through there where I sell my socks, hats and things. A friend looked after it while I was in Courtenay this morning, but another ferry docked fifteen minutes ago and I want to be there when the last wave of tourists arrive. Do you need help finding anything?'

"No. I'm grand. I'm just here to collect the messages."

"The what?"

"Ah, sorry, the groceries," recalls Mary.

"Come by my place tomorrow and I'll show you around. Give me your arm." Flower pulls a pen from her pocket, licks the nub and writes her address on the inside of Mary's arm. It's slightly painful. Flower leans over, kisses Mary's forehead and floats away through the myriad brightly coloured cottons. Mary puts her lips round the straw and takes a sip, conscious of a surge in her heartbeat and heat mottling her throat and breast.

Something is different already.

ADVANCE GUARD

T HERE IS A KNOCK AT THE DOOR and Bruce cautiously opens it.
"Hi. Catriona Doyle, Cat. I'm not sure I gave ye my name last night. Here, love." She pushes a pineapple upside-down cake into his hands and looks him up and down. "Jay – sus," she breathes, crossing herself swiftly. "Ye're foreign, alright. I didn't get a clear view of ye in the dark. Yer long hair, that smile. I wouldn't blow ye away, boys-a-boys."

"Thank you," Bruce says, laughing.

She reaches up and touches his necklace. "Those wooden beads are a lovely colour against yer skin, lad. And I love the bright weave of yer vest. I'd say, from the look o' yer clothes, aye . . . South America? Such interestin' pants," she says, giving him another nod, head to toe.

"Canada. Hornby Island. A friend made my pants. The vest is from Peru though. You were right there. It was made by workers in a collective."

"Jesus." Cat crosses herself again. "Canada. O' course. At the sight of ye I forgot everythin' Mary said. This is a fair leap to come all the way here. Not that we aren't glad t' have ye." Cat pushes past Bruce and motions for him to follow her down the hall to the kitchen. She takes back the cake, reaches in the cupboard for plates and cuts two slices.

Bruce takes the plates she hands him and places them on the glass kitchen table by the back sliding door.

Cutlery tinkles as she rummages in a drawer for forks. "Placemats," she says, with a nod of her head. "Left hand cupboard in the pine hutch," indicating the corner of the dining-nook with a nudge of her head.

Cat is around five-foot-two and reminds him of a professional figure skater. Her medium-blond bob swings forward in a smooth wedge as she reaches further into the recesses of the drawer next to the sink. "Do ye know ye have carrots in yer cutlery drawer, so?"

"Those must belong to the gentleman from last night."

"Ahh. Makes sense. I'll return 'em to him."

"You seem to know your way around the place. You must know Mary and Martin well."

"That I do. Mary's my best friend. As far as knowin' my way around, it's not hard. Everythin' is always in its place round here. Not so at mine. My Michael, the bank manager, is far too busy a man t' be tellin' me what to put where and how. And I wouldn't listen to 'im if he tried."

Bruce pulls out a white metal chair upholstered in turquoise and peach swirls and offers it to Cat. He takes a seat across from her and accepts a fork.

"So — what are ye doin' here with us?"

"My father was born in Ballycanew. I came to find out more about my grandparents and, truthfully, what it is to be Irish," says Bruce, popping a piece of cake in his mouth.

"Ye'll want t' talk to Father Fingal about yer grandparents," offers Cat. "See what it is to be Irish, though. Ye'll be watchin' us like we're specimens in the zoo, will ya, so? I hate to disappoint, but I think ye'll find we're pretty much like everyone else, lad."

"Sure. Sorry. That didn't come off the way I meant it," says Bruce, swallowing. "This cake is delicious, by the way. Thanks for bringing it."

"Ye're welcome." Cat whistles, "Lad, ye're out o' place. Yer like a shaman and sexy Fabio rolled into one. I think ye're goin' to be as much of a spectacle to us as we are to ye."

"Well, as you say, we're mostly the same underneath," says Bruce. "That being said, you've got a very happy aura."

"That's gas. What do ye mean, my aura?"

"Our body, it's like the wick of a candle and our aura glows all around us. Not everyone's is visible. But yours — it's not to be missed. It shimmers with pink and violet."

"Oh, get on with ye," says Cat. "Ye're serious?"

WELCOME COMMITTEE

THE DOORBELL RINGS as Bruce is slipping on his sandals to go out. "Twice in two days?" he says to himself.
Cat stands on the stoop flanked by three smiling women. They're arm in arm like teenagers, but Bruce guesses they're in their thirties and early forties. A mixture of perfume wafts in with the breeze. Each is holding a casserole dish.

"These are yer other neighbours. We've brought yer tea," says Cat. "This is Joan. With her big perm we tease her she's our *cool* Sandy from the final scene of Greace, the American film. She's yer neighbour on the left, married t' Séamus. This is Margaret, Mags. She's two doors down on yer right. And Claire, our princess Di. We don't hold it against her that she looks like an *English* princess. She's across and three doors down on yer left if ye look out yer front door. And I'm across. Ye know that. Should we come in?"

"Of course," says Bruce, kicking off his sandals and moving out of their way.

He takes the dish from Mags, who's struggling to remove her stiletto heels one handed. She's almost six-feet tall with them on. He's struck by how she resembles his boyhood fantasy pin-up girl, the likes of which he's never actually met in person. Auburn hair surrounds her face in large waves that hold their shape as she leans forward. He peaks under the clear film wrap on the dish and inhales. Lemon bars. She straightens up and their eyes lock awkwardly.

"I, uhm," Mags nods toward the kitchen.

"Right. After you. I'm in the way," he says. "These bars look delicious."

Cat turns his oven on and slides a pair of foil-covered dishes inside. "We thought it would be good for ye to get t' know the village. These are my close friends, and fellow thespians."

The four of them bow dramatically.

"They also happen t' be village know-it-alls. Mags, ye might have guessed with that doo, is a hairdresser, and ladies love t' gossip in her chair. Claire's our post-mistress-slash-newspaper editor — self-explanatory. And Joan and her husband, Séamus, own the Pub. Together they see and hear everythin', aye."

"I was the one who put yer advert in the paper," says Claire. "I've been excited t' see what ye're like." She looks him over with open curiosity, and he want to laugh.

"I hope I live up to your expectations," he says.

"Not at all. What? No — I mean, yes we do. Ye do. I love yer hair," Claire says.

"Jaysus Claire. And you write for the paper," says Cat and then turns to Bruce. "Will ye still be here end o' July? The twenty-nineth?"

"I leave August first, so yeah."

"We'll get ye tickets to the play," says Mags. "It's goin' to be massively class. Ye can't miss it."

"Do ye know *A Thousand and One Arabian Nights*?" asks Claire.

"I do."

"We're only doin' one o' the tales, *Ali Baba and the Forty Thieves*, so, it should be called *Arabian Night*," says Mags. "I play the Sultan's first wife. The one he kills, aye, for havin' an affair? And then I play Ali Baba's wife. Cat is the slave girl, Morgiana, since she's our best dancer. Claire's Scheherazade's younger sister, and two of the main thieves. And Joanie's the wife of Ali Baba's brother, Cassim."

"Who's playing Scheherazade?" asks Bruce.

"That'll be Bridget, sure. She already has the play memorized. She starred as Scheherazade forty year ago when it first ran in Ballycanew. None o' us could learn that many lines if we were given a year, so she was a shoe-in," says Cat.

"Forty years? How old is she?" says Bruce.

"Eighty-two," says Joan.

"With a wig, tight ponytail and make-up as thick as plaster she won't look a day over sixty," laughs Mags. "Although I say it myself, I am a wiz at make-overs. I sell Beauty Girl products at home parties on the side. I've been asked t' do all the hair and makeup for the show, so I have."

"We're short o' lads if ye want a role. Just say the word," says Cat.

"Do you sing or play, Bruce?" asks Joan. "Down the pub we're always lookin' to hear new music from away. My Séamus sings a lovely ballad and there's usually someone with a fiddle. If the spirit grabs ye, come sing for us one evenin'. That is, if there's no Hurley match on, mind, like there is today."

"I do sing. And play a little flute. I brought one with me, as a matter of fact," says Bruce.

"Ye may so, then, lad. I'll let my Séamus know t' expect a tune or two," says Joan.

"Boy," says Bruce, "whatever's in the oven smells great. Do you do this for all new people to the neighbourhood?"

"We don't get new people in the neighbourhood," says Mags. "This is a real treat for us havin' someone like you here."

"It's a treat for me being here."

"Ye're lookin' for family are ye?" asks Mags.

"I am. The only thing I have to go on is my grandfather's name, James Connors. I'll find out if he had any siblings and go from there I guess."

"If he was Catholic ye may find out he had a whole lot o' siblings. Are ye prepared for that?" says Cat. "Come t' think of it, there's Davey Connors that owns the garage center o' the village. He's got a few brothers that I know of."

"The more the merrier," says Bruce. "Do you four have children then?"

"I have twins, a boy and a girl, off at Uni," says Joan.

"You don't look old enough," chides Bruce. She swats him and laughs. "It's true," he says honestly.

"Michael and I are just startin' to try," says Cat. "It'll be down to Mary alone to supply these two with the condoms from now on," she adds, indicating Mags and Claire. "The doctor's not likely to keep givin' me a script if I get pregnant."

"Claire and I aren't married, ye see," says Mags. "Not that I haven't been lookin', but the choice bein' slim in the village . . . ye know. And it's only down t' Cat and Mary that we haven't had an accident. Knock on wood, hey Claire? I'd love t' have a family though. One day."

"I'm sure we can rely on Mary as long as we need to," says Claire. "Martin's never goin' to let her off the pill. As long as he doesn't insist on fillin' the prescription himself she can keep askin' for a couple o' condoms when she collects it."

"I wouldn't put it past 'im," says Mags.

"So long story long," says Cat, "three of us don't have children yet."

Bruce laughs.

Mags, Joan and Claire fall silent. Mags clicks her fingernails up and down the edge of the linoleum counter then nudges Cat.

Claire clears her throat. "Will ye ask him, then?" she says, indicating Bruce with a nod of her head.

"I told them what ye said about my aura," says Cat. "They're wonderin' whether ye can see their's."

Bruce smiles and looks each of them up and down. "Well, I might be able to do one better. I can help you see them yourselves."

"Jasus! The oven," exclaims Claire, crossing herself, grabbing a dishtowel and throwing open the oven door.

FLOWER TEA

IT ONLY TAKES MARY half-an-hour to walk to Flower's place on Downes Point Rd. Situated in a grove of trees, the house is covered in roughly hewn boards like the stalls in the Co-op parking lot. Painted wooden flowers and butterflies are nailed to the outer walls and a kiwi vine encircles the front porch.

Before Mary reaches the walkway, the door flies open and Flower runs to meet her, hazel eyes creased in triangles. Her skin is the warm colour of Kalua liqueur. Her light brown hair, streaked with blond, drapes across her shoulders; loosely braided bangs, finished with rows of coloured beads, dance as she talks.

"You found me!"

"Easily, aye," says Mary. "And it was such a beautiful walk."

Flower takes her hand and leads her into the foyer. An unexpected tang hits the back of Mary's throat. She spies the source — dozens of woolen skeins hang from the rafters, newly dyed.

Flower follows Mary's eyes. "Do you knit?" she asks.

"I do. We're overrun wi' sheep back home," says Mary, tugging off her loafers and placing them by the door.

She follows Flower down the hall to an airy hexagonal room with windows on four sides. Here, the pungent air of the foyer is replaced by the earthy scent of drying herbs and flowers that dangle from the ceiling. The room serves as living room, kitchen, dining room and bedroom, with a narrow bed tight against one of the floor-to-ceiling windows. The décor is similar to that in Bruce's cottage — pine wood panelled walls, rag rugs and riotously colourful patterned fabrics.

"That cot with the old quilts is for Joni and Mitchel," says Flower, following her gaze. "My room is off the hall."

"Oh," says Mary. "Joni and Mitchel are yer? ..."

As if conjured, two large white dogs, both missing numerous patches of fur, lope in through the open patio door and jump onto the bed. They circle one another and then flop down on the fraying patchwork quilts.

"Dogs. Yes. Tea? I make my own. I've got marigold, dandelion, mint, camomile, rose hip and fermented blackberry leaf. Take your pick, or I can mix them," says Flower.

"Which do ye recommend?"

Flower steps out from around the counter and places her hands on Mary's waist. She slides her left palm to Mary's belly button. Mary tenses with surprise. Flowers gaze is so intimate that Mary has to resist closing her eyes.

"Do you have any soreness in your throat? Any menstrual cramping?"

"No," says Mary, feeling heat rise across her chest and up her neck.

"You've had a long journey. I'd recommend Chamomile to reduce bloating and gassiness, with a dash of rose hips to boost your immunity with vitamins C and A, and a touch of marigold to relax you." Flower releases her and turns to the kitchen. She pulls jars of dried flowers and fruits from the shelf and fills the kettle.

"Sounds grand t' me. Ye seem to know what ye're doin'," says Mary uncertainly. "I just drink plain old Bewley's at home."

A spinning wheel and stool sit next to the dogs' bed. "Do ye spin yer own yarn?" Mary asks.

"And dye it too, with natural dyes. I have a lot of knitting to do for the Filberg Festival. I pay for a booth there. It's coming up in a month and I'm really running behind. When I asked you before if you knit, It wasn't just curiosity. I'd be willing to pay you to help, if you're interested — if you're any good. Oops. I should have asked you that part first."

"Yes. And sure now, I'm a fair hand at it."

"Can you come by again tomorrow? I'll put you to work if you can prove you know what you're doing."

"I should ask Martin, my husband. This is our honeymoon. I don't want t' make too many plans, in case he's got somethin' romantic planned."

"Of course. I remember you saying so," says Flower. "I'll write down my number. There's no pressure. If you can't get any time away, I understand. This isn't your emergency, after all. I just really need the help and got excited."

"I'd like t' help. I'll see what Martin says, yeah?"

They drink their tea swinging in a pair of hammock chairs suspended along the back porch. Mary takes in the spectacular view afforded by their position on the high bluff. Beyond the tall firs, the ocean is sapphire blue and the mountains of Vancouver Island snow-capped, despite the summer heat."

"Ye get snow in the summer?" asks Mary.

"That's the Comox Glacier. Beautiful, isn't it? Have you been to the beach yet?"

"Not yet. Is it far?"

"After we finish our tea, we can walk down along the cliff to Tribune Bay."

A white cat materializes from nowhere and jumps in Flower's lap, lifting its chin in search of scratches. It's as mangey as the dogs. Patches of fur are missing up and down its sides.

"This is Garfunkel."

"He's very affectionate, aye?" says Mary taking another sip of her tea. It's slightly astringent. She takes milk in it at home but isn't sure if it's proper to combine milk and marigold. She doesn't risk offending Flower and asks instead, "You mentioned a festival — Filbert?"

Flower laughs. "Filberg. Ten years ago, Filberg Park was a private garden surrounding a home built in the '30's from hand-hewn logs. It's been open to the public since Mr. Filberg died. He was a multi-millionaire with no surviving family. Kind of sad that he outlived his children. If your husband likes gardens, he would absolutely love it there. Loads of different species. And it's on the water with a great view of the glacier. Their tea house hosts live classical music on the lawn every second Sunday. Take the early ferry and you can make a day of it. It could be the romantic outing your husband was wanting to arrange, don't you think?"

"Martin loves gardens. Ferries — that's another thing."

"The festival happens the first weekend of August every year, with people like me bringing our hand-made creations to sell to the public. You can find anything from felted hats like mine, to metal work, to dried wild mushrooms. Anything you can imagine someone making by hand. The co-op market, but much bigger."

The cat jumps off Flower's lap and winds itself around Mary's bare legs. Its long hair is surprisingly soft, but Mary tucks her legs up into the hammock just in case. The last thing she needs is to start her holiday with ring worm or scabies.

"Have ye lived here a long time?"

"Almost fourteen years. It was my uncle's holiday place. He was a biology professor."

"Where were ye before?" Asks Mary, setting her empty cup down on the porch.

"A long way away. My uncle saved me, letting me come here. I slowly bought the place from him with what I could earn each year. Eventually when he passed, he left it to me free and clear."

"It's a beautiful place," says Mary. "Magical. It must be nice to have a home that's all yer own."

"It is. I have a good life."

Mary looks thoughtfully through the windows to the disarray of the living room.

"If you're finished your tea, let's go. I'll show you the beach," says Flower.

REVEALING

MARY AND FLOWER FOLLOW a narrow path strewn with fir and hemlock needles across a wooded spit of land and then veer left along the edge of a cliff. The warm dry air is redolent with the scent of sap mingling with the salty breeze. Joni and Mitchel bound ahead, cut back, then tear away excitedly again through the undergrowth of salal, huckleberry and fern.

At the bottom of a hill, they pass through several private gardens and a farm, before a sharp right steers them onto an overgrown path. Sunlight leaking through the wild-rose and arbutus saplings sprinkles the ground with light. Mary's eyes have only just adjusted when suddenly they emerge into daylight and they're confronted by a barrier of driftwood logs, two feet or more in diameter, that the currents roughly shouldered onto the shore.

Hopping from the last log, Mary is surprised to land on a sandstone shelf rather than a sandy beach. The tan surface is dotted with hoodoos and pockmarked by broad tide pools brimming with purple starfish and bright green and pink anemones. Bending, she pokes one of the anemones with her finger. Its sticky tentacles shrink into a tight knot.

"Did you ever notice anemones look like cervixes?" says Flower.

"Oh, uh, aye," says Mary. "I just wouldn't 'a thought t' say it out loud."

"Why not?"

"It's indecent — isn't it?"

"Are you shocked by me?" laughs Flower.

"No. Not shocked. I like that ye say what ye want. I wish I could.

I just don't feel comfortable talkin' t' others about anatomy, ye know, sex. I've got a close friend that's pretty spunky, aye, but I don't think even she would make mention o' cervixes."

"It's not a big deal to me. We all have them, and I don't get worked up talking about noses and toes, why get worked up about cervixes and vaginas?"

"I guess." Mary studies Flower's face, untrammeled by any hint of self-consciousness.

The sandstone gives way to a fine white powder as they continue along the shore. The water is a brilliant turquoise. In the curve of the bay, people frolic in the water. Onshore, sunbathers, spread-eagle on the sand, willingly sacrifice themselves to the afternoon heat.

It's only as she and Flower get closer that Mary notices no one is wearing any clothes. She tactfully averts her gaze as they step over logs within a stone's throw of the bathers and head toward a long point of land.

"This is Little Tribune Bay," says Flower. "When we get to the end of Spray Point, you'll see the bigger Tribune Bay on the other side. It gets busy with tourists this time of year. Little Tribune's much better."

Flower halts, picks up a thin piece of driftwood, and begins to dig a long, tough looking grass out of the sand. "Wild garlic. I'll give you some to take home." She shakes the bulbs clean and pops them into the macramé bag she has slung across her body. Getting to her feet, she waves excitedly to a figure on the beach.

Mary chances an embarrassed look. The man is trim and tanned, and wearing nothing but a grin. He waves enthusiastically and starts toward them. Mary turns her full attention to the nearby forest, conducting a thorough accounting of its trees.

"We'll catch up later," Flower calls to him. "That's Nick. From the Co-op. You gave him a ride, remember?"

"Oh, sure, yes." Mary waves without looking back. "He also rang my groceries through the first time I did a shop."

They finally reach the point, unaccosted by any further hikers, nudes or otherwise, and find a well-used path meandering through an underbrush of knee-high, berry covered plants.

"If I give you one of these Tupperware, will you help me pick?" asks Flower, batting her eyelashes. "I want to make Oregon grape jelly. I promise you a jar, if you do."

"I don't mind doin' it for free. There's nothin' else I need t' do today. Martin'll be in the garden 'til supper."

Flower bends to pull clusters of small, purple berries from the prickly shrubs. Light penetrates the orange cotton of her skirt, casting her legs in shapely silhouettes. Her pale blue crop-top hangs open from neck to waist, revealing breasts of honey gold. Mary turns away to preserve Flower's modesty, wishing at the same time that she had a figure like hers.

Mary takes a deep breath, expanding her chest against the constricting elastic of her bra. The lack of give in her clothes suddenly makes itself known and she resents their confinement like a long-shackled prisoner.

When their containers are full, Mary follows Flower the rest of the way across Spray Point. As they pop through the treeline, she is struck by the long crescent of white sand edging the aquamarine water. It could be a tropical beach scene from the travel agency posters. But Flower is right, it *is* a busy place. The scene is frenetic with swimmers, sailboats, jet-skis and yachts. The sand is an explosion of colourful beach umbrellas, inflatable toys and coolers. The distant notes of Madonna's 'Holiday' reach her ears, tinny on the salty breeze.

PARISH PÈRE

BRUCE STEPS FROM THE church vestibule into the nave. Notes of wax, furniture polish and fading roses mingle in the gloom, their scents amplified by the stillness of the air. Rainbow coloured saints, perched in the windows high above, filter the incoming light, turning dust motes, freshly disturbed, into fireflies that dance and lift as he treads softly on the carpeted aisle. A gray-haired woman kneeling in the front pew turns her eyes to him. He lifts a hand in greeting. She hunches her shoulders and resumes her conversation with God. To his left, a young couple, hand in hand, light a votive candle.

"Hello?" he calls hesitantly, into the silence. The couple turns to look at him and he mouths an apology.

When no one appears, Bruce considers his own foolishness. He imagined he'd find the priest standing at the ready, waiting to be called upon.

He moves to leave but turns again when he hears clanking and the squeal of tortured hinges. A figure robed in a stiff, black cassock emerges from a doorway set into the rear corner of the sanctuary. The priest locks the door behind him and pockets an ancient-looking key. He turns, spies Bruce and, leading with a broad smile, glides towards him.

"Welcome, my son. I'm Father Fingal."

He's in his late-sixties, hair neatly combed, with a complexion that suggests his office, like the weather outside, is rarely warm.

Bruce starts to bend on one knee, uncertain what to do, but fearful of offending. "I'm Bruce. Mary Hughes said you would be expecting me."

"Up ye get, lad, I'm not marryin' ye," Father Fingal chuckles. "Glad t' meet ye, sure. We weren't sure when ye'd arrive. Ye're lookin' for records on yer father, or grandfather. Isn't that right?"

"Yes. Both. I'm hoping to look through your birth, death and marriage records?" says Bruce, looking around for the doorway to an archive. The church is exactly as he hoped it would be; a peaceful, meditative space in which to meet the ghosts of his father's past.

"Those records have been kept at the public records office in Dublin since the late 1800's," says Father Fingal, watching Bruce closely. "Fortunately," his expression quickly lightens, "we still have our own parish records. Most of our parish priests are avid record keepers, ye see."

"My Dad was born in 1930. I don't know much as far as dates beyond that."

"Our records go back a sight further than 1930, so no need t' worry."

"When Dad died last year at fifty-seven, I regretted not having pressed him for more details about his family. He was pretty tight-lipped, other than saying his father was a great man in the village. Perhaps he didn't know much more himself. He was transported to Vancouver Island by boat at the age of five."

"Ye've come a long way for answers. Let's hope we find what ye're lookin' for. Follow me." Father Fingal turns with a sweep of his cassock. "Everythin's over at the church hall, so it is. We'll walk together."

Father Fingal swings the heavy door wide and ushers Bruce through. Visible from the side of the church, beyond the stone wall at the back of the church, a worn path cuts through the field toward Bruce's new home on the other side of the village.

"Do you think there's anyone in the village that would still remember my grandparents?" asks Bruce. "I suppose it might be too much to hope, but maybe I have some relatives here? I'm told there is someone that owns the garage with the same last name."

"I haven't been in the village more than twelve year, myself. I'm sorry son, but what was yer last name? I'm afraid Mary just gave me yer first."

"Connors."

"Connors, sure now. I can't say, lad. The Connors that own the garage aren't Catholics I'm afraid, so I can't tell ye too much about them."

"Is there any way of finding out where my grandfather lived?" says Bruce.

"That would be the census. We can see what we find there," says Father Fingal. "The last census would be 1911. Depends on when yer grandparents were born. Were they born in the village?"

"I don't know for sure. I just know that Dad came from here."

"Ye've not much to go on, but don't let that dampen yer hopes. We'll see what we find o'er at the hall."

As they walk, Bruce feels a knot growing in his stomach. What if there's nothing here? What if there's no family to find. What if he has just crossed an ocean for no reason? Is he truly alone in the world? To tamp the anxiety, he asks an idle question.

"Are the church services busy? It looks like there must be a lot of traffic through the field."

"Not so. Not like the old days," says Father Fingal. "Not many o' the young folks are weekly regulars. Monthly, more like. Even biannual, some. We see more when there's been a big hooley and they've lots t' confess. No, that path's well-trod not 'cause o' the church, but more 'cause o' the popularity o' the hall. Always somethin' going on. They're rehearsing for a play, now so."

"A neighbour where I'm staying mentioned it," says Bruce.

"Ahh, and who will that be?"

"Catriona? She introduced herself as Cat," says Bruce.

"Oh. Good girl, Cat. She and her husband, Michael, regular comers, along with Mary and Martin. Never a foot out a' line."

Father Fingal raises his hand in greeting to a hunched old man inching along the far sidewalk with his walker. The man doesn't acknowledge the gesture. Father Fingal grabs Bruce's elbow to stop him crossing the hall parking lot, "We'll tarry a while. Have a quick word with 'im."

The man could be walking backward; his gait is glacial. Bruce suddenly recognizes old Desmond by his scowl and oversized glasses.

With relief Father Fingal finally relents. "Ahh, sorry now, I've a meetin' with 'im. He's one o' my parishioners. I think it's safe t' say I can show ye the records and still make it back t' the church before he does."

Father Fingal opens the door to the hall, then glances over his shoulder once again to judge Desmond's progress. "Bless 'im for still gettin' around on his own two pins."

It took Bruce ten minutes to walk from Village Gate to the church. At Desmond's pace he must have been at it for hours.

CHURCH HALL BINGO

THE HALL SMELLS OF WARM bodies, wet socks and burnt coffee. At the far end, on an elevated stage, rehearsal is in full swing for *Arabian Nights*. Bruce recognizes Cat and her girlfriends waiting stage left while a stringy young man belts out his lines. Alibaba at the cave of wonder.

A barrel-shaped woman in her sixties, tightly wound in a tweed skirt and jacket launches herself on an intercept course with him and Father Fingal, as they cross the back of the hall. The Father's radar picks her up, and he quickens his pace. She accelerates to match.

"Father Fingal? Oh, Father Fingal? It's me."

Suddenly she is upon them. Iron-grey curls foam at her prow. Chalky pink lipstick cracks and flakes from her rusty smile.

Father Fingal, reluctant to yield, tries to sidestep her, but only manages to stumble over his hem. Bruce deftly grabs his elbow.

"Yes, Geraldine? Ye've been well since this mornin'?"

She pulls tight alongside Father Fingal, parking herself beneath his chin. He nearly disjoints his neck trying to address her.

"Geraldine, let me introduce to ye Bruce Connors, all the way from Canada t' find his family." Father Fingal takes a step back. "Bruce, this is Geraldine Cousins. She does my ironin', keeps the church clean, and spoils me with her bakin'."

Her smile slackens as she drops her gaze to Bruce's sandaled feet. Her nostrils quiver then clamp tight. She stares so long he has to look down to check if he unknowingly stepped in dog poo.

"Nice to meet you," says Bruce. He brings his hands together in prayer position and bows respectfully to her.

Nostrils relaxed, she turns back to Father Fingal.

"Father, ye must help us. Ye must." She fingers the priest's vestment coyly.

He inches backward again. A more robust colour blooms in his cheeks.

"Father, Padraig is threatenin' to drop out o' the play after a week o' rehearsals if I don't give 'im more lines. I'd consider, if he showed any ability t' remember the ones he already has. And, I've told him just so. Would ye consider, Father, bein' in the play? Fine voice as ye have. Everyone's already playin' several parts. We won't have enough men if he leaves."

"Nooo — it wouldn't be proper for me to take part," says Father Fingal. He takes her hands in his and politely steps her back to an appropriate distance. "I'm still not convinced this is a play to be stagin' in a Catholic Church Hall."

"Well, I tried to say so myself, didn't I, Father," says Geraldine, shaking her head.

Father Fingal tugs Bruce's sleeve gently and sidesteps with him until they have fully revolved around Geraldine.

"We best get on. Young Bruce has come a long way. And I've someone waitin' at the church."

Geraldine pouts. On stage behind her, the rehearsal has stalled.

Father Fingal opens the door to a narrow room running along the far side of the hall. Inside, a glass book cabinet stands floor to ceiling on the nearest wall. A plywood tabletop sits on folding metal legs in the centre, and beyond it juts a Formica counter used for brewing coffee and washing up. The far end of the room is a jumble of janitorial supplies, stacks of spare chairs and cardboard boxes. There is little room to maneuver. The only window in the room is dripping with condensation. Bruce peels off his vest and slings it around the back of the plastic chair nearest the door.

With a jingle of keys, Father Fingal unlocks the bookcase and slides the glass open. "I'll leave ye to it then."

"Thank you, Father."

Bruce takes down a soft leather book marked *Births 1925-1940* and begins thumbing through it.

From the other room he hears young Ali Baba stop his

performance mid-line.

"What is it now, Eoghan?" says Geraldine, exasperated.

"I think Ali Baba should kiss his wife hello when he returns. That would be more convincin' to —."

Geraldine cuts him off, "C'm'ere to me, Eoghan, lad. I'm sore tired of ye tryin' to turn that stage into a den of iniquity. Do ye think Mags is goin' to kiss an eegit like you?"

"It would improve the show," argues Eoghan.

Another male voice cuts in, "Either ye leave off a' Mags, or I'll fecken hammer ye."

"Feck off, Callum," says Eoghan.

Bruce hears a scuffle and pokes his head out.

The two roll on the floor — Callum in a headlock — then as quickly as it began, they break off.

Eoghan musses Callum's hair and says, "I won't hurt y' o'er a woman."

"As if ye could," laughs Callum.

They punch each other's shoulders good naturedly and saunter back to their marks.

"You've not the full shilling between ye," sputters Geraldine. "Mags, lass, ye can continue the scene for us. Places everybody!"

Before long Bruce finds his dad's birth entry, Ambrose Finbar Connors, Feb 26, 1930. Born at home. Father's name, James Ambrose Connors. Profession, Pauper. Mother's name, Violet Virginia Pillow. His father's age is forty-five. His mother's, twenty. Bingo! He can't believe he found it so easily. He scribbles in his journal and circles Violet Virginia Pillow. His father has never mentioned her by name. It's an unusual name, at that. His grandmother. He pictures a soft, violet throw pillow. He closes the registry, shelves it and then scans the leather spines for Death Records, 1935. He struggles through the first ten pages before realizing the job is bigger than he thought. Without a better idea of the timing of his grandparents' deaths, he could be searching for days. Whenever it was, it must have been before the boat left for Canada.

He leans back on his chair again so that he can see the stage through the open doorway. He waves at Cat. She and the other ladies are practicing a belly dance. A piper plays a Persian melody.

He traces the names on a dozen more pages of death registrations in 1935 searching for Connors. The faded brown ink is hard to read.

An hour into the search Father Fingal pops his head around the jamb. "Findin' what ye need?"

"The birth record for my father lists my grandfather's profession as pauper. What does that mean exactly?"

"It means that the church was providin' them with some charity. Occasional unemployment and hard times have been a part o' life here for centuries, lad."

Bruce rubs his eyes roughly. "I'm not sure how to go about searching for my grandparents' deaths. I'd like to find clues as to when and why my orphaned father was sent all the way to Canada. For it to have happened I assume there was no other family here, but maybe the death record lists someone. Is my grandmother's last name, Pillow, a common one?"

"It's not common in this parish, per se. As far as the date o' their passin', have ye tried the graveyard?" says Father Fingal.

"No. I didn't think of that. So simple." Bruce jumps to his feet and slides his notepad and pen into the pockets of the hand-quilted bag his friend, Jeana, made for him. She'll be happy for him if he finally manages to get answers.

As he crosses the hall, he catches Cat's eye and nods. He gives them all two thumbs up.

"Don't be runnin' off Bruce Connors. We could use ye in the play," Cat yells, interrupting someone's lines.

"Trust me. I'm no good."

"I'm not buyin' it. Don't pretend ye're in there doin' research. Ye're listenin' to every word we say. Probably memorized yer lines already." Cat winks. "You'll be a great Ali Baba. Won't he gals?"

"People, please!" barks Geraldine.

"I'm Ali Baba," says Eoghan, the underfed twenty-year-old.

"Don't worry, Eoghan. I'm kidding," says Cat, mouthing to Bruce that she's not.

"Back t' work," the iron haired Geraldine snaps, glowering at Bruce.

MINT

MARY PICKS HER WAY around the small piles of branches and weeds already scraped together in Bruce's back garden. Martin, humming while he prunes flowering currant, has his back to her. She taps his shoulder, then, just in case he startles, hops out of range of the garden shears.

"Chuir tú eagla orm," he says crossly. "Be more careful, Mary."

"Sorry, love. I promised t' go over t' Flower's house today t' help with the knittin'. But I can cancel if ye want t' go out and explore with me."

"Have ye seen the magnitude o' what I'm dealin' with here? Bruce is goin' to be over the moon when he sees what I'm makin' o' this tangled mess. Whole thing likely got away on 'im, and poor lad didn't have the experience t' get it back under control."

"Flower showed me a beautiful beach yesterday. There's a path to it at the end of our street. We shouldn't be missin' things like this," says Mary. "Will ye take breaks so we can go for a swim together and see the island? I've seen people out paddlin' kayaks. I'd love to do somethin' like that."

"This is a challenge that can really prove a gardener's worth. Not many like it come along in life, Mary. If ye're goin' out, pick me up one o' them disposable cameras, will ye? I need it t' take *before* photos, today — or tomorrow, at the latest. Sure, I've already missed documentin' the full extent o' the change," says Martin, waving the shears between a blackberry and ivy-covered Holly tree, and the numerous piles dotting the landscape.

"I thought ye'd be disappointed when ye saw the garden," says Mary. "Ye get so upset at the neighbours for lettin' their gardens go to seed."

"Sure. I near took the rickets. But, Jesus!" His shears inscribe a cross in the air. "This is practically a blank canvas. And I have the chance here t' make a lad really happy." His chest expands. "Ye go now and have a bit o' fun and bring me the news o' it. But first, you'll leave my tea, aye?"

"I'll leave a sandwich in the fridge and a tray o' biscuits by the kettle."

"Good girl."

Mary heads back inside and checks her appearance in the bathroom mirror. She smooths her hair, applies frosted pink lipstick and a little blue shadow. She glances at her watch. She told Flower eleven o'clock. She'll be late by the time she gets Martin's tea.

She takes a shortcut across the farm, as Flower suggested. The grass is nicer against her sandaled feet than the gravel of the road. She watches three eagles circle overhead looking for a meal. Two parents and a juvenile. One of the parents swoops down, and with a beat of its massive wings, grasps a rabbit in its talons and flies away. Mary's breath catches in her throat. Her sympathy is with the rabbit, but she's awe-struck by the beauty of the bird and how close it came to her. If only there had been someone to witness it with her.

At the far edge of the field, Flower emerges through the trees just seconds too late.

"I thought I'd meet you to make sure you didn't get lost," she calls.

She is wearing cut-off jeans and a beige cotton long-sleeve blouse with a draw-string neck. The beads hanging from the open drawstring match the blue and red ones dangling from the loose pigtail braids framing her face.

Mary is suddenly self-conscious in her powder-blue polo shirt and knee length pleated shorts. She thought she looked cute when she checked herself in the full-length mirror. She was pleased with how smooth her long strawberry-blond hair looked, waves held back with a headband that matches both her polo shirt and eyes. Now her outfit feels square and uptight.

"How'd ye know I'd be comin' this way?" says Mary, shielding her eyes.

"Lucky guess. Why come by the road when this is such a great view?"

"Ye wouldn't believe what just happened. An eagle, big as can be, came down right in front o' me."

"There's a nest over in those trees. Lucky you, to have seen one so close."

Flower's hand, warm and gentle, takes hers; the edges of Mary's thoughts dissolve like a mint on her tongue.

"You've got such a lovely smile," says Flower leading her through the opening in the trees.

"Thank you," says Mary.

"I mean it. You're so pretty," says Flower, stopping on the wooded path to take in Mary's face. "I love the freckles across your nose. And I'd love to have perfect brows like yours."

"Ye do have perfect brows," says Mary. She makes no move to let go of Flower's hand.

They climb to the bluff together, sweating in the rising heat of the morning. Dust from the track sticks to Mary's exposed toes.

When they reach the house, Flower motions for them to go around to the back veranda. "We can knit first," she says. "I've got a sock started for you already."

"My feet are really dirty, sorry. Is there somewhere I can wash first?"

"The hose at the side of the house. Follow me."

Flower waits with the hose nozzle in hand for Mary to remove her sandals.

"I can wash them myself, so," says Mary reaching for the hose.

"Don't be silly." Flower sprays Mary's feet and then quickly splashes her outfit with a squirt of the hose. Mary shrieks, with surprise as much as indignation.

"Why —?"

"You look hot," giggles Flower, aiming another quick jet of water at her.

Mary lunges for the hose and wrestles if from Flower's grasp, turning the hose on Flower and giving her backside a thorough soaking.

"Hey. I only squirted you," says Flower, trying to regain

possession of the hose.

"You looked hotter," Mary says ruefully, giving Flower another spray as she continues to wrestle for the nozzle. Flower gives up and runs for the tap to shut it off.

They both stand dripping and laughing.

"I'll get you a towel," says Flower. "Admit it. You're cooler."

Taking the offered towel with her, Mary settles into a hammock chair and picks up the knitting needles. She *is* cooler. And her shirt and shorts are drying quickly.

"If you continue on with knitting that sock, we'll see if I can tell where my stitches end and yours pick up," says Flower. "Do you forgive me for spraying you?"

"Maybe I do." She hadn't expected to find a friend here, especially one she likes as much as Flower. She has only known her a few days, and yet can say she is drawn to her more than to anyone she's ever met. Flower is how she imagines an angel — shimmeringly beautiful, unfettered, and the physical embodiment of joy. She wonders what Flower could possibly get in return for spending time with her. Someone as amazing as Flower probably has lots of close friends. At the thought, a small bubble of inadequacy surfaces and she presses it down, vowing to take every moment with Flower as it comes and enjoy the warm feeling it gives her.

Holding the sock up to the light, Mary closely examines Flower's stitch pattern and tension and then settles the balls of wool on either side of her lap. She occasionally glances at the view and at Flower, who is sitting on the nearby picnic table knitting small, coloured flowers.

Half-an-hour later Mary checks her own work one last time and triumphantly says, "done." She hasn't knit socks in a while so is surprised at how quickly and easily she finished. Martin has all the sweaters, socks and scarves he needs, so most of the knitting she does these days is for her grandmother, who finds winters increasingly cold.

"Hey, you are fast," says Flower, taking the newly finished sock. "But, are you good?"

Mary waits anxiously as Flower holds the sock up to the sun, stretching the wool, feeling inside from toe to band. She puts the sock down and smiles. "Fast and good — and hired." Flower pulls Mary to her feet and gives her a tight hug and kiss on the cheek. "You are going to make my life so much easier."

When Flower releases Mary she tosses two new balls of yarn at her. "How about we make two pairs of socks each and then have some fun."

CHINK IN ONE'S STONE

AFTER SEARCHING EVERY headstone Bruce packs it in for the day, disappointed by how little he has accomplished. Before walking back to Number 8 he decides to check with Father Fingal one more time. He pulls on the heavy oak door of the church and carefully re-latches it behind him. The atmosphere is hushed. The light outside has faded and the stained-glass refractions have been replaced by the flicker of prayer candles jittering on the stone walls. He brings his thumb and the tip of his middle finger together on each hand in Shuni Mudra, a recall to peace and strength. He breathes deeply, and the smell of burning paraffin transports him unexpectedly to his boyhood. A happy memory flits across his consciousness, of walking hand-in-hand with his parents up the aisle of a church. His family didn't normally attend church, and he tries hard to recall what the occasion would have been.

"I don't wish to interrupt. Ye seem deep in thought," says Father Fingal quietly. "Did ye find what ye were lookin' for?"

"I searched every headstone and nothing. I don't understand. They *did* live here."

"I hate t' ask, but were they perhaps Jewish, or Protestant?"

"Catholic. I'm certain."

"Ye may not have seen every headstone," says Father Fingal.

"No, I was very thorough. Except, I didn't check the sarcophagi. Dad said his father was important in the village, or a hero, maybe a war hero? But could he have been wealthy enough to afford one of those? He was listed as a pauper, remember. Do you think I should have checked?"

"Well, he may have been a grand hero, lad. It's possible. What I mean though is that the *new* graveyard used to be where the hall is now. The church was beginnin' to sink beneath the weight of all the souls planted round it, ye see. The church had a good plan when they started a new plot, yet that new graveyard didn't last seventy year before it was dug up in 1968 and all of the headstones brought back to this side. They were handled very carefully, I'm sure, but some were broken in the process. Even some of the newest ones. These broken ones are lined, or stacked, against the back o' the church. I'll get my torch and switch the light on o'er the rear door. We might find somethin' yet."

Bruce wonders what happened to the bodies, maybe even his grandparents' bodies, as they were moved. He's picturing a large front-end loader jumbling parts of Mrs. M's with Mr. C's.

The fractured headstones, overgrown with grasses and creeping brambles, are well disguised. Bruce has to stub his toe on one before he sees them. Father Fingal grabs a hoe so that Bruce can clear the growth. When he's done, Father Fingal exchanges the hoe for a second torch. They start at opposite ends.

It's properly dark when Bruce lifts a heavy, lichen-covered slab sideways to reveal a brighter marble one beneath. His heart leaps.

>James Ambrose Connors
>Born September 19, 1885
>Died August 31, 1947
>His Beloved Wife Violet Virginia Pillow
>Born January 18, 1910
>Died February

The stone is broken. If only it had broken a few inches lower. Working quickly, he begins sliding the other stones aside. He reaches for the hoe and pulls a web of white grass roots from the lower most stones half-buried in mud. And there he finds it. The same fresh marble.

>26, 1930
>And His Second Wife Nellie Vera Larkin
>Born April 6, 1895
>Died June 4, 1935

Bruce drags the pieces together and props them against the wall.

"Died February 26, 1930. That's the day my dad was born."

"Ah. I'm sorry lad. Childbirth could be a sad business back then."

"And what does this mean — a second wife? Died 1935. Jesus — Pardon me, Father," says Bruce, looking skyward. "That was the year my father was sent away. Look at these dates. *His* father was still alive! His father lived another twelve years. Could this be right? He never sent for him or checked on him once. This can't be right. Could there have been another James and Violet Connors?"

"I'm sorry, my son."

Bruce spits on his finger and rubs the chiselled surface of the gravestone along his grandfather's year of death. "Maybe this four is a two? Maybe he died in '27."

"I'm afraid that would be an impossibility, wouldn't it lad?" says Father Fingal. "Ye look a touch shaken, ye do. Would ye like to come in and talk about it?"

"No. But, thank you. Here's your torch back."

Bruce is struggling, overwhelmed by anger and disbelief. Even though he knew nothing he found on this trip would change his own childhood, or that of his father, discovering *this* now makes what happened to his father feel exponentially more unjust, and unnecessary. He was drawn to Ireland by some ineffable connection to his grandfather. Now, learning how heartless that man must have been, he wonders if he shouldn't just chuck it all in and go home.

He sighs heavily and squeezes through an opening in the churchyard wall to strike out across the field. Still within hailing distance of the church, he stubs his toe again, and barely manages to corral the curse that springs to his lips. The path, already deep in night shadows, shrinks into invisibility as his vision tunnels. His chakras are shrinking. He needs to get back to Martin and Mary's, fast.

CONNECTED

EVEN IN THE SHADE OF Flower's porch, Mary is feeling the heat. They've been knitting for two hours and the wool is itchy against her skin. With relief she finishes the last pair of socks. Flower ties a paper tag to it, then scribbles on the price and washing instructions.

"Don't bother putting anything away," says Flower. "I can do that later." She takes the balls of wool and needles from Mary and tosses them back into the swinging chair.

Flower's hand, moist and warm, grasps hers and she allows herself to be led to a smooth patch of yellow grass atop the bluff, beyond the firs and twisted pink arbutus, where the view of Vancouver Island and the glacier is uninterrupted. As they appreciate the view, her hand is still nestled in Flower's, and she is struck by how special it feels to be taken by the hand and led in this way. Flower only releases her to flop down, spread eagle, near her feet.

Flower is Eve, haloed by the golden garden.

Mary follows, dropping to the ground as she did as a child to carve angels in the snow. Her spirit feels hampered by some unseen force and she wishes everything about Flower was contagious. She would lick her and magically be transformed into the same child of nature, with smooth caramel skin and untameable hair, free of a dogged self-consciousness, and full of love for everyone.

Mary turns sideways, shielding her eyes to look at Flower. "Ye'd like the views of the coast near Ballycanew. I hope you'll visit someday."

"I imagine Martin will be excited about that," laughs Flower. "I think he's scared of me."

"Oh, stuff what Martin wants." A pang of disloyalty pricks her, but she feels powerless against the resentment slow boiling inside her since their arrival. "He's too busy prunin' bushes into somethin' they're not. Ye know . . . I feel like this is the first time I've been able to grow — I don't know — a little wild. His rules, his cautions — what a holy weight," she blurts out.

It feels good just to say it. She couldn't say it to her friends back home. They would look at her marriage differently from there on out.

"Have you told him you feel like that?"

"O' course not. It wouldn't make any difference. He isn't gonna change who he is. Maybe I should've stood up to him more when we were first married. It's just not done though. Ye obey and serve yer husband and all that." Mary sits up. "I've only known ye a few days. It must seem weird I'm telling ye all this. Must be I'm on edge. And it feels like we've been friends forever." She holds her breath, realizing that she has just told Flower how much she likes her, without any clue it will be reciprocated.

"I feel like I've known you forever too."

Mary exhales. "Ye do?"

Flower rolls toward her with a mischievous smile and pulls a thin home-made cigarette from her pocket. "This will help." She lights the cigarette, takes a puff and gently blows a sour cloud of smoke into Mary's face. Mary pinches her nose shut and waves the smoke away. Flower smiles beatifically, takes another puff and offers it to Mary.

"Oh, I don't smoke. But, thanks anyway."

"This isn't a normal cigarette, babe. It's Hornby grown weed. A joint." Flower takes another slow drag and passes it to Mary. "Open your mind and become one with all that's wild within and around you," she says, dramatically enough that she bursts into giggles.

"Isn't this illegal?" says Mary, reluctantly taking the joint.

"Just take one drag."

Mary puts the dry paper to her lips and inhales. "Satisfied?"

"Very."

Mary inhales again, deeply, and holds her breath until she

coughs. She hands the joint back and waits, wondering what will happen to her. The joint is back in her hand. She takes another drag and laughs. It's so funny she can't stop.

Flower leans close and takes a puff without taking the joint from Mary's hand. In slow-motion Mary watches Flower's moist lips slowly lock on the narrow fuselage. She stares in fascination as the muscles in Flower's neck tighten, hold, as though poised on some precipice, then sweetly slacken. She sees the pout of her lips relax to eject a billowing, lingering cloud.

Mary takes another drag. "Do I look different? I feel like I'm revertin' to my natural state," she giggles. "This is wild, it is."

Flower is propped on one elbow, legs stretched to the horizon, toe rings sparkling silver against the cerulean sky.

"I wish I had a picture of ye as ye look right now," says Mary.

Mary kicks off her sandals and flips on her stomach. A beetle is struggling up a nearby blade of dry grass. She lowers her head and closes one eye. The world of the beetle stretches on for beetle-miles, an impenetrable straw jungle. The beetle lands on the jungle floor and weaves between the trampled blades. A spider crosses the beetle's path, pauses on its angular stilts to assess the interloper against some mysterious set of criteria, then continues on its way.

"Have ye ever thought, Flower, of how alien insects look? How scary it would be if they were the size o' dogs and cats, or horses and cows?" says Mary, lifting her head and looking at Flower seriously. "Each one is so completely different from another. Imagine how many life forms there are in the universe, if all o' the insects and, come to think o' it, all the animals, have unique bodies — just on earth."

Flower takes the dwindling joint from Mary's hand and examines it. "If insects were the size of rabbits, mice even, there would be no room for anything else. There are one-and-a-half-billion insects for every human. Imagine," says Flower, putting her lips to the joint. "Worse, imagine a world without them, or without bacteria and fungi. There would be dead bodies and dead plants piled so high we'd be sinking in them. And without decomposition, there would be no nutrients for plants, and therefore nothing for animals to eat. Mother Nature got it just right. Wouldn't you say?"

Flower puts her hands together in prayer position. "All we have to do is not screw it up." She flashes a white smile at Mary and winks.

"How do ye know all o' this, like how many insects there are in the world?"

"I remember it, from university. I took ecology classes. Some physics and chemistry as well," says Flower.

"Sure. I had no idea."

"Yeah. Physics and chemistry were just as interesting as ecology. Roll closer, Mary. Put your hand against mine. Although we feel solid to each other, at a subatomic level, the building blocks that make up everything we think of as our body are just dancing points of energy, surrounded by larger clouds of energy that are mostly made up of space. And these balls of energy move so fast they're both everywhere and nowhere all at once. If it was possible for every ball of energy in our bodies to be nowhere at the same time, I wonder if we could disappear."

"Brilliant," says Mary. "Is that real?"

"Yeah. The tiny points of energy are called quarks and they are held together by forces stronger than gravity or magnetism. All true, except the disappearing, of course. Every atom makes sure its neighbouring atom's energies are *not* all positioned nowhere at once." Flower releases Mary's hand and flops back onto the grass. "Everything my mind sees is just energy, even though it looks and feels like something distinct. We think we as humans are unique and deserve to dominate the earth. But at a sub-atomic level, we aren't. All of nature and the world are one.

"That's heavy."

"But reassuring too, hey? I'm connected to everything and everyone because the energy stored in our atoms is continually shared. In a year, most of the energy in my body will have spread to the world around me. Some of me is becoming you right now, as I exhale and you inhale. It's why we need to take better care of not just other life on earth, even life like bacteria, fungi and insects, but the non-living earth as well." Flower reaches for Mary's hand in the grass and gives it a squeeze. "I'm rambling. Call it a side-effect of the weed."

"I like it," says Mary. "The ramblin'."

Flower digs her hand into the back pocket of her jean shorts and pulls out another joint. She places it between her lips and flicks the lighter. Squinting through the smoke she crawls on her elbows toward Mary and hands it to her.

Mary takes another toke and watches with fascination as Flower straddles her hips and leans forward, a hand on either side of Mary's shoulders. Her hair draws a curtain around them, blocking out the sun. Mary feels intensely giddy. She quickly inhales the tangy resin and lets it out through pursed lips. The smoke hovers, rolling faintly in the air between them. She puts the joint to Flower's lips and the end glows red. Mary notices the fine smile lines at the corners of Flower's eyes. She has a chicken-pox scar on her forehead. The vermillion border of her lips is a browner pink than the rest of her lips, as though she is wearing lip-liner, which she isn't. Her only makeup is a daub of light brown eyeshadow and a hint of mascara. They pass the joint back and forth until it's reduced to a short hot nub.

Flower stares so deeply into Mary's eyes that she has to close them, but not before emitting an awkward squeak.

Flower takes the joint from Mary and pinches it out with a wet finger. She rolls off into the grass. "You have very fine skin. I can see the blood pumping through it where it hugs your cheek bones and forehead. And, you blush easily."

"And I'm sure ye can also see how freckled it is," says Mary. She draws her finger over the bridge of her nose and across her cheeks. "I'm probably sproutin' more freckles by the minute, lying out like this."

"Do you want to roll with me to the shade?" says Flower, rolling back and forth like a child readying to roll downhill.

"No. I like it here. I like the smell o' baking grass. Everythin' is so grand, so beautiful. If we stay like this maybe my atoms will take off and become part o' that tree, or a bird. Maybe this sweet grass is becomin' part o' me. The longer we lie out here the wilder I'll become." Mary rolls onto her stomach and lifts onto her elbows. A wave of dizziness washes over her.

"True," Flower laughs. "Mary, has anyone every told you, you have beautiful energy. I'm glad you're here with me. Bruce would have loved you. He really picks up on people's energy."

"Here I am wishin' I had *better* energy — somethin' you have; I can't put my finger on it. It's warmth and honey. When I'm with ye I feel like I can trust in the way I did when I was four, before anyone had pushed me down in the school yard. Plus, ye inspire me to be as wild as the livin' things on this hillside. To live in my natural state." Mary checks herself. She's never spoken to anyone like this. "I'm soundin' daft. Sure, I'm embarrassin' myself. What will ye think o' me?"

"If you mean what you said, it's not daft. I'm happy you said it. I meant everything I said to you," says Flower.

Flower stands and hauls Mary to her feet by both hands. "Come to the beach with me."

KI

BRUCE IS IN HIS BEDROOM when the front bell trills. He peeks out the window. Cat, Joan, Mags and Claire are on the doorstep with a casserole, still steaming. Mags is swinging a bag of white rolls. Claire is gripping the neck of a rum bottle. All four wear determined expressions. Bruce senses something is up and tucks the jar of his father's ashes back into his suitcase.

"Mags heard from Father Fingal, on her way past the church, so, that things didn't go well for ye with yer research," says Cat.

"We're comin' in." Claire thrusts the bottle into his hand like a chicken needing to be plucked.

"Ladies, I appreciate this, but would you take it the wrong way if I want to be alone? I was just about to meditate. My chakras are out of balance. In particular, sahasrara and anahata, my crown and heart chakra."

"We are not goin' anywhere," says Cat. "First, we eat. Then we drink. And then, and only then can ye explain what a sahata and an anarara are and how we help."

"You shouldn't have gone to all this trouble. You don't have to keep bringing food over," says Bruce, as he is swept down the hall.

In the kitchen the women immediately get to work pulling plates, glasses and cutlery from the cupboards and drawers.

"It wasn't any trouble, to start with," says Cat. "I pulled the casserole out o' the freezer and popped it in the microwave while I waited for the gals. I hope ye like fish pie."

"I love it."

Joan heaps steaming casserole onto Corian plates retrieved from the cupboard. Mags adds a buttered roll to each and carries them to the coffee table in the front room.

Cat is rummaging through the hutch in the corner of the breakfast nook. "I don't understand it. Martin always keeps a box o' matches in the front right corner o' this drawer."

"I used them to light some incense. Sandalwood and lavender — it helps my focus when I meditate," says Bruce. "They're on the bread box."

"Well, it smells nice in here," says Cat. "Ladies, what do ye think? Should we do Mary a favour and finally light those candles she bought last year. Martin hasn't let her take the plastic wrap off. I mean, Jesus, how much is it to buy new candles?" Cat accepts the matches from Bruce and crosses herself.

"Do ye have any cola in the house?" Claire asks, holding a glass up to eyeball the measure of rum she's just poured.

"I'm not sure. I'm a tea drinker, mostly," replies Bruce, moving into the kitchen and pulling open the lower cupboard doors. "This do?" he says. A half-dozen cans dangle from his finger.

"If the cola runs out, we'll do shots," says Claire. She pops the tab and starts to pour. "This one's yers, love," she says, handing it to Bruce. She fills the remainder of the waiting glasses and pushes them to the end of the counter. "Have a gargle, girls."

"That's the fastest I've ever gotten a drink in this house," says Mags. "Martin has t' go through a whole shebang with that damn drinks trolley every time I'm over."

The four women stand in a semi-circle, glasses raised.

Claire says, "Sleep well auld spirits hauntin' Bruce tonight. Sláinte." She takes a big gulp. Bruce pretends to drink.

A few drinks in, meal finished, and dishes tossed in the sink, Cat sits beside Bruce on the couch and takes his hand. "Tell us what happened."

Bruce lifts his glass to take a drink and remembers it's rum and coke. "Well . . . I thought my dad was sent to Canada when his parents died, but I found a gravestone today that proves my grandfather lived another twelve years after sending him away. Dad grew up on Vancouver Island in what was essentially a child labour camp dressed up as a school. He was tormented and abused by the older boys and pervert caregivers that came and went. He never knew what it was to be protected and loved by a parent. I felt bad enough for him when I thought he was an orphan. Now it feels nothing short of criminal that this was his fate. There was no need for it. It turns out, the grandparents I came here wanting to connect with were horrible people. Well, my grandfather was. My grandmother died in childbirth."

"Oh, Bruce," says Joan. "You've had a bad dose. And you've come all this way. A shame it must feel. But we'll set ye right."

"Tell us what we can do," says Cat, releasing his hand and briskly rubbing his upper arm. "Tell us 'bout this chakra thing."

"What about your husbands? Do you have time?"

"They're down the pub watchin' hurley. Semi-finals," says Joan. "Depending on the outcome they could be out till wee hours."

"In that case, how much do you know about healing chakras and Reiki?" asks Bruce.

The ladies look at each other.

"Nothin'," says Mags.

"It's straight forward if you understand the science. It all starts with energy. Energy is everything. Physical matter and free energy, just two forms of the same thing. Yeah?"

"Grand," says Cat. "Maybe I've had a few too many o' these," she says, swirling her rum and coke. "I'm lost already. Are ye still explainin' what chakra is?"

"Of course he is. Don't be rude, so, Cat," says Mags.

Bruce looks from one to the other but sees eager, open faces. "Well, because everything is energy, and trust me it is, an electromagnetic field surrounds and interpenetrates our body, and from that, each of us has an aura and electrical energy as unique as a fingerprint. It's not just true of us, but of all living things. This energy concentrates in our bodies at certain vortices or 'chakras'. The chakras are analogous to the brain and organs. And, just as we have veins and arteries to carry blood to our organs, we have something called meridians and nadis to carry our Ki, our life energy."

"Ye seem to know a lot about this," says Mags. "It sounds very ancient, even though ye're talkin' about science. I think I might've heard of it on the tele."

Cat raises her eyebrows at Mags. A look Mags ignores.

Bruce is spurred on by Mag's rapt attention. "Reiki is our spiritual energy. It expands when we're healthy and happy and contracts and blocks when we're hurt or unhappy. Before I found that headstone, I was hoping to confer a blessing of peace and rest on my ancestors. But this discovery has flooded my chakras, causing them to draw inward. It's a bad state for me. I'm not myself."

"Sounds like ye need a hug for starters," says Cat, swinging her arms around him as far as she can and rocking him side to side. "That's what I need when I'm not at myself."

"Me next," says Joan. "Bring yerself in here. I'll give ye a big old squeeze that'll set ye t' right."

Claire and Mags hug him more timidly.

"Thank you so much, ladies. It was great of you to bring the drinks and dinner. I think, though, what I really need to do is recharge. I have some music I use to help me awaken each chakra, and then through breathing and meditation I restore energy flow from my root chakra to the chakra we carry above our heads."

"We'll stay and do it with ye," offers Cat. "Ye're a great lummox if ye think we're abandonin' ye."

"True, we're not leavin'," affirms Mags.

"If you really don't mind, yes, stay. I can talk you through it. Your positive auras and free-flowing Ki will be good for me."

"Of course they will," says Claire brightly. "Ye'll see. Ye won't be sorry we forced ourselves on ye."

"Look at us, givin' this a lash," says Mags with a slightly intoxicated laugh. "Nothin' like this ever happens in Ballycanew."

"I'm still not sure what it is we're doin'," says Joan. "But so long as it's not occult, and Father Fingal never finds out, then I'm up for anythin' that'll help ye."

"He is obviously not a devil worshiper," says Mags. "And he needs our help."

"He does, so. And I'm eager to, for one," says Cat.

BLOOMING

MARY IS FLYING HIGH. Dizzy and giddy, she and Flower stumble over the logs at Little Tribune Bay and flop down cross-legged in the sand.

"I don't have a swimsuit," says Mary. "I forgot to bring my suit."

Flower grins at her. "You didn't know we were coming." She pulls off her top and lies back on the hot sand with her legs still crossed. "You don't need a swimsuit. No one here will care if you're naked."

To demonstrate, Flower leaps to her feet and shimmies off her jean shorts. She smiles down at Mary and slowly turns, arms open wide, bottom gyrating.

Not only does Flower not wear shoes, it's confirmed that she doesn't believe in wearing underclothes either. Mary sneaks quick short glances at Flower as she turns, admiring the silky sheen of her skin and the toned, smooth curves of her breasts and hips.

Mary checks no one is watching them. When she gets over her embarrassment for Flower, she makes a split-second decision to lift off her polo shirt. Kneeling in the sand, back turned, she nervously fiddles with it, arranging it on the driftwood, ostensibly to keep it from getting sandy. When she glances over her shoulder, Flower is standing above her with a cocked eyebrow and a daring smile. Her finger inscribes circles in the air over Mary's bottom-half.

Still emboldened by the pot, and not wanting to disappoint Flower, Mary flips onto her back and hastily undoes her shorts, sashaying left and right until she can slip them over her ankles. Flat on the sand, still clad in bra and panties, she feels utterly exposed.

Her underclothes don't match. No one will ever believe she's wearing a bathing suit.

"My God! What are those? Your grandmother's bloomers?" blurts Flower.

Mary lunges for her shorts and hides beneath them. "What?"

"You'd be better off nude than wearing those. They come up to your nipples," Flower teases. "Natural state, remember."

"Did I say that?"

"I believe you did. And I am going to be your official ambassador to all things natural on the island."

"I hope ye understand how hard this is for me. I don't even take my clothes off in front o' other women at Wexford public pool. I'll already have t' confess to the Priest for takin' this much off in mixed company, so."

"Heaven forbid God sees one of his children naked," laughs Flower. "Come on, Mary, take it all off. You'll thank me for it."

Mary scans the beach again. A pair of well-basted sunbathers are dug in about twenty feet from them, lying on their backs, eyes screwed tight against the sun. Further down, a man with red hair is reading a book with his back to them. Beyond that, there's only a handful of people on the beach and in the water. All of them, like Flower, nude.

"Natural state," whispers Mary. She reaches behind her back and undoes her bra. She lets it fall forward, exposing her breasts. She avoids making eye contact with Flower until she has the bra tucked under her polo, out of sight. "Satisfied?" she says, grinning with embarrassment.

"Better. Although, if I were you, I would have ditched the underwear first." Flower flops back on the sand, chuckling, and closes her eyes.

Mary stretches out beside her and lets the soft sand run through her fingers. The air is heavy with the taste of salt and parched seaweed.

After half-an-hour Mary is uncomfortably hot, the snow-white skin on her breasts now pink and prickly.

Flower senses her discomfort and squints sideways. "Wanna swim?"

"I do, but I can't walk past everyone like this."

"Your modesty is cute," Flower says, getting up and dusting the sand from her behind. "Walk behind me, then. Because I'm definitely not letting you put that girdle-like bra back on."

Mary stands and covers her breasts with her hands. She walks as close behind Flower as she can without treading on her.

The water, when they reach it, is a shock to her hot feet. When it reaches her knees, she runs forward and dives under, swimming until she's neck deep.

Flower's sleek head pops up nearby. Mary catches a devilish look and paddles to escape.

"Now the granny pants," Flower says, hand outstretched, still trying to catch Mary.

"I'm not givin 'em to ye. I don't trust ye yet," Mary laughs. "I'll do it. But ye need to stay back."

She gets her panties off and holds them in a tight fist.

"Are they off?"

She flashes the evidence at Flower by whirling them briefly above her head. Drops of water fly all around her, their little trajectories describing a tale of infinite happiness. Unprepared for how good she feels, Mary is suspended in a moment of joy.

CHO KU REI

Bruce drops a cassette into the stereo in the corner of the sitting room and pushes rewind. The candles flicker.
"We can spread one of the quilts on the carpet if we slide the coffee table to the corner," he says.

The whirring stereo snaps to an abrupt halt, announcing the tape's readiness. Once they've smoothed the quilt across the carpet, Bruce pauses with his finger over the play button. "Ok. Here we go. The first music will be loud. Our root chakra, at the base of our spine, and our sacral chakra in our groin are activated by music like rock. High energy sound. I focus my energy on each chakra, moving from my root to my crown. As they activate and begin to flow, the music changes. Our chakra in the solar plexus, for instance, is stimulated by string instruments, like classical guitar. And then the heart, flute. The throat, cello. Our third eye, Anja, chimes. And the crown above our heads, soothing sounds like ocean waves. Ready?"

"Grand. We're ready," says Cat, nodding to the others.

Bruce pushes play and static hums through the speakers.

"I'll sit in the centre of the blanket and you can surround me, extending your palms over each of my chakras, about twelve inches from my body. Think of peace and positivity, feel your connection with the universe, imagine opening.

Cat is momentarily distracted by the flutter of candlelight on Bruce's unbound waves. She wonders, 'Is this really the same room she and Mary had tea and biscuits in last week'?

She tunes him back in. "Visualize unblocking the vortices at each point so that they can swirl clockwise and reach outward. As we progress, you may feel my aura envelop yours. If this happens, it's natural to feel your own aura swell."

Cat, Mags, Joan and Claire exchange glances as 'Peace Sells' by Megadeth blares from the cassette tape. Cat lifts her hands and links her thumbs as though she is going to make a shadow puppet dove. The other three nod and do the same. Cat timidly kneels in front of Bruce and leans forward over his crossed legs to hover her linked hands over his groin. Joan reddens and does the same. Mags starts moving her palms in a clockwise direction and elbows Claire beside her to do the same. Like the wave at a sporting match, they sway, and flutter over Bruce's groin.

The heavy metal is beginning to affect Cat's sacral chakra. It's that, or the tanned skin on Bruce's smooth bare chest. She notices for the first time that he has a small gold chain and cross tangled up with his wooden bead necklace.

Joan is blushing, moving from a tomato red to a worrying eggplant.

The music changes. Spanish guitar music softly replaces the bone-jarring metal. Claire moves first, raising her hands to the level of Bruce's naval, closer than she should. Cat, Joan and Mags move to match her circles. Cat's wondering if they could be accused of performing some satanic ritual, the kind of kinky ritual she sometimes fantasizes about. Except, in her fantasies, she's always the naked one in the centre of a constellation of eager, patient men. She has the urge to cross herself. There's no way she's telling Michael what she did tonight.

The music switches again. Bruce's palms are together in prayer position with his thumbs to his heart. The flute is distant and reedy, haunting. They move their hands higher, careful not to bump Bruce's. Cat's feet are falling asleep and she glances down in order to shift without knocking Bruce's knees. She catches movement in the rough cotton of his pants. A circus tent in Mary's living room. She decides it's too risky to move. She might fall on him; they've had a lot of rum. Her sacral chakra starts to vibrate and perhaps even her solar plexus.

As the flute plays on, Bruce whispers, "Place your fingertips on my fingers, chant with me – cho ku rei . . . cho ku rei . . . bring me power."

Cat realizes that Mags has also seen the tent. Her face is red. Mag's eyes close and she chants more fervently.

The music changes. The tinkling of chimes in the wind signals the movement to Bruce's throat chakra. They bring their hands higher. Cat stands.

Cat sways. She, Joan, Mags and Claire sway. They chant, "hon sha ze sho."

Bruce's lips part in a beatific smile. Cat closes her eyes again and tries to recapture the tingling in her groin and belly. She is not quite at peace, but she is enjoying the trip there.

Without noticing, the chimes have become a bell. A tinkling bell. Her hands rise to Bruce's forehead. She makes large circles. She recalls why they're doing this and focuses her mind on Bruce's need to find peace and love for his ancestors.

The sound of waves, rolling on a pebbled beach, fills the room. They rock out, and in, like the tide. They surround him now, their hands above his head are almost touching as the music pulls them in tighter. Cat would like it very much if her blouse fell open and her nipple happened to fall against Bruce's wet lips. Parts of her are swelling. Maybe it's her aura.

The tape clicks off and starts to auto-rewind. They are still swaying when Bruce speaks, "The light and love in me honours, respects and sees the light and love in each of you. Namaste." He bows his head over his praying hands and then opens his eyes, startlingly green in the candlelight.

Cat can't speak. It seems wrong to disturb the peace. Without premeditation they all grasp hands. Joan starts to chatter nervously. Bruce eases himself to his feet and pulls the four of them into a hug. His penis knocks into Cat's stomach and then is gone as he pulls away and stretches, unashamed that the front of his pants is swinging.

Joan says, "We'll leave ye now that ye're feelin' better. Shouldn't we? Besides, Séamus might need me down the pub t' help close up. The walk 'll clear my head some. It's hot as a skillet in here."

"I'm much better," says Bruce.

"I really felt somethin' there," says Mags.

"Sure. Didn't I feel it too. That was brilliant," says Claire, running her fingers through her hair to re-feather the sides.

"Is é an fear is gnéasaí dá bhfaca mé riamh é," says Mags, slowly exhaling through her pursed lips.

"Tá sé," says Cat.

"What does that mean? It sounds beautiful," says Bruce.

"I'm sorry. That was rude o' us. I was just sayin' how moved I was," says Mags.

"Jasus," says Cat, crossing her bosom. "That was savage. I'd be up to doin' it again sometime, I would, so."

SKINNY SPLASHING

NEVER BEFORE HAS MARY felt so ambivalent with regard to sin. Even though she knows God can see what she's up to, she doubts He cares as much as Father Fingal would. And he's not here right now.

So it's with abandon that she immerses herself in this new pleasure. Her heart races with titillation as the hour approaches, and she celebrates the sensation. There is a pleasure in naughtiness and secrets that she had forgotten, or perhaps never knew.

Once she and Flower finish knitting and Flower leaves for her stall at the Co-op, Mary cuts through the field at the bottom of the hill and follows the path to the beach. After skinny-dipping with Flower, she hadn't planned to return on her own, but the very next day she ended up here instead of home with Martin.

The first day alone, she forced herself to be brave. Hiding at the edge of the path, partly concealed by wild rose, she noted the sex and location of each bather, calculating where to sit and be least observed. She stealthily approached this ideal spot, then lifted her top as she lowered herself to the sand. Her bra came off next — swiftly, before she lost her nerve. Her skirt she left on; no need to get crazy the first day. Fifteen minutes later, half of that spent with her hands covering her sunburnt breasts, she dressed and headed back to the path.

That night, to her amazement, she didn't burst into flames. Father Fingal didn't show up at the door. And from her conscience, not a single prick or pang of remorse. Instead, she felt exhilarated. And proud. Proud that she had defied the naysayer in her head.

Today is her fourth afternoon in the regular spot. She is getting better at this. She remembered a towel, wide-brimmed hat and sunscreen. She dispensed with underclothing too, thinking the gawky struggle to get them off was likely to earn more stares than her simple nudeness. Plus, her underwear were always full of sand when she re-dressed.

She squirts Coppertone into her hand and rubs it over her breasts in wide circles. This suddenly strikes her as sexual so she hunches her shoulders and keeps a narrow eye on fellow nudes until her burnt skin is covered. She spends five minutes lying on her back and then, because her breasts are so badly burned, flips to her stomach. She squirts another dollop of sunscreen onto her hand and awkwardly reaches back to apply it.

"Want help with that?"

At the sound of the voice she mentally dissolves into the sand.

"The sunscreen. I can help you put it on."

She squints up at a vague male shadow haloed in sunlight. She fumbles with the floppy brim of her hat, twisting to look up at him without elevating her breasts. The man is standing over her. Surely this breaches the etiquette of nude bathing. Nudists should avoid openly looking at each other, or should pretend to, shouldn't they?

"No — thank ye. I'm managin'."

"You'll end up with handprints on your ass. I've seen it before."

"No. I'm fine. I was just goin' for a swim."

All she can see of him is a penis scrunched tight in a collar of wet brown curls. His silhouette shimmers. Sunlight crowns him.

"I was just in. The water's great," the stranger says. "Can I join you afterward?"

She isn't ready for this. Not on day four. She lowers her eyes. Her best chance of getting out of the conversation is to follow through with her stated intention to swim. But this means standing. He is hovering, waiting for an answer, and shows no sign of leaving.

Her back to him, she slides up onto all fours, preparing to rise. Oh God, is he going to think this an invitation to take her from behind? She quickly changes position, dropping her bottom and casually twisting her hips to the side. From here, she realizes she'll have no chance of getting up gracefully. She gamely contorts again, managing to half rise with one shoulder in the air. Quasimodo at the beach. Hiding her face behind her hat brim, she prays he is no longer looking at her. She bends down and tugs the towel, but it's held fast, pinned beneath the stranger's toes.

"I can watch your stuff for you if you want," he offers.

"Oh. No! I mean, I like to dry off right away." She tugs again with her back to him. "Ye're on my towel. Do ye mind?"

He laughs.

Other people on the beach are looking at them. A few wave. She politely lifts her hand to wave back. Perhaps for the best. The stranger will see that she isn't someone new to this, someone naïve, someone battling shame with a sprinkling of self-loathing, someone currently experiencing intense stage fright — despite how brave she thought she was — how brave she wants to be.

She channels Flower's energy: Carefree, comfortable in body and spirit. Without overthinking it, she drops the towel and takes a step, her back straight, chin lifted, toes pointed and hips swinging. She waves and greets the others on the beach as she strolls to the water. If he is watching her, it no longer matters.

GUIDE TO SELFCARE

THE HANDLE ON THE FRONT door rattles. Old Desmond is cursing on the stoop. Bruce looks up at the clock in the kitchen. Right on time. Desmond goes for a walk, gets confused and rattles the knob every morning at 11:09.

Bruce empties the Brown Betty teapot into the sink and stares out the back window at the garden. The topiary are shaggy. He flips through the forty-page instruction booklet he discovered beside the breadbox this morning. Addressed to him, the instructions reference various pruning shears and a 'patent-pending chemical cocktail'. Bruce glances at the bearded giraffe stretching its neck above the other plants forming the border of his host's monoculture lawn. He feels his heart rate quicken.

He practices box breathing. In for four, hold for four, out for four, hold for four. The force of Martin's expectations is embedded with inky jabbing keystrokes into every page of, 'Guide to Garden Care Number 8 Village Gate'.

Bruce's spiking blood pressure has nothing to do with gardening and everything to do with not living up to expectations. His Dad's, specifically. He loved his dad, absolutely, and can't blame him. If his dad hadn't felt like such a failure himself, if he had had parents of his own, perhaps he would not have demanded so much of Bruce, not driven him to excel at everything. But he had, and Bruce had let him down. He hadn't become a doctor or a lawyer or an entrepreneur. He wasn't chosen to captain sports teams or ranked top in his class.

Slipping into his flip-flops, he opens the patio door and scans the sum of his responsibilities. Maybe looking after the garden won't be onerous after all.

The garden shears are hanging in the shed, exactly as per the guide. Behind each tool, Martin has painted a bright orange outline, so none could possibly suffer the ignominy of misplacement. Smaller than any he's seen before, the shears are more suited to toenail trimming than gardening. Bruce handles the smallest of them, snips an imaginary branch in the air, then replaces them on their outline. He realizes that for many reasons, not least among them his lack of interest in this form of gardening, he'll be on the back foot against a month's worth of growth. He came all this way to discover his heritage, not do Martin's yard work.

Despite the initial disappointment over his grandfather, he woke this morning still wanting to find out more about him, and more about the village that might have been his Dad's, had he not been sent away. There still may be people in the village that knew his grandparents. Aunts, uncles, cousins. Even a single relative would be a one-hundred-percent improvement over the number of family he currently has.

After yoga and lunch, he'll strike for the village and resume the search.

Bruce heads inside briefly to pull an old quilt from the couch. He spreads it on the back lawn. Hands together in Anjali mudra, prayer position, he steps to the centre of his makeshift yoga mat. Folding forward, he wraps his hands around his ankles. Slowly he walks his fingers forward to Downward Dog. He swings low into Cobra. Deep breath, then Plank.

He cocks his head to the side. Not only is the grass lush and even, but the entire lawn appears combed to the right. He releases from Plank and arches into Upward Facing Dog. A face peers at him over the shoulder of the giraffe.

"Hi ya, lad. What ye be doin'?"

Séamus, Joan's husband, pushes greenery aside and rests an elbow on the fence.

"Yoga," says Bruce.

"Ye do it in yer briefs then? Naked?"

"It's cooler and easier to move," says Bruce. "I keep a couple of pairs just for yoga."

"Jesus, yes." The shrubs rustle. "What I wouldn't give to walk around the back garden in my briefs. I tell Joanie they aren't much different from bathers, but she worries old man Desmond will pop his clog if he sees me in 'em. Daft old git."

"Have you done yoga before? Do you want to join me?" asks Bruce.

"Can't say as I have. But I'm always one for new things. Ye can't say I'm not," says Séamus. "I'll grab a sheet, yeah? And put on a fresh pair."

ARE YOU MY . . . ?

THE BELL CHIMES AS BRUCE pulls open the smudged glass door of Connors' garage and filling station. There is a line of customers and it gives Bruce time to look around. The walls are hung with a series of pictures of the owner and his employees, perhaps family members, from over the years. Bruce takes a closer look to see if he can detect a resemblance to himself or his dad. Judging from the photos the garage has been owned by the Connors since the '40's.

The last person ahead of Bruce finishes paying and Bruce is face to face with a young woman resembling the owner, his daughter perhaps.

"Hi," he says. "May I speak to Mr. Connors? I'm Bruce Connors."

"Ye are, are ye?" she says, opening the till and straightening the bills. Over her shoulder she yells, "Da!"

Through a small square cut-out to the bay of the garage he sees Davey Connors slide out from under a hoisted vehicle, put down his wrench and wipe his hands. He is about 5'6" with dark wavy hair and a complexion lined with grease.

"Yer car won't be ready till next week," he says gruffly when he trudges through the swinging door to reception.

"I haven't got a car," says Bruce.

Davey raises his eyes for the first time and registers just a flicker of surprise quickly doused with disinterest.

"Well, then," he says, and lays a hand back on the swinging door.

"I just need a minute of your time, sir. I'm Bruce Connors. I've come from Canada and I'm looking for family. My grandfather was

James Connors. Could he have been a brother to your father or your grandfather, or a cousin — any relation at all?"

"No."

"Do you have any other family in town that might know?"

"He wasn't."

"Da," the young woman behind the counter chides. "Yer bein' rude."

Davey takes his hand from the door and comes over to plant both hands on the reception desk. He heaves a sigh and glances sideways at his daughter. "Let's see now, lad — as it's important — since ye've come a long way . . . James Connors, only son o' Finlay Connors, no relation t' us. They're what *we* call the *bad* Connors, terrorists they were, chose the wrong side. That answer yer question?"

Bruce is too taken back to respond at first. The daughter gives him a weak smile.

"It does, thank you," Bruce says as Davey is disappearing through the swinging door.

"Sorry, love," says the daughter. "Don't take it personally. They're all still messed up with stories from the war, even though they weren't even born yet. My generation's not so daft. Good luck with yer search. I like yer outfit, by the bye."

The bell rings above the door and a customer nods to the young woman and positions himself behind Bruce.

"Thanks. Have a good day," says Bruce.

The door closes behind him and Bruce squints up at the large sign over the station bearing his name. It was worth a try. Nothing lost. Something gained, however. He now has the name of his great-grandfather. Finlay. As for terrorists — can he take the word of a guy like that. It's almost a relief not to be related to him. He'd like to find family, yes, but he's not desperate.

THE RESISTANCE

MARTIN'S DAILY FIELD briefing on the war against foreign invaders has begun. Mary blows on her coffee and peers over the brim as she walks. The wild grasses and flowers that managed to parachute onto Bruce's lawn over the years have been mowed to stubble. A recent area-bombing with herbicide ensured nothing but a few blades of green were left standing. Buttercup, clover, daisy, dandelion, plantain and creeping Charlie shrivel on the wasteland. Mary read somewhere that in the heat of battle men experience a manic high. Martin is buzzing.

"It's a good job I brought everythin' I did from home. It would've cost a punt or two to buy it here. By the way, how do y' think we should ask Bruce t' pay us back for the plants I'll be needin'?"

"You can't ask him to pay ye back. I'm not sure about anythin' ye're doin' here, to be honest, Martin. Maybe he liked it the way it was."

Martin turns a cool gaze on her. "Be serious, Mary. Who could be happy livin' with that riot in the back garden. What are ye sayin' exactly?"

"Nothin' at all, dear." She scans the desert and wonders how Martin is going to rebuild before Bruce returns. Wasn't the aim to improve the yard? She buries her face in her cup until he resumes his stride.

Martin pauses by a heap of tree branches to wait for her to catch up. Spikes of yellow goldenrod and the disembodied limbs of black cherry and fragrant elderberry protrude at odd angles from the pile.

"I'll need yer help gettin' rid o' this. The pile grew this much yesterday," says Martin raising his hand from chest level to eight inches above his head.

She doesn't respond. She is swallowing coffee.

He raises his bushy brows, "I am makin' progress here. Are ye in a bad mood or somethin'? You've been silent and sullen since we started our stroll."

"I'm fine," says Mary. The phone is ringing in the house.

"That better not be yer hippy friend again," says Martin, glaring at the open sliding door. "She's the type that'll have lice and you'll be bringin' 'em home if ye spend any more time together. Maybe ye're willin' to take that chance, but I'm not. Ye need t' do somethin' more sensible with yer time. I can find somethin' for ye if ye can't think of somethin' yerself."

The phone is still ringing. Mary sprints for it, sloshing the remains of her tepid coffee.

"Hello?" she puffs into the receiver.

"Hi ya. It's me." Mary can hear Flower smiling on the other end of the line. "Is it too much to ask you to pick up a bag of wool from my friend on your way over? He's the farmer whose field you cut through."

"Not at all. I'll see ye soon."

"He knows you're coming. He'll leave it by the door. And Mary — don't freak out when you see it. It's big, but light."

"At last! I find the source o' yer especially soft yarn," Mary chortles.

KINDLY INVITATION

WHEN BRUCE POKES HIS head into the research room of the community hall there's nowhere to sit. All the furniture has been removed to the main auditorium behind him, and now sits arranged in a rough circle. He takes a seat facing the stage and stacks a selection of church and town records on the chairs either side of him. His mug of highly concentrated black coffee doused with powdered creamer is tucked behind the leg of his chair. Births and Deaths creaks open on his lap.

On stage Bridget's hips weave a tale of Arabian nights as she criss-crosses the stage. Her voice, high and raspy, shimmers with the crackling clarity of an early century radio actress. A long, black wig compliments the ruby red of her lips.

Below stage, directress Geraldine is reading from a crumpled copy of the script, mouthing Bridget's lines. She suddenly stabs the page and barks, "Stop!"

Bruce catches his book mid-slide before it hits the floor.

"Ye missed the same bloody line again, Bridget," Geraldine says. "Get back t' yer startin' position beside the Sultan. And take off that wig. We aren't in dress rehearsal yet."

"It helps me stay in character," Bridget says, sticking her tongue out at Geraldine. "And it would be a lot easier without this damn walker." Bridget lifts the walker and shakes it at Geraldine.

"We don't want ye t' break a hip before the big night. Do we, aye? Ye'll use it!" Geraldine glowers at Bridget over the rims of her spectacles. "Places!"

Bruce looks down at the open page of Births 1900 to 1925. His attention fastens on a familiar name, Nellie Vera Larkin. The first line on the page is a birth, June 5, 1923, Delia Mary Larkin; sex, female; father, unknown; mother, Nellie Vera Larkin.

"I wonder if it's a common name?" he mutters.

If this is his grandfather's second wife, she had a daughter — an illegitimate daughter. Bruce calculates the child's age. She would have been twelve when they deported his father. Was this child deported with him? He slaps the book closed. Why should he care about his grandfather's second wife. He should be looking for more information on his grandmother, Violet Pillow.

An echoing crash and the clatter of metal reverberates around the hall.

The cast rushes to the front of the stage. Geraldine and the piper are blocking his view of whoever fell. Bruce quickly scans the stage for dear old Bridget. He's halfway to the stage before he sees her, healthy and happy, reclined on a cushion stage left.

"Is it broken?" Bridget asks hopefully.

"Ye old wagon," Geraldine yells, "That's my sister-in-law's walker. I promised we'd be careful with it."

"It was an accident," says Bridget. "I must've knocked it with my foot. Oh, dear. Is it whole?"

Geraldine lifts the walker from the floor and stands it on its feet. She rolls it back and forth. "You're lucky. I think it's fine."

"We need a break, Geraldine," says Cat sighing. At mention of a break the cast heads for the stairs without waiting for Geraldine's okay.

Cat takes Bridget on her arm and they follow.

Bruce knows half the cast now. As they file past, they pat him on the shoulder or poke his ribs and joke about him joining the show.

"Want a cuppa?" asks Joan.

Against the back wall the tin coffee urn is bubbling and spurting, ejecting dollops of hot coffee onto the creamer-dusted table.

"Got one, thanks," says Bruce. He reaches under his chair and holds up the evidence. A blotchy film has formed on its surface.

Cat and Bridget shuffle toward him.

"I thought I might introduce ye t' our star," says Cat as they get closer. "Bruce Connors, this is Bridget Larkin."

Bridget beams and adjusts her wig. "Connors ye say? I've known a few Connors in my time. Where are ye from, son?"

"Here, well, I mean my father, Ambrose, and my grandfather, James Connors, are from here. I'm over from Canada looking for information now that my dad's passed. Information on my grandmother, Violet, too. She died giving birth to my father."

"Ay, she did. A sad t'ing," tuts Bridget.

Joan, Mags, and Claire join them. Joan hands a steaming paper cup to Bridget. "Tea, one sugar," says Joan. "The coffee was thick enough to stand a spoon."

Bridget passes the tea to Cat. "Help me sit, love, before I take that. And, Bruce, dear, I'd like ye to come by my farm. Cat can give ye directions. This is no place to properly meet someone new."

MOSQUITO FARMER

THE WOOL ISN'T ON THE front stoop of the farmhouse as expected. Mary rings the bell. A dog barks and Mary steps back to wait for the door to open. The dog eventually quiets, but there is still no sound of footsteps. She rings again. The dog whines and scratches at the other side of the door. She looks around and decides against trying the bell a third time.

A half-filled watering can sits next to the entry, teeming with mosquito larvae. She tips it over.

The sound of bleating sheep echoes from behind the house. Maybe Flower meant the barn door.

Several more vessels line the path between the house and barn, each filled to the brim with water — and squiggling larvae. "No wonder there are so many mosquitoes." She tips each one over, watching the larvae squirm into the muck.

The bag of wool isn't at the barn door either. She ducks through the horizontal rails of the metal gate and wanders along the alleyway between two sheep pens. The sheep startle in her presence, amplifying the smell of lanolin and sheep dung. It's intoxicatingly familiar and she suddenly misses home. Leaning over the edge of the pen on her right she clucks calmly at the yews. They compete with one another for the far corner. Twelve twitchy pairs of eyes watch her warily. Something isn't right with one of those sets of eyes.

She lifts the loop of rope securing the door to the pen and lets herself in. The one she is interested in disappears behind the others. Edging along the side of the pen so that the sheep are forced to break single file for the opposite corner, she picks out the ailing ewe and grabs hold. The ewe submits, and warily lets Mary check her gums and the lids of her eyes. Mary lifts her tail and inspects her vulva.

"Hmph," she says.

She scoots the rest of the sheep away from the gate and lets herself out. She peaks into the pen opposite. They all look good. One is slightly lame, favoring its back left hoof. That isn't unusual. A glance at any flock of sheep back home will tell you their legs and hooves are not their strongest attribute.

"What are you doing in here?"

Mary stiffens to attention. "I was lookin' for the farmer. I'm here to collect the wool," she says. "Is he here?"

"I'm the farmer. You're scaring my sheep. Maybe you didn't notice the lock on the gate?" He steps aside and motions for her to leave.

He is in his early thirties, tanned, and stripped to the waist. His pants are made of a rough pili material held up by a worn, brown leather belt. His boots are caked in dung. He hasn't shaved; a day's growth of light-brown stubble catches the light slanting through the crack in the barn doors. He makes a sweeping motion with his arms again, trying to herd her like one of his flock.

"Ye needn't fuss. I was raised lookin' after sheep," Mary says, "I know what I'm doin'." She puts her hands on her waist and plants her feet shoulder width apart, undaunted.

"Is that so?" he says. "Well, you'll know then you've stressed them. It's sheering day. I've still half of them to do — and you're not helping." His wide mouth is stern. He flicks his head to toss back his straight brown bangs. His hazel eyes, flecked with amber, would be beautiful if they weren't glowering at her.

"Flower sent me. She said the farmer was a friend of hers — so I obviously have the wrong farm," says Mary peevishly, squeezing past him and starting for the front of the house and the path back to the field.

"Flower's wool is by the shed door."

Mary glances around. "I don't see a shed, so."

"I'll show you then — and you can be on your way." The farmer passes her with long easy strides.

He nudges an inverted bowl with a muddy boot. "Did you dump

all the water out of my pots?"

"Yes. They were breedin' muiscit, though I suppose ye knew that, yer bein' a great sheep and muiscit breeder," says Mary. "Ye're welcome."

"You numbskull. I just refilled those this morning. It's dry. The animals, birds and insects need water."

"Surely they can drink from ponds and rivers," says Mary.

"Do you see a pond or river?" says the farmer.

In the front yard, across from the house, he points to a small wooden hut with a steeply pitched roof. It's poppy red, painted with huge yellow sunflowers. Real sunflowers hang their heavy heads alongside their painted upright rivals. The bag of wool is slumped against the royal blue door.

"I didn't see it," says Mary.

"I think I liked you better the first time we met," he says, turning back toward the barn. "Give my regards to Flower."

"We haven't met. And one of yer sheep has worms. She's anemic."

He stops, but doesn't turn around. "We *have*. And I don't need you telling me about my sheep. I would have noticed if one of them wasn't well."

BLACK AND WHITES

B RUCE BENDS TO HELP Bridget remove her muddy Wellingtons, and receives a swat in thanks. "Wow, you're a very spirited lady," he says, examining his own shoes before removing them. It rained overnight and Bridget's dooryard is deep with muck.

"I do this every day, boy'o. Don't need yer help. But Aye, I was spirited in the day. There's far more to this old lady than meets the eye."

Bruce's shoulders scrape the narrow walls of Bridget's entry. She removes her coat and hangs it on a peg behind his elbow.

"Come in. Come in. I'm glad ye've finally come t' pay me a visit." She clutches the overstuffed furniture for support as she wobbles through the sitting room and into the kitchen at the rear of the cottage. Shelves overflowing with papers, books and photographs stretch floor-to-ceiling. Bruce ducks his head to avoid the low beams and follows Bridget to the kitchen.

"I'm puttin' a kettle on," says Bridget, roughly handling the tea tin as though it is trying to escape.

"Let me make the tea, at least," says Bruce. He pulls Bridget's tea pot from a low shelf and gently sets it on the counter. The tea tray is at hand beside the stove and he gathers cups, sugar and the tea cozy.

When the kettle begins to whistle, Bridget's uncertain pour splashes milk into the creamer and onto the counter. "Oh, bother," she says grabbing a cloth from the sink. "You're managin' the rest, are ye, lad? Bring it on it when ye're ready."

"I love your cottage," Bruce says poking his head around to the sitting room. "It's very homey."

"It's been a home for sure. It had a rough beginnin', but we turned it right in the end."

"Who is we?" says Bruce

"Myself and my sister. That's why ye're here today. I've been alive a long time. It feels good t' be able t' share with someone who'll appreciate the story I have t' tell."

"If you don't mind me asking — do you look after all of those sheep out there yourself?"

"I did, sure. I've got a shepherdess to help now, so. I do the cheese myself; on rare occasion a young gal from the village comes t' help. Ye can buy my cheese in the local shop. It's a beauty, it is."

"You're full of surprises," says Bruce, setting the tea tray on a cushioned ottoman between them and pouring Bridget a cup.

"Now bring me those albums from the shelf over there, lad, the ones wi' the purple covers."

Bridget flips open the first page of each of three albums until she finds what she's looking for among the old black and whites. "Come closer, dear. Ye see this? This is my sister. I want to be tellin' ye about her."

Bridget pulls a photo from the album and presents it to him in the palms of her hands. Three women, arms linked, stare back at him with sunken, owl-like eyes. Sharp collar bones are visible above the narrow lace trimming of their blouses.

"That's her, the one in the middle. This was taken 1914 — she was just nineteen. This is right after her release from Tullamore Prison. She and her fellow suffragettes went on a hunger strike. It would have been bad press t' have Irish political prisoners die in custody . . . especially women, but they made sure to let 'em get awful close t' it before lettin' them go. I'm very proud o' her. She was a militant member o' Cumann na mBan all her life. When we finally got the vote in 1918, it was because of women like her."

Bridget replaces the photo in Bruce's hands with another. Men clad in suits and flat caps stand together, some reclining in front as though posing at a picnic. A few women dressed in long narrow skirts, belted hip-length jackets and pith hats are interspersed with them. It's not a Sunday outing. Half are carrying rifles.

"A hunting party?" he says.

"Easter Rising, 1916. That's Nellie," says Bridget. "That, in the shadow, is our older brother, Tom. But this isn't about him. Nellie, she helped liberate weapons from the RIC barracks in Ballycanew night o' the rising. She was there with the men when the IRA burned it to the ground."

"Wow," says Bruce. "How old were you?"

"I was just gone ten. My parents were active as well, good Catholics and supporters of an Irish Free Republic." Bridget flips the pages and then brings her finger down sharply on the glossy paper, rotating the book for Bruce to see. "These were my parents. There were years o' reprisals. They knew Da was a member o' Sinn Fein. One night, on his way home from pub, the RIC ambushed Da. He was beaten — hit on the head. That was early 1918. We lost Ma t' the flu three months later. Nellie was twenty-three, workin' in a factory in Wexford, supportin' the war effort. She came home to look after me. Then, when my brother returned from the war, he got the farm."

"I'm sorry for your losses. That must have been difficult. I guess you might have heard that my father was sent away as a boy." Bruce smiles slightly. "Are you . . . are you telling me this so I don't feel as bad about what happened to him?"

"No, that's not the reason, son. It's true, though, to say that happiness and fairness were rare things back then. Now look here and drink yer tea."

She produces a photo of a beautiful young woman in her mid-twenties, lipstick, wavy dark hair and a tight knit sweater.

"War of Independence, 1921. That's Nellie. Still smugglin' guns, ammunition, messages. Would ye suspect that pretty girl? She got away with a fair lot. She was a good soldier. Out any time o' day and night when called upon by the IRA or the Cumann na mBan. Men were being shot, executed, blown up. Sometimes on purpose, sometimes accidentally. There was no peace here in County Wexford, I tell ye. But, this wasn't as bad as what came after."

"The village is so peaceful, so friendly. Most of it," says Bruce, adding that last bit for the Connor at the garage. "I can't imagine any of this in such a beautiful place."

"We came out o' that war on top, almost. I was sixteen. Nellie was twenty-seven. Unfortunately, with the signing of the Anglo-Irish Treaty, the country was torn in two. Civil war broke out, sure it did. Ye didn't know which neighbours t' trust — nor which family members, neither. Nellie continued to support Cumann na mBan and de Valera's IRA forces, against the treaty. She became a deft hand at makin' Irish Cheddar," says Bridget, checking his face for understanding. "That's not cheese, love. It's an Irish grown explosive."

"That sounds rather dangerous to be attempted as an amateur," says Bruce.

"She was no amateur. But, it was dangerous — for her. Our brother, ye see, he was pro-treaty." Bridget looks him squarely in the eye. "Things I'm tellin' ye are goin' to get dark, Bruce. But I think ye can handle it."

Bruce pours more tea for them both, even though it's gone cold.

"The Irish Free State showed up at the door one night, knockin' and hollerin'. Tom let 'em in. Nellie and I shared a room. They kicked us from our beds into the yard. The sheep were bleatin' t' raise all hell. They beat Nellie, threatened to beat me if she didn't confess. We were dragged by our hair t' that big chestnut tree across the door yard, and then, they shaved off our beautiful locks. Bobbin', it was called. One o' them took our hair as a souvenir."

"Again, I'm so sorry. You are always smiling and upbeat. I had no idea you'd had such a hard life," says Bruce.

"I'm not finished. So stop interruptin'." Bridget picks at the fraying fabric on the arm of her chair. "Nellie was raped. Worse, Tom was one o' those that did it." Bridget spits on the carpet.

"After that, Bridget never left me alone. I joined her on missions. Helped her make the cheddar. Two months later, Nellie knew she was pregnant and Tom, the shitehawk, suffered an accident. Blown up when his car hit a mine on the road home."

Bruce sits quietly observing Bridget. She takes a long sip of her cold tea and grimaces. She seems almost to have forgotten him.

"Not long after, the Cause was lost," she says, placing her cup carefully back in its saucer. "The IRA surrendered. Life moved on. Nellie had her daughter, Delia. Beautiful thing. We got the farm.

And the sheep. Nellie went back to the factory to make ends meet. She had t'. Little ones cost money, don't they lad? And just so, we were fine, until the '30's, when de Valera betrayed women across Ireland who'd fought for The Cause, turning industry against 'em. Now, do ye know why I'm tellin' ye this Bruce?"

"Well, it's a story that needs telling, isn't it? And to give me a history of Ireland around the time my grandfather was here, I suppose?"

"Partly. Ye see, I knew yer grandfather. Nellie was yer grandfather's second wife. Furthermore, her daughter Delia was raised by me after her passing. Delia grew up and had a daughter. That daughter is Mary. Ye're stayin' in her house."

WOOLLY BITS

MARY DROPS THE cumbersome sack of wool onto the tiled floor of Flower's entry and flicks off her shoes. The dogs lick her ears and hands in a frenzied greeting then excitedly waddle ahead of her down the hallway.

"Hi. I'm here."

Flower's living room glows with late morning sun. Colourful hats and socks for the Filberg Festival are spread out across the kitchen table and living room furniture.

Joni and Mitchel give her hands one last lick and jump onto their cot. They've both received rather bad haircuts since she saw them yesterday. Electric razor tracks meet at odd angles across their sides and back. As much as she detests the farmer, Mary thinks he could give Flower lessons in shearing. Of all Flower's many talents, dog grooming is not among them.

Flower steps in from the back porch, her figure a lean silhouette beneath a white cotton ankle-length dress. "Sorry for asking you to pick up the wool. I wanted to organize what we have before we start on the final batch. I'm spinning more yarn, so we'll have to decide what colours we need before I prepare the dye. Have a seat. I'll make tea."

Mary pulls an ottoman out from under the coffee table and plunks down on it. She picks up an unfinished hat and resumes Flower's seed stitch. The sunlight is warm on her legs and she closes her eyes for an instant, willing away the itch of anxiety still clinging to her from the farm.

"How did you make out with Sam? Was he there when you

picked up the wool?" asks Flower.

"He was there. Thick as manure," says Mary, not opening her eyes.

Flower sets a big mug down on the table at Mary's elbow and plants a kiss on the top of her head. She gathers Mary's hair into a ponytail. "You should let me braid your hair before you go. The red would look so pretty with a green feather in it. Hey, are you alright? You're so tense."

"It's nothin'. I just haven't had a great start to the day."

"Martin?"

"Not just him. Yer farmer too."

"I'm surprised. It's not like Sam to cross anyone."

Flower runs her fingernails across Mary's scalp causing the corners of her lips to lift involuntarily. A shiver runs through her.

"That's so nice," Mary sighs.

"Anytime." Flower kisses the top of her head again and crosses to the spinning wheel by the window. She has a basket of fuchsia wool at each knee. As she pumps the treadle she feeds handfuls of wool from the larger basket through the orifice in the flyer, occasionally twisting small bits of wool from the second basket in with it.

"Why the two different baskets?" asks Mary.

"That's *my* secret," says Flower with a grin.

"I thought ye would be using the wool I just picked up from the farm."

"No," sighs Flower. Her shoulders droop. "That needs to be washed, combed and dyed first. I'll be up most of the night."

"I'll ring Martin and ask can I stay and help ye."

"No need. You've already helped so much. And I don't need to give Martin another excuse not to like me," says Flower, ruefully.

"I'll be happy t' do it, if ye change yer mind," says Mary. "This is a hard way to make a livin'. Ye've a great deal more energy than some."

"I don't just knit. In the spring before the tourist season peaks, I tree-plant. It's good exercise, and good money. Enough to get by on for the rest of the year if I need. The worst part is that it's usually wet, the bugs are bad, and there are no showers for weeks on end.

Plus, I don't sleep well out in the bush on rough ground. But as I say, it's good money."

"Does everyone on the island have different jobs summer and winter?"

"Sam doesn't. Bruce helps on the herring boats seasonally. That can be good money too. If you're willing to do the rough jobs, you can get by with an easy life the rest of the time. And who could ask for better? We get to work out in the forest, or on the ocean, surrounded by wildlife and these crazy views."

"Did ye not want to use yer science degree?" says Mary.

"I gave you a false impression the other day. I never finished it. I dropped out, and afterward, because of everything that was happening in my life then, my uncle offered me his cottage here."

"I remember. Ye said he saved ye from a bad situation."

"He did."

SLUGS

THANKS TO SÉAMUS, word spread and men's yoga is now, improbably, a regular event at Number 8. Bruce knows most of the men now spreading their oversize towels on Martin's back lawn: Eoghan, who plays Ali Baba in the play; his best friend Callum, who plays Cassim; Paul, the piper; and Padraig, who plays the Sultan. Others, including Michael, Cat's husband, he's meeting for the first time. With a steady climb in membership, they've reached their limit, unless Bruce moves the class to the grassy commons out front.

"This is a real treat," says Michael. "Martin chewed my head off last time I was in their back garden. All I did was walk across the grass t' look at his roses. He ran out o' the kitchen, knife in his hand, bellowin', 'use the fricken steppin' stones'."

"Aye, did the same t' me," says Paul. "I had the temerity to touch that deer over there. Always wondered if it was plastic," says Paul.

"We'll have to be careful then," says Bruce. "Lift to Plank, and hold."

"I think ye've a slug problem," says Séamus, inspecting the ground near his towel.

"Focus, gentlemen. Open to Side Plank. Breathing. Count down from twenty. Holding. You're doing great."

"They're on my blanket!" shrieks Eoghan, jumping to his feet and shaking his towel.

A slug lands on Callum's back.

"Watch it, gobshite," hollers Callum.

Towels fly like sails as ten men in white briefs scamper to the safety of the concrete patio. Crouching in a line, they examine the grass.

"Aye, ye've got real problems here," says Michael. "The local garden store sells a good slug killer. Might be the answer to it."

"I'd say chemicals are likely the cause," says Bruce. "What we need are more birds, and insects like beetles. A more varied planting that includes slug repellent plants like rosemary and lavender would help."

"I'm sure Martin has somethin' in the shed for it," says Séamus. "Ye won't have to purchase a thing, if ye're worried about that."

"I'm just a guest here. I couldn't put chemicals on Martin's lawn even if I wasn't against them."

"I've got left-over chips I brought home from pub last night. If we throw those on the lawn, we'll have gulls all over this in minutes. I'll go get 'em," says Séamus, wrapping his towel around his waist and disappearing into the house.

A minute later, Séamus pops up on his side of the fence and handfuls of chips, launched over the giraffe's back, begin to rain down onto the grass.

The class stares up at the sky, waiting.

"Don't know if I've seen any gulls lately," says Michael.

"Ravens then. Do ravens eat slugs, Bruce?" says Eoghan.

"Sure. I think they'll prefer the chips though. We're going to need a lot of ravens. And, they probably won't come while we're standing here watching. Should we move the class out front?"

"Yeah, sure lad," says Séamus. "Let's leave the birds to their chips and slugs. Sure's a good thing Joan isn't home this mornin'. Can ye imagine what she'd say if she caught me out dressed like this." He chuckles.

Unfortunately for Séamus, Cat *is* home, *is* looking out her window as they file past, and will *definitely* be giving Joan the full report later. In fact, Bruce muses, ten men in their tighty-whities doing a Downward Dog on beach towels is unlikely to go unnoticed by anyone.

Assembling on the common, Bruce carefully lays out his newly purchased yoga mat — a low-pile carpet runner — and the class resumes.

"From Downward Dog, left foot forward, rise to Warrior One.

Hold. Cross your arms, Eagle Arms, inhale, lift your elbows. Exhale, rounding through the back. Has anyone ever thought of planting wildflowers on the green? Now twist to Triangle, front leg straightens. I teach something called wilding back home. You could do that here, maybe mix it with communal fruit and vegetable growing. Open your chest. Now come up. Bring your feet together on the towel and — Chair Pose. Feel those thighs burn and reach high with your arms. As you inhale, check in with how you're feeling. What are you carrying around with you today? As you exhale, choose what you keep and what you let go of."

"Council would never approve it. This is village land," says Séamus, screwing up his face with the effort to hold the pose.

"Come back up, forward fold grasping your ankles. I could do up a plan for you to submit to them if you're interested. They may be green, but these open spaces are still deserts for our non-human friends. We need to be thinking about habitat creation and sustainable healthy ecosystems. Walk your fingers forward to return to Downward Dog."

"Somethin' to think about," says Michael. "The common's been this way since forever. And there are some real shites on that council. They haven't approved a thing in years — 'cept their own reappointment."

"Plank."

"We don't have water out here for fruit and veg," says Séamus. "Wildflowers would be nice though, I guess."

"Open to Side Plank. Focus on your breathing."

"Jesus, God, it's killin' me," says Callum, one leg up in the air for some reason.

"This is a piece a piss," retorts Eoghan. "You've got the muscles of an auld woman."

"How 'bout we yoga free-style, and I twist ya into a pretzel so tight Fiona won't be able to find yer willy come weddin' night," sneers Callum.

"That's enough guys," says Bruce. "Anyone else getting tired?"

There is an affirmative rumbling and nodding of heads.

"Let's come to the centre of our . . . towels, and take our bodies from Extended Puppy, knees apart, into Child's Pose. Listen to the sounds around you. Hear the flap of bird's wings, insects buzzing above the grass. We are grateful to Mother Earth for all she provides.

"Except the bloody slugs, eh Bruce!" yells Eogan.

"Thank you, Eogan. When you're ready, move with me into Hero Pose. Deep breath in. Big sigh out. I thank you. Namaste. The divine spark in me bows to and sees the divine spark in you."

"Namaste," repeats the class.

A THOUSAND CUTS

MARY SLIDES MARTIN'S egg onto a plate and nudges his bacon and fried tomato to separate corners so the yoke won't touch them when it runs. The toast pops and she cuts it into four triangles.

"I'll be havin' the raspberry jam this mornin'," says Martin. He refolds his newspaper and tucks it beside his placemat.

"Comin'." Mary places the warm plate in front of him and returns to the kitchen for the butter and jam. Her toast pops and she tosses it onto a side plate, burning her fingers on the metal in her haste. She spins the kitchen tap and thrusts her fingers under the cool stream.

"My toast's goin' t' be cold by the time ye get here with my jam," reminds Martin.

"I burned myself. I need a minute."

Martin shakes his head in a way that implies burning herself is the result, once again, of complete incompetence. She sees him and her mood drops a stitch.

"Were yer own legs sawed off in the night?" Mary shuts off the tap, grabs the butter and jam and sets them down hard in front of Martin. "Here ye go."

She sits down with her own plate and stares at it. She's forgotten something. The coffee. She returns to the kitchen and pours two cups. She takes a big gulp of her own while her back is turned. A comforting heat spreads through her chest. She takes one more. She can't remember when she started doing this. Why should she feel guilty about enjoying a small part of her own breakfast while it's still warm?

"Do we have more o' this jam?" says Martin.

"It's good, isn't it? I bought it at the market. Made right here on the Island," says Mary, coming back to the table, coffees in hand, feeling calmer.

"This butter is hard as clay." Martin holds up a triangle of scraped toast with one hand and his knife, a pat of butter stuck to its tip, with the other. "Ye know better, sure, than to wait till mornin' to refill the butter dish."

Mary responds automatically, rising from her chair and reaching out in a long-practiced manner. "Here. Give it t' me. I'll warm the butter in the oven a minute." Her coffee cools on the table.

"Why bother. Ye'll probably melt the whole lot. I'll just have my toast without butter this mornin'."

Mary thinks of responding, then shrugs and sits down. Her toast is stone cold. She reconsiders. "Well, I want butter, so I'm warmin' it for my own." She takes her coffee and the butter back to the kitchen and turns on the broiler. She pulls a cookie sheet from Bruce's oven drawer and puts the butter dish in the centre. Watching the butter through the glass, she takes two more sips and then quickly flicks the oven off.

"Have ye overdone it?" asks Martin.

Without replying, Mary sits back down at the table and butters her toast. She drops a generous spoonful of jam on top and takes an angry bite. Slowly, her shoulders relax. Her eyes close as she takes another long, languorous sip of coffee.

"What are ye up to today?" asks Martin, swirling a forkful of tomato through his egg yolk.

"I'm not sure yet."

"Ye should try stayin' here with me. I could use yer help in the garden — if ye can be careful with me shears. There's nothin' technical about this stage."

"Ye know I'm not that interested in gardenin'."

"Not that interested. Jaysus sake, where do ye go all day? For all I know ye could be shaggin' some bloke, lettin' him feel up yer jelliers."

"Don't be so crass, Martin. Ye're ruinin' the mornin'. I'm just not willin' to help ye turn what looked like a perfectly good garden

. . . oh forget it."

"Ye're the one ruinin' the mornin', Mary. Are ye insultin' my gardenin' just so that I'll be happy to be rid o' ye today? Maybe ye fancy yer new girlfriend. Is that it? The two o' ye off friggin' your gees." Martin laughs.

"Stop, Martin. You're meltin' my head. And ye wonder why I don't want t' spend the day with ye."

"It's all in good banter, Mary. All in good banter." He reaches across the table to her with a big grin on his face. "You've never had a sense o' humour."

Mary pushes back from the table, grabbing the empty plates and cups. She drops them roughly into the sink. The clatter makes her think better of it and she separates Bruce's plates to make sure she hasn't broken anything. A throb ignites behind her eyes and suddenly she can hardly think straight. She looks over the sink, through the window. The calming meadow view of their first days is gone; she shudders at the new vista, sheared, shaped, wasted.

In the bathroom she splashes cool water on her face and drinks from the faucet. Martin loops his arms around her waist from behind, placing his head between her shoulder blades.

"Ye aren't mad are ye? I'm just bein' funny, Mary. We'll spend the day together. Just you and me."

"That wasn't funny, Martin. I don't know why ye think it was."

"Come on. This is our holiday. Let's work on this project together," says Martin, tickling her ribs to make her squirm.

She smiles, and it makes her madder.

"I don't want t' work on Bruce's garden. I'd rather we went for a walk and explored. Can we not do somethin' that I want to do?"

"Walks are a useless waste o' energy. We can get our exercise in the garden. It's because ye have no imagination for this kind o' thing, ye can't see the vision, Mary. It's just like when we redecorated the house. Trust me. Bruce is goin' to be very happy. And I can use yer help."

"Excuse me, I have t' dry my face." Mary wiggles out of Martin's grasp and buries her face in the towel, taking as much time as possible. "I'm goin' to use the washroom. I'll be out in a minute."

She closes the door behind Martin and sits down on the toilet to rest her face in her hands. She's been sitting like this for a while when the doorbell rings.

She can hear Martin talking. Perhaps it's someone selling door-to-door because he sends them away. She sighs and gets up. She flushes the toilet, even though she hasn't used it, and then washes her hands, taking a few more sips from the tap.

"Who was that?" she says, coming into the living room.

"Just that hippy, Flower. She wanted to know could ye come out t' play, but I let her know ye were helpin' me in the garden today."

"Ye shouldn't have done that." Mary yanks open the front door and runs up the walkway.

"Flower?"

She runs to the road and looks both ways. Flower has already disappeared.

A roiling, blistering anger fulminates within her. She's ready to push Martin over when she returns to the living room. Stopping just short of him, she yells, "How dare ye do that. Ye could've come t' get me. Ye had no right. Flower is *my friend*!"

"Sure I have a right. This is my house. Ye're my wife. I set the rules."

"What the feck?" She is surprised by her own cursing. "God damn ye to hell." Why should she control herself? "And this is Bruce's house, not yer's. And I am not yer property." She backs away and grabs her hat and shoes from the door, not bothering to put them on until she's outside.

Mary starts walking and turns left instead of right at the end of the drive. No destination in mind, she simply has to move, her rage is so incandescent it feels as though it could consume her if she stops.

By the time she settles she finds herself at the market. The sun is hot overhead and she has no money to buy a drink. She remembers the fountain in the library. After using the washroom, she takes a long drink in the foyer, enjoying the library's cool, slightly musty scent of ink, leather and paper.

A table near the checkout desk hosts a colourful display. A large sign reading *SPECIES AT RISK* is tacked to the bulletin board above it. Mary picks up pamphlets and unfolds them randomly. There are several on whales, glossy and professionally printed. Another describes the local herring stocks, still more on native plants, one on invasive species, and a how-to pamphlet on raising bees. Alongside the pamphlets are a collection of books on the same topics. One cover photo looks vaguely familiar.

"Welcome to the Library."

Mary jumps. A green-haired woman, visible from the nose up, has been sitting behind the counter just a few feet away.

"Hi ye, sorry. I didn't see ye. I hope this is alright. I just came in to get a drink and then noticed yer display."

"It's there to be noticed. You're welcome to the water, but we also have books, and you're welcome to use some of those as well," she says. We have romance in the back, mystery here at the front, local history to your left, and picture books in our reading room to the right. It's a good place to sit on a hot day. Stay as long as you like."

"Thanks." Mary looks at the large black and white clock on the wall behind the librarian. It's not yet gone noon. "Do you have a phone I could borrow?"

"Of course. Local call?"

"Yes," says Mary. She takes the receiver from the smiling woman and puts her finger in the rotary dialer. As she spins the first number she realizes she can't recall the last four digits of Flower's phone number. Because the librarian is now watching, she dials a random seven-digit number and then places her finger on the cradle to end the call. She holds the phone to her ear and waits. After the count of ten she hangs up the phone. "Thank you. No one there."

She's not ready to go home, but now it's too hot to be aimlessly walking outside.

"Is there something particular you might be interested in?" says the Librarian, pulling Mary out of her thoughts.

"I think I'll just browse."

"Alright then. I'll be here if you need any help."

The reading room is bright, with four comfortable leather chairs. Mary pulls a large picture book of Vancouver Island from the shelf and melts into the soft cushions. She is still angry. Not only would she have preferred seeing Flower today to spending her day alone in a library, but Martin bloody embarrassed her in front of her friend. She doesn't need Flower to draw conclusions about her and Martin, beyond what she has chosen to share already.

Not even Cat knows how much Martin drives her mad, how less than perfect everything has turned out to be. The marriage course, when they took it, promised she and Martin would be on the same page, that they would collaborate, and continue to share the same values. If she had been upfront then, not acquiesced to everything he wanted, pretending she wanted the same, she might have a family now. Or maybe a job like some of her friends.

She sinks deeper into the soft leather of the easy-chair and spins toward the window. Friends and couples pass by, unaware she's watching them, watching their faces, deep in conversation. She watches their body language, their natural drawing together as they talk. She really hoped this honeymoon would fix what was broken, but she's fighting with Martin more than ever. She needs Father Fingal's advice. It's just not right that she can only see herself, her real self, when Martin's not around.

CANDLELIGHT DINNER

SEVERAL HOURS LATER Mary says goodbye to the librarian and heads home, via the most indirect route. The heat of the day has ebbed and her temper with it. She wants to lie down but is in no hurry to face Martin. With any luck he'll be in the garden when she returns. Maybe she can sleep before making supper.

Dragging her feet up the drive she listens for the sound of chopping or digging in the backyard, but the garden is quiet. She puts her hand on the doorknob, steeling herself for another confrontation. Among other things, Martin will be unhappy about having had to make his own tea.

She flips off her shoes and hangs her hat on the peg. All is quiet. She may get her nap after all.

"Finally. Ye're back," Martin calls from the dining room. He doesn't sound angry.

Mary pokes her head around the corner. Martin has set the table and lit two tapered candles. A box of pizza is open on one end.

"I made ye dinner. Can ye forgive me, Mary?"

He pulls out her chair. His smile is warm. Unexpected. She doesn't know what to say.

"Aren't ye goin' to sit down? It's still warm, and yer favourite."

"But ye don't like pineapple."

"I'll live. I wanted t' do somethin' special for ye. I don't know what I did this mornin' to make ye so mad . . . but I did somethin'. I love ye, Mary. Will ye smile for me again, let us go back t' how things were?"

Out of energy, Mary accepts the offered chair. A cacophony of thoughts and feelings reverberates in her head.

"There ye go. That's my girl," Martin coos. He sits opposite her and slides a piece of pizza onto each of their plates. "Now doesn't this remind ye of how it was when we were first married? Ye were a terrible cook and a special night used to be take-away with candles."

Mary bursts into tears. Is that how it used to be? Who was she when she fell in love with Martin?

"What's wrong? Don't tell me I said somethin' wrong again. Jaysus," says Martin. He isn't mad. He sounds confused. She feels bad for him.

"No. Ye didn't. I'm tired. I'm disappointed, maybe, that this doesn't seem like much of a honeymoon so far."

"It was yer idea t' call it a honeymoon. I didn't really want t' come. The summer is when I most like to be in my own garden. Ye can't blame me for wantin' to at least spend my time in Bruce's. It's what makes me happy. One look at the misfits on this Island and, no offence Mary, I was grateful I'd somethin' t' do."

"Misfits?" The word irks Mary with its pettiness. "Everyone I've met is really nice, Martin. I think ye're just makin' excuses to avoid spendin' time with me. If it wasn't for Flower, I'd be completely alone."

"I'm not goin' to be convinced t' start goin' barefoot, wear burlap and not wash my hair, if that's what yer expectin' o' me." Martin takes a big bite of pizza and stares at her inquisitively. "I'm not goin' to change who I am," he mumbles.

"I'm not expectin' ye to. Could we not plan t' go out together, try doin' somethin' different than what we do at home?"

"What is wrong with what we do at home? I'm quite happy with our life. We have our hobbies. I have my work. We have a good community wit' the church. We're good people."

Mary takes a bite and chews slowly, thinking. Martin does the same. They watch the candles flicker. The fading sun paints their rosy silhouettes on the far wall.

"I'm not happy," Mary whispers.

"What?"

"I've no hobbies of my own and I don't have a job. My life always revolves around yers."

"Are ye jokin'? Ye seem happy t' me. I think I give ye a pretty good life."

"Don't get mad, Martin. I think I should be able to say that. If ye don't think so, then maybe we should meet with Father Fingal. He holds marriage-counsellin' classes at the church. I've been thinkin' a lot about it this afternoon. There's no point in just me goin' to see him."

"Wow." Martin throws down his napkin. "While I've been home thinkin' o' how to make ye happy, ye've been thinkin' about how bad our marriage is?"

"No."

"I'm sorry this holiday's a disappointment to ye," says Martin. "I'll spend more time with ye if ye want, but ye have t' meet me part-way. Ye spend time in the garden with me, doin' what I want t' do, and I'll spend time doin' whatever crazy hippy thing you've come up with, within limits."

Mary pictures herself on the beach, naked, staring up into a strange man's groin. Definitely out of limits.

"Martin, I'm not goin' to make ye do somethin' ye'll just complain about the whole time." Mary stands, abruptly, smothering the candles with dry fingers. "I can see ye still have a lot to do in Bruce's garden. And I've been fine explorin' on my own. How about, for now, we keep doin' what we've been doin'. When we get home, we can talk about seein' Father Fingal. Agreed?"

"What are ye puttin' the candles out for? We still have dessert," says Martin going to the kitchen for the lighter. He relights the candles and lifts the lid off of a Sara Lee chocolate cake. "Will ye sit down a little longer?"

Mary sighs and takes her seat. The cake is good.

"Ye haven't answered me, Martin."

"I'm not goin' to counsellin'. Word will get out that there is somethin' wrong with us. We won't be able to show our faces in church again. What if the teachers at school find out? End o' story."

"Cat and Michael did counsellin' with Father Fingal."

"Ye see? Nothin' stays private. I think what ye really need is for me to take ye to bed and prove to ye how much I care about ye. Isn't that right?"

ENERGETIC EMBRASE

THE MOON IS JUST SETTING on Village Gate. Earlier than usual, Bruce shuts the front door behind him and steps into the pre-dawn air. Mornings he explores the countryside, timing his arrival in the village with the first delivery of ginger cookies to the general shop. Today, he'll have to collect his cookie late. Today he's fulfilling a promise to Cat and the gals.

With three pairs of divining rods tucked into his coat he waits in the middle of the road for the others. He'll leave a gift, perhaps a plant, for Mary and Martin — an apology for destroying their coat hangers.

Joan's door opens and she backs out, shushing Séamus with a finger to her lips. Cat's shadowy figure approaches from across the way, Claire on her heals.

"We'll meet Mags and another friend at the graveyard," whispers Joan. "Keep yer torches off til we're beyond the bend."

As they swing their legs over the graveyard wall, bird song fills the void left by the lazy retreat of the fog. Bruce's pants are wet to the knee. Long grassy clumps twinkle pink and orange with dew; the thinnest sliver of sun breaks over the horizon.

"Why all the secrecy?" he asks.

"Genuinely . . . if someone sees us, we'll be accused o' witchcraft," says Cat.

Bruce chuckles.

"She's dead serious," says Claire.

"Are you sure you want to do this then?"

"Are ye jokin'?" they say in unison.

"I don't want to get you in trouble."

Mags and a short rotund woman reminiscent of a dinner roll appear around the wall of the church parking lot and begin picking their way between the headstones.

"Bruce, this is Fiona, she works in the salon with me," says Mags.

"Nice to meet you, Fiona," says Bruce, bowing.

Fiona giggles. Bruce takes the soft hand she offers, marvels at its rainbow-coloured fingernails and gives it a squeeze. Her hair, arranged in various top knots and ponytails, matches the sunrise.

"Our Fiona is young and naïve, so, and we've taken her under our wing before her big weddin' in August," laughs Cat. "With any luck, this should help corrupt her."

The six of them form a semi-circle around Bruce, each with their hands clasped nervously in front of them.

"Go ahead and pair up," says Bruce. "We'll spread out across the graveyard. An aura's outer layer can be anywhere from five to fifty feet beyond our physical body, intermingling with those close to us. I'll demonstrate and then let you do it," says Bruce, separating out a pair of wires from the bundle he's holding and handing the rest to Mags.

"Hold the divining rods in a loose fist with your thumb on top so that the protruding ends can swivel like a hinged gate," says Bruce. "Do you want to be my model, Cat?"

"Of course I do."

"Great. Okay, move down that way about thirty paces, to the furthest headstone."

Cat takes her position.

"To find our auras we first have to calibrate the divining rods," says Bruce. "You ask 'what is positive' and watch which way the rods move. We must use our energy force and intention to detect what we wish to find. You next say, for instance, 'I am looking for Cat's aura'." Bruce aligns himself with Cat.

The others squeeze in to watch the rods.

"It would be better if you moved back so we don't confuse the rods." Bruce starts again. "What is positive?" The rods cross. "What is negative?" The rods swing wide.

"Jesus!" says Claire, crossing herself. "It *is* witchcraft."

There is a tremble in her voice and Bruce turns to look at her.

The others shift from foot to foot, either with nerves or damp cold. He smiles reassuringly.

"I am looking for Cat's aura," he says.

Behind Bruce all six now cross themselves. He steps slowly toward Cat. The rods swing outward, waver, and then when Bruce reaches a spot on the grass ten feet from Cat the rods swing toward one another. The others rush up behind him. Bruce continues to close in on Cat. When he's a foot away they cross completely to form an X. Smiling, he hands the divining rods to a shocked Cat. "And there you have it," he says, pleased. "Everybody, now it's your turns."

Cat, Mags and Joan nervously chatter and giggle as they find positions along the top of the graveyard. Their earlier fears forgotten, they cackle like tv witches, pretending to cast spells on one another. Claire, Fiona and Séamus wend their way to the bottom, spreading out like players on a hurley pitch, the better to separate their auras from one another.

Next to Bruce, Mags hesitantly says, "What is positive?" and then lets the rods drop to her side. "Are ye sure 'bout this? Don't ye think we might be conjurin' up evil spirits? How can a coat hanger be doin' this without spirits at play? Unless ye were makin' the rods move yerself?"

"Nope. It's not me. It's the energy that makes them move. Try it and see. I promise no harm will come of it. It's science not magic. Although, I confess, I don't know how it actually works."

Cat and Joan march between the headstones, divining rods thrust straight out at chest height.

"It's workin'. I found Séamus's," squeals Joan. Séamus lets her get a little closer and then rushes forward to take a turn.

"It does work!" shouts Mags. "Here, Fiona. Do me. I swear to ye, I wasn't movin' 'em. They move on their own."

"It's like Ouija board," says Fiona, hushed. "This is too craic. Wait till I show Eoghan."

They skip up and down between the gravestones, compare the size of their auras, switch places, run to opposite corners of the graveyard and start again.

"Before we're done, gather round me with just the outer edges of your auras touching mine," says Cat. "It'll be like ye're givin' me a giant energy hug."

Out of the corner of his eye, Bruce sees someone slip behind the walnut tree at the back of the church and then trot off around the far side and out of sight.

"That's the spirit," says Bruce. "You'd better measure mine, in that case, so all six of us can gather 'round you."

IN THE FLESH

MARY SPREADS HER BEACH blanket and kicks off her sandals. She hasn't had as much time for the beach this week. The day Martin turned Flower away, Flower hadn't just been making a social call.

Thanks to a customer at Flower's Co-op stall buying a large order of hats, she was suddenly short of stock for the festival. Flower had come to beg Mary to put in extra hours replenishing their supply. Mary gladly agreed, but it meant knitting at home with Martin, instead of coming to the beach. This morning, together, she and Flower finally completed and tagged the last of it.

Mary hops from foot to foot on the hot beach sand until she has the corners of her blanket square. It's been sunny and warm every day since their arrival. She has a great tan. Better than when she and Cat used to lie out in the garden, covered in cooking oil and surrounded by tinfoil like the Sunday bird.

She unbuttons her skirt and blouse, neatly folds them, and dons her floppy hat. She brought a summer romance novel retrieved from a cute book swap hiding among the trees at the corner of Central and Seawright Road. The book stays unopened as she lazily watches the play of sunlight dancing on the water. A dog cavorts along the water's edge before rushing the shore and trampling blankets with sandy feet and comical, lettuce-spinning convulsions. Mary figures he is likely an escapee from greater Tribune Bay, as no one here seems interested in reining him in. She picks up her book and is soon mid-way through the second chapter.

She listens with half an ear to the gulls overhead. It's warm. Her eyelids are heavy. Words backstroke across the page.

She shakes her head and refocuses. Her eyes high dive off the end of each sentence.

A splash of sand on her body jolts her awake. Fine grains slithers down the page of her book to settle in the gutter. She shakes the paperback, twisting up and cursing the darn dog. But in place of a guileless retriever, a naked man is settling down beside her, his body sharing her narrow blanket.

"Hi ya, sugar tits," he says playfully

He is young and smoothly muscled. His shoulder length hair is thick, straight, and sandy blond, as is his cropped beard and mustache. A silver cross, strung on a black leather cord, glints against his tanned skin. They are almost touching.

"Excuse me? Sorry?" Mary stammers, attempting to tug the blanket out from under him and drape it over herself. This fails. Instead, she's dragged him closer. Their knees touch and she jerks but doesn't pull away.

"I thought I should say hi. We haven't seen you for a few days." He brushes his hair back over his ears. "I'll introduce you to some of the others. You remember me, right? Nick. From the ferry? You gave me a ride."

"No, I mean — sugar tits," Mary says, not liking how breathy her voice has become.

"Well, you've got great perky tits. And I love those freckles. Really cute."

Mary finally sits up and draws her knees to her chest.

"Thanks, I guess. You've got nice — hair," she says, her cheeks flushing.

Nick motions the others over to her blanket.

"Hey there, I'm Blue," says a woman with a great afro. Mary has been waving casually to her since the early days on the beach.

A bald man in his sixties with a snow-white beard introduces himself as Frank. Jeana is a slender wiry woman in her early fifties with tight salt and pepper curls. Luc, like Mary, is a redhead. He is in his mid-twenties, freckled, with a prominent nose and a French accent.

At first, she simply cannot believe she's meeting people — *meeting them!* — while not wearing any clothes. But in shaking hands, so familiar and formal a gesture, she somehow feels less naked. She relaxes.

"Hey, you should come out with us sometime," offers Blue. "We're going mushroom hunting on Saturday if you want to join."

"Yeah, come along. We'll meet at the library around ten," says Nick, giving her an appreciative look.

He is stunningly attractive. She mustn't encourage him. She pulls her knees up to her chest again and directs her answer at Blue.

"I'm helpin' Flower get ready for Filberg. I should check with her first," she says, hoping to be free, mostly because she has never been mushroom picking.

Nick is still looking at her. She flashes him a smile, despite herself.

"Sure. But we've let her know about it, and she usually comes along. A few others will be there too," says Jeana.

"Where are you from?" asks Blue. "Is that an Australian accent? We get a lot of Aussies."

"Ireland. I'm just visitin' for a month. We're stayin' at Bruce Connor's house. Do ye know him?"

"Of course we know Bruce. Great guy. He worked day and night to help me put in a new septic tank before he left. He'd do anything for anyone," says Frank. "Say, Sweetheart, do you like red wine?"

"Sure, aye."

"You just wait then. I've brought some of the best wine you'll ever taste. I make it myself. We'll have a drink in honour of meeting you properly." Frank springs nimbly to his feet. Skin drapes in thin folds over his wiry muscles.

All of her new friends are in excellent shape. Tanned, wild and — she thinks of the dog on the beach — joyful. They have the same free-spirited quality that attracted her to Flower. In a flash of enlightenment Mary realizes it's more than a lack of self-consciousness, it's more than just nudity, it's a complete abandonment of an entire social convention. Without it they seem . . . lighter. She is seized by a deep yearning. She wants to be one of them, whatever it is.

THE DEVIL YOU DON'T

BRUCE DRAGS OPEN THE HEAVY wooden door of St. Moling's church. Cat, Mags, Joan, Séamus, Claire and Fiona file past him. The silence inside has a weight of its own. Prayer candles flicker in dim alcoves. The ceiling is a well of darkness. Light spilling from Father Fingal's open door is the only interruption to the gloom. Bruce leads the way and the rest shuffle forward behind him. They've been summoned. It's evening. Séamus and Joan have left an underling in charge of the pub over the late-supper hour.

"Whatever this is about, I'll take the blame," says Bruce.

"No, you won't, bye" says Séamus.

Father Fingal is slow to greet them when he emerges from his quarters. He is waiting for Geraldine, who emerges in a frenzy of curl adjusting, jacket tugging and skirt brushing. Her movements are especially curt, her expression especially serious. Father Fingal locks the door behind her and deposits the key within the folds of his vestment. The church is cast in greater gloom.

Father Fingal intercepts them half-way down the aisle and raises his hand. Geraldine kneels in a front pew. Her head is turned slightly and Bruce suspects it's not God she is listening to.

"Take a seat," Father Fingal says ominously.

Bruce's spirit slumps. Upon his arrival in Ballycanew, Father Fingal extended him such a warm welcome and spent so much time helping him. Now, he's let the Priest down — he's just not sure how.

Bruce slides heavily into the wooden pew next to Cat. She is shaking and on the verge of tears.

"I've been informed, by a reliable source, o' somethin' deeply disturbin'," Father Fingal says. "I shall ask ye t' pray wit' me now."

> God be with you, brethren; stop, ye thieves,
> robbers, murderers, horsemen and soldiers, in
> all humility, for we have tasted the rosy blood of Jesus.
> Your rifles and guns will be stopped up with the Holy blood of Jesus;
> and all swords and arms are made harmless by
> the five holy wounds of Jesus.
> There are three roses upon the heart of God;
> The first is beneficent,
> The other is omnipotent,
> The third is his holy will.
> You thieves must therefore stand under it,
> Standing still as long as I will.
> In the name of God the Father, Son and Holy Ghost,
> You are commanded and made to stop!

The seven of them exchange glances, confused. No one speaks for a long moment.

"Father, forgive us," says Cat.

Mags puts a hand on Cat's knee. "Honestly Father, we didn't think we were doin' anythin' wrong. Look at Mother Mary for instance, she's got one."

"Got one? There is no connection between the Virgin Mary and the sin for which ye're guilty, young lady," says Father Fingal.

"Her halo," says Mags.

"It's my fault," Bruce says, "I put them up to it. They warned me someone might think it was devil worship. It's not. I'm a spiritual person despite — ."

"Devil worship?" says Father Fingal, touching a thumb to his forehead, lips and chest. "When Geraldine came t' me, we checked that none o' the graves were disturbed. We surmised ye'd be returnin' in the dark o' night. Now, Lord have Mercy upon ye, am I t' assume this is tied t' somethin' more sinister, like Devil worship?"

"That Holy Joe! The brass neck on her," curses Cat. "I can't pardon it. Anythin' to get in with ye Father."

Bruce takes Cat's hand and gives it a squeeze.

"Can ye spell it out for us Father, what is our sin?" asks Séamus.

"Grave robbery. Treasure huntin', some call it." Father Fingal's voice echoes in the vaulted beams.

"You'll forgive us, Father," says Séamus, biting back a laugh, his fist between his teeth.

A jet of air shoots from Cat's flared nostrils. She erupts into hysterics.

Bruce relaxes with relief, but then Cat's laughter infects him as well.

Father Fingal gapes.

Geraldine rises from her prayers. "Father, look upon them, see their wickedness! It's the foreigner that put them up to this." Her heavy tread thumps the red carpet. "Have ye no shame? Laughin'? It's him, Father. What do we really know of him? I'll tell you what."

She shakes her finger in Bruce's face, so close that he pulls back to avoid being beat on the nose.

"Ye heard them say it. Devil worship. They want t' pluck our poor, departed Christian souls from eternal rest and defile them for their dark purposes. Ye've seen the way he dresses, Father. Sure as the nose on ye, he's a coven master back in 'is own country."

"I hardly think —," Father Fingal starts to say.

"Jesus! Sorry Father. For to start with, we weren't treasure huntin'," interrupts Joan. "And we certainly weren't plannin' on raisin' a corpse from eternal rest. Bruce was showin' us how to use divinin' rods." She nods at the rest of them.

"That's not what Geraldine saw and heard," says Father Fingal. "Ye were searchin' for somethin' above the graves and then convened in a circle."

"It was a pentagon, Father. A pentagon," corrects Geraldine. "Ye were chantin'. And usin' metal detectors."

"It was a hexagon, actually," says Bruce. "No chanting that I can recall. Chattering possibly. It was a chilly morning."

"Geraldine, ye need yer eyes checked," says Cat. "Where do ye get off accusin' us o' devil worship. Ye've known me all my life. I come to church regular, so. For all o' the right reasons, too, mind. Can ye say the same? Ye might as well accuse us o' being from Mars."

"I can assure you, we were only using divining rods," Bruce says, sensing that the full truth may not get the others out of this scrape.

"Fie, Father! Ye don't believe 'im, do ye?" says Geraldine. "He'll cause nothin' but trouble while he's here."

Father Fingal folds his arms. His hands disappear into the sleeves of his cassock. His look of disappointment remains, but its edges have softened considerably. "So, the seven of ye are tellin' me I have no one to task with scrubbin' the gravestones?"

"No, Father."

"Go without penance. Best stick to the fields from now on. There is no sense lookin' for water among the dead."

"Thank you, Father."

"It was a simple mistake on Geraldine's part, mind. Ye mustn't hold it against her," says Father Fingal.

"No, Father."

PAPER OR PLASTIC?

MARY'S GROCERIES WOBBLE along the Co-op's check-out conveyor. The elderly man ahead of her pulls out his cheque book. He focuses his attention squarely on the top right corner of the cheque, hovering his pen above the date box. He looks helplessly at Mary.

"It's July 22nd," she says, giving him a reassuring nod.

"Thank you, dear. Seems only yesterday it was March." He fills in the date.

Mary nervously eyes the shoppers passing the checkout line. A man emerges from the aisle opposite with a full trolley and she crosses her fingers he doesn't join the line behind her. The new her can undress on the beach but, when it comes to feminine hygiene products, she feels the less the other sex is reminded of her monthlies the better. Her family size box of Raisin Bran doesn't fully cover the seven boxes of tampons hidden beneath it.

The cheque-writer looks at the total on the register, makes another doodle on the cheque, then squints up at the register again.

Mary sighs with giddy relief when a woman in her early 50's reaches for the plastic divider and lifts milk, vegetables and a gardening magazine onto the belt.

"I love that garden shed on the cover of yer magazine," Mary says, "I almost bought it just for that."

"It's whimsical isn't it. I'd need to be a damn sight better painter to reproduce it though."

Seeing the shed, Mary is reminded of the farmer and his brightly painted one. The conveyor belt lurches into action. The cheque has been completed, its author now shuffling to the exit. Mary turns, digging her wallet from her purse.

She looks up. There's been a crew change. Nick is now standing at the till, slipping a new cash box into the register. Her breath catches. He looks good. She can't believe his warm naked body was inches from hers just the other day. She quickly grabs a second plastic divider, sweeps the tampons out from under the cereal box and hopes she can be out of the store before the woman behind her notices the addition.

Nick starts scanning her groceries. "Nice to see ya, gorgeous."

Mary pulls random bills from her wallet and holds them out, a silly grin on her face.

His hand rests on the divider. He looks at her inquiringly, "Do you want these on a separate bill?"

Mary contemplates ignorance of the tampons, but the woman with the magazine is looking at her. "A separate bill, yes, please."

"Ok, that will be twenty dollars and seventy-nine cents for this first lot then," says Nick, giving her a wink. While he waits for her to fish coins from her wallet, she can see him studying the tampons. "Weren't you just in here buying tampons two and a half weeks ago?"

"What, so?" Mary says, holding out the cash. She realizes he even looks good in a Co-op uniform.

"The tampons. You bought a box when you arrived," says Nick.

"Ye mean male cashiers actually keep track? I thought I was just bein' paranoid." Mary's face is hot.

"Twenty-six dollars, sixty-five for the tampons," he says.

She is having trouble counting the sixty-five cents in coins. A nickel falls to the floor and rolls under the counter.

"We can't get these at home," she says defensively. "That's why I'm buying so many."

"May I make a suggestion? Hold on to your money for now and switch these for the ones with paper applicators."

Nick leans backward to speak to the teenager bagging groceries at the next till. "Will you get us seven boxes of super-size Tampax please. Thanks, John."

"You'll like these other ones just as much *and* they're way better for the environment. You wouldn't believe how many plastic applicators get washed up on the beach. It says on the box not to flush them but, somehow, they end up there anyway."

"It's fine actually," Mary stammers.

"It's no trouble. He'll be back in a jiff."

Mary's pulse pounds in her ear. Her role in environmental destruction is the furthest thing from her mind as Nick continues to chat about tampons. She pictures the young John rushing to the feminine hygiene aisle, scanning the shelves for her super-size paper applicator Tampax, his face lighting up as he finally finds them, and she thinks about what she just said in defence of buying so many boxes.

She looks to the woman drumming her fingers on the conveyor belt behind her, then back to Nick. "When I said we couldn't get these in Ireland, I didn't mean we couldn't get tampons."

The woman behind Mary clears her throat, "I'm in a bit of a hurry today, Nick."

"This is good information for you too, June. I saw you buy a box of plastic last month. Wouldn't hurt you to switch to cardboard."

"That's what he thinks," says the woman leaning toward Mary's ear, "I'm peri menopausal. Just you wait."

The stock boy dumps the new tampons on the conveyor and scoops up the beach polluters. Nick scans and bags them.

Mary hands Nick thirty dollars and waits for her change.

"See you Saturday, Sugar t —" Nick calls out behind her.

She is through the automatic door with her arms full of cereal and tampons before she can hear the rest.

GO WILD

SÉAMUS INVITES BRUCE IN for a celebratory cup of tea. They've just returned from town council. Michael and Séamus, convinced by Cat and Joan to give the application for rewilding the green at least one effort, succeeded in getting approval, conditional on collecting the signature of every resident.

Bruce attended the meeting as a bystander, sitting quietly at the back of the hall while Séamus and Michael presented the schematic he'd created. Sensitive to the idea that this isn't Hornby, he sectioned the beds of herbaceous plants into distinct traditional borders. He researched native trees and shrubs in a book picked up at the county library and photocopied pictures of each they proposed to use. He thought it a good presentation, and thankfully so did council.

Standing in Séamus and Joan's front entry, Séamus indicates a corner where Bruce should toss his shoes.

"Hang on," says Séamus taking a few steps up the narrow staircase. "I'll just let Joan know ye're here, so." He hollers up to the rafters, "Joanie, Bruce has come t' pay us a visit."

Bruce hears the bathroom door open and the sound of the shower.

"I can't come down, ye eejit. Tell him hallo," says Joan.

"She's just gettin' freshened for the pub. Always got to look her best. I think she worries she has t' complete with all the younger lassies comin' in wit' their lycra, half a ton o' black all around and four sets o' lashes. I don't go in for all that," says Séamus.

"No. I prefer the natural look, myself," says Bruce. "Well done today, by the way. You'd had me convinced there was no hope."

"Well, it's thanks to yerself. Ye did a good job puttin' everythin' together. Come through. Come through. I'll put the kettle on."

Séamus moves a small stack of magazines from the kitchen chair, and Bruce takes a seat. As much as he has grown comfortable with Martin and Mary's pink and orange sitting room, and teal and peach kitchen, this room is much easier on the eyes. The walls of Joan and Séamus's kitchen are covered with the same pine tongue and groove he has in his own kitchen back home. The countertop is a goldenrod yellow laminate and the cupboards a moss green.

Séamus plunks a steaming cup of tea down in front of him. "Milk?"

"Sure. Thank you. Should I worry about leaving a ring on your table?"

"No. We've had that an age. Sure it can take a cup a tea. Here ye go, lad. I'll let ye add yer own milk. So, what d' ye recon? I think Michael and myself should go door t' door explainin' what the petition's all about. Michael's a big man in the village. I don't imagine any would say no, but just so, it wouldn't hurt t' give the project a name. What did ye call this stuff we're doin'?"

"Wilding. It's introducing native species, especially those that provide fruit, seeds and nectar to insects and birds. If you design twisting pathways through the trees and meadow plantings, you'll be able to wander and observe the variety of creatures that use the space through the seasons. You'll be amazed at how beautiful that green will become."

"It sounds like a lot o' work, Bruce. Ye've convinced me, but ye're only with us a few more weeks. I'm concerned we won't know what t' do once ye've gone. Ye've seen my garden. I'm no Martin."

"You'll do alright. Just don't follow Martin's example. This is the opposite of what Martin's garden is. I'll leave a guide, some suggestions for species and the sample garden plan I drew up for the council. If anyone is handy, you could think about installing bird and bat houses in the trees along the pasture line. Start by imagining all the animals and insects you share your villages with and what they need to thrive — you won't go wrong. Whatever you do, though, no pesticides and no fertilizers. If you keep a patch of grass to do yoga on make sure the village council knows not to add chemicals to it."

"Sure now. I can do that. Let's think on a name. How's about we call ourselves, the Society for Wild Things. SFWT. No one round here is goin' to know what wildin' is and I like the idea of us bein' a proper society."

"Great," says Bruce. "We could start the membership with the men in the yoga class, plus the gals. The more the better. You'll need lots of hands initially to collect seeds, perennials and saplings. Even if we don't get the signatures, try planting some berry producing vines in an unused corner. There is that hedgerow over against the field. No one would notice if you plucked a few brambleberry vines from the country roads and stuck them in there. If we get approval soon enough, I can help dig up some of the turf and start beds of native meadow grasses and flowers."

"Ye'll have us raisin' fox and deer before we know it," says Séamus.

"That would be great," laughs Bruce.

"For now, though, let's focus on gettin' these signatures," says Séamus, "for the SFWT."

"I won't mislead you. It will be a lot of work to do the planting, but it's going to be so worth it."

"You've got me rare excited. I might even overhaul my own little patch o' grass."

Bruce looks over his shoulder to where Séamus is pointing. Most of the back garden is grass. It is unmown and dotted with dandelion. There is a narrow border of foxglove, lupin and lavender along the back fence. With so little, there is still more life in this garden than the one next door at Martin's.

"You've got good plants back there for bees and butterflies. You should think of dividing the perennials and donating them to the new society," says Bruce, smiling.

"Joanie's been talkin' with ye and wants me t' break up the concrete out front o' the house and plant veg, edible flowers and our own little apple tree. I didn't know there was such a thing as edible flowers. She's goin' to feed 'em t' the customers down the pub. You've had quite an impact on us Bruce. You stay a year and we won't recognize ourselves."

"Make sure you keep in touch after I leave, will ya?"

"No worries there, lad. O'course we will. Another cuppa?"

"I'd better get going."

Séamus gets up and collects the mugs, moving the petition to the centre of the table. "Ahh shite!" he says, pointing at one of the many addresses.

SECRET SHOPPER

MARY ZIPS UP A PAIR OF pleated jean-shorts, puts on a hot pink polo shirt and stares into the mirror. Ever since her first day on Hornby she's been feeling less and less like the woman staring back at her. Whose clothes are these now?

It's a Wednesday. The co-op market won't be too busy. She'll walk up and see what the stalls at the far end are selling. It's been ages since she bought herself new clothes.

She parts the bedroom curtains and looks outside. Martin has pulled Bruce's chainsaw from the garage and is struggling to start it. They've never had one at home. No need. He yanks the starter cord. The engine hiccups and the blade slews drunkenly sideways. He yanks the cord again. The hiccup becomes a cough. She ought to open the window and holler at him to be careful. She knows from his current expression, and past experience, that her telling him anything, including to be careful, will trigger a long, drawn-out argument about whether she does or does not have respect for his pride. They have only just healed from their big argument and she'd like to keep the peace if she can.

She makes him a sandwich and leaves it in the fridge, then scribbles a note.

The market is busier than she expected. She scans the dresses, skirts and tops waving in the breeze above her head and strung along the walls. She has no idea where to start. What she is wearing isn't her, but how does she find what is? She rummages in her wallet. She only has the money she's earned working for Flower. If she spends more, Martin will notice. She has one crack at this.

A gust of wind suddenly wraps a dress around her head. She spins to free herself from its clutches, but almost falls into a table. She is overwhelmed and realizes that putting together a whole new look with such unfamiliar clothing and fabric is not going to happen today. She weaves between tourists toward Flower's stall, hoping for a brief visit before walking home.

"Mary, is that you?" calls a voice in the crowd.

Mary stands on her toes and searches for a face she recognizes. "Over here."

Perched on a stool outside one of the shops, Jeana from the beach is waving at her. As Mary gets closer, Jeana jumps down and throws her arms out.

Mary sinks into the embrace. "Hi! I didn't know ye had a clothes shop, so. Do ye make these?" Mary looks around with fresh eyes, impressed.

"Some. I import the rest." Jeana takes both of Mary's hands in hers. "Are you looking forward to Saturday? Make sure you bring a basket or bag. We collect all sorts of wild edibles. Not just mushrooms."

"I can't wait, actually. Thank ye so much for invitin' me." Mary looks more closely at the clothes lining the wall behind Jeana. "Hey, this feels silly, but I came t' buy somethin' that's more like what ye and Flower wear. But, now I'm here, so, I don't know how t' find things that go together. I have fifty-four dollars. Do ye think ye can help me?"

"Are you kidding, girl? With your cute little frame, it'll be like dressing a doll." Jeana moves to the far side of her racks and starts pulling hangers and draping clothes over her arm. She sorts through the folded tops on the tables, grabs one of everything in Mary's size, then thrusts the collection at Mary.

In the dressing room with a curtain that doesn't fully close, Mary strips off her top and shorts and pulls on a skirt and top from the top of the pile. She barely has them on when Jeana pokes her head in.

"Great! Do you like them?" Jeana directs her by the shoulders to the narrow mirror just outside the change room. "Beautiful, huh? Let me see that shirt with the orange maxi skirt." She drives Mary back into the change room. Out and in, out and in. There isn't an outfit Mary doesn't like.

In the end she decides on a powder-blue poet's shirt she tried on at the beginning, paired with lavender bubble-leg overalls, two skirts of various lengths, a crop top and a pair of paisley wrap pants. It all comes to sixty-one dollars. She hands over her fifty-four dollars plus seven of the grocery money. She is enraptured by her new clothes, and the way she feels in them will be worth the earful she'll get from Martin when he goes over the receipts next week.

Once home, she stuffs her purchases under the bed. On the walk back, it dawned on her that if Flower pays her again before Friday, she might be able to replace the extra seven dollars before Martin finds out. Until then, it'll just be easier for both of them if he doesn't know she went shopping. She won't need to justify herself. Besides, he made fun of her all evening when she came home from Flower's house with a feather in her hair. He hates it if she changes how she looks.

She'll just dress twice each day — once when she gets up to make his breakfast, and the second time when she leaves the house.

PARTY PLANNING

Bruce presses dirt firmly around the roots of a Marigold and inserts his spade a foot to the right. The border is a small gesture to thank Martin and Mary, and repay them for having destroyed their coat hangers.

The phone rings in the kitchen. Bruce wipes his hands on his pants and rushes for the receiver.

"Bruce, lad, it's Séamus."

"Hi Séamus. How are you?"

"I'm doin' just well, 'tanks. Wondered if ye were wantin' an update on society business. *Project Wild Things* has now got twelve of the sixteen signatures we need. Everyone's well boosted, son. People's been sharin' stories of when they were young and playin' in the trees and riverbank or catchin' butterflies in the fields. They want that for their own wee'uns. It turns out our young'uns don't play on the green as much as their parents hoped they might. They go up the school and hang out where they can't be seen. Our local geriatrics, too, want a place t' walk the dogs and sit and watch birdies. Good reception all 'round, son."

"That's great news," says Bruce. "But what are we going to do about our main problem?"

"Yer guess is as good as mine. I can tell ye, we've no hope o' gettin' Martin to sign this petition. And sure, so, he won't be home in time for the deadline."

"I don't suppose we could call Martin and Mary and fax it to them?"

"I'm tellin' ye, Martin won't put a drop a ink on this. Mary though — if we could get it t' Mary, she would. Accordin' t' Joan, anythin' we send, Martin'll intercept. Mary hasn't signed a thing in her life without his say so."

"Well, let's cross this bridge when we have the rest of the signatures we need."

"I'll keep ye in the loop. Ye really started somethin'. The neighbours livin' around the green at the other end o' the lane are asking how they can get permission t' do the same."

"If I can't save the money for a second trip to Ballycanew, I'm going to want pictures — before and after," says Bruce. "I might even be able to use them in my next book."

"No worries. I'll put Joanie or Cat on it. They're mad into amateur photography. Gotta ring off. Headin' down the pub. Thanks for gettin' the ball rollin'."

"Thanks, yeah. Keep me informed," says Bruce, hanging up the phone. Buoyed by the good news, he heads back to the garden. He digs another hole, smiles as he tosses a chip missed by the seagulls into the bottom and plops a marigold on top. He's been looking for hidden places to improve the diversity of the garden. Martin has a certain ethos at work here that's hard to crack. The fence behind the topiary animals is so clean he suspects Martin of regularly vacuuming it. It occurs to Bruce, he hasn't seen a single spider web.

The phone rings again. He wipes his hands and dashes inside, catching it on the fifth ring.

"Hi Bruce. It's Mags."

"Hey there. This is my second phone call in ten minutes. I must be gaining in popularity," says Bruce.

"O' course ye're popular. Listen now, I'm kind o' short o' time on this. I hate to be botherin' ye, but ye know how I sell makeup? Like, the parties I hold at women's houses, so?"

"I think I recall you mentioning it. Beauty Girl?"

"Yeah, that's right. Fiona is gettin' married soon and we want t' throw her a bridal shower this week. The rehearsals for the play are rampin' up. Startin' Monday, they're every evenin' till openin' night."

"You're all going to do great. I'm enjoying watching."

"You're suppose t' tell us t' break a leg. Thanks a lot," says Mags, in mock exasperation. "Sure now, the reason I'm callin' … we need somewhere t' throw the hooley."

"uhm."

"We can promise not t' break anythin' or get out a hand. We're hopin' ye'll let us do it at Mary's house. Ye wouldn't even have t' leave if ye didn't want — but maybe just stay out o' the way, hang out in the kitchen or somethin'."

"Isn't there anywhere else you can hold it? I want to help, but it's not my house to offer."

"Mary wouldn't mind. In fact, she'll hate that she missed it. The thing is, it's kind of a ladies only type a thing — though, as I say, we don't mind if ye stay — honorary girlfriend and all that. To put it plain, Fiona doesn't know the first thing about sex and we've invited a woman that does a gettin' to know yer body and sexuality thing. She sells things too. Like Beauty Girl but different. We'd really rather not hold it at one o' our houses. Those of us who are single don't have the room and those of us with husbands don't want to be interrupted."

"When?" asks Bruce.

"Saturday night."

"Who is Fiona marrying again? Did you already tell me?"

"Sorry yeah. Eoghan. Ali Baba in the play. Ye met him."

"Oh right. I know Eoghan," says Bruce, looking around the kitchen. It's not a big space. The front room isn't much bigger.

"How many?"

"About t'irteen of us, plus the woman I mentioned, the consultant. We supply all the food, drink, everythin'. Ye just have to open the door. Can we? Please?"

"Sure. Why not? How wild can a wedding shower get?"

NEO WHAT?

MARY WIPES A DIRTY GLOVE across her brow, leaving a smear of mud, sweat and tangled hair. Martin has hired a man with a truck to haul the pile of brush and vegetation to the local recycling depot. She and Martin just need to load the truck themselves. Taking time to roll down the sleeves of a shirt borrowed from Martin, she gingerly lifts stalks of blackberry bramble into a wheelbarrow already heavy with the remains of slashed cabbages, goldenrod and wilted lupin. It's a cool, grey day, which one thing she is grateful for.

Bruce's back garden looks much bigger than it did when they arrived. The ground is dry and bare, except for scattered clumps of daisy and buttercup that stubbornly survived several poisonings. The previously overgrown hedges are smaller and shapelier, but bald in places where Martin's pruning was especially zealous. The fir trees bordering the garden are limbed to eight feet and the forest floor is raked clean.

They have little over ten days left on the Island and she can't imagine how Martin is going to transform this demolition site into anything remotely resembling the garden he promised.

"Hurry back with the wheelbarrow," Martin calls as she starts toward the truck parked on the drive.

She slows. There are large snails all over what used to be the meadow and it takes time to weave around them. As careful as she is she hears a crunching under the front wheel and squirm with guilt. She dodges another, but the wheelbarrow hits a rut and the whole thing tips.

"Oh damn!" she says.

She rights the wheelbarrow and begins reloading it. A blackberry thorn pierces her gloved finger.

"Damn again!"

She whips off the glove to suck her finger, her tongue probing for the thorn. Satisfied nothing has broken off beneath the skin, she carefully puts her glove back on and reaches down to collect another armload of vegetation. Her fingers close unexpectedly on something soft. She pulls her hand free of the branches and opens it. It's a bird; it's head dangles between her fingers. Recoiling, she drops it. Her heel lands on another soft lump. She stares down. There are dead birds all over the side yard.

"Martin!"

"What?"

"You have to come here! What is going on?"

"What? Did you hurt yourself?" says Martin, running over. He peers into her downturned face, his hand on her back.

"There are dead birds everywhere. What could have done this? It's like they all fell out of the sky." She's shaking and squints through tears to find a path back to the house through the bird corpses and crunchy snails.

"It's likely just the new pesticide, it's got neonicotinoids for added punch. I needed to get things growing more quickly and get on top of any remaining weeds before we left. I cleared a few birds off the back patch before you came out and I guess I didn't see these. There haven't been any new ones since — so no harm done. It's just a few birds."

She shakes his hand from her back. "No harm done? This isn't just a few birds! It's a horror show out here. That's it! I'm going in. And you wonder why I don't like helping you in the garden."

Inside, she scrubs her hands and face then makes herself a cup of tea. She watches Martin through the back window. He is red and winded. Then she thinks of the beautiful birds, their colourful plumage covered in dust. "Jesus, what a mess." She crosses herself. "The garden was *so* much prettier when we arrived."

INVASION OF THE BODY SNATCHERS

B RUCE TUCKS HIS FLUTE securely into his vest pocket. It's a short walk to Séamus and Joan's pub on Killenagh Rd. He took the route through the field and as he crosses the churchyard is he reminded of his misdirection to Father Fingal about their early-morning presence in the graveyard. A pang of guilt makes him look over to the bench by the back door, but Father Fingal is nowhere to be seen.

It's bright for 8:00 p.m.. The streets are strangely crowded. As he nears the Wexford crossroad, he notices people weaving back and forth over a stretch of road and sidewalk. It seems early for so many drunks. There must be a special event on. Joan mentioned there would be fiddlers. Would they draw this many people? Or perhaps he got the night wrong, and it's a hurley night.

Nearer, it's clear the drunkards are not drunk. They're young people, walking toward each other, and then abruptly changing course. They're everywhere, little metal rods swinging them hither and thither. His first thought is of Father Fingal as these teens toddle around like Frankensteins and zombies; Father Fingal will understandably jump to the fresh conclusion that the village is possessed. And he'll be to blame.

Bruce stops between two young men. "Excuse me. Hi, excuse me."

"Wah?" the young men say in unison. Intent on every quiver, they don't look up from the rods.

"Can I ask what the rods are for?"

"A friend, sorry yah, showed us how to, like, find force fields usin' coat hangers. We're practicin'. Every now 'n then it works," says the tall, bushy haired youth of about seventeen. "Cool outfit, by the bye."

"Thanks. How did your friend learn how to do it?" asks Bruce.

"From his friend, Callum, who learnt it from his friend's fiancé, who saw a proper warlock do it. I can show ye, if ye'd like."

"That's okay, thanks. I'm meeting friends," says Bruce.

The youth spins and follows his divining rods across the road, without once taking his eyes off the metal.

Bruce has a bad feeling. Is it possible Father Fingal comes into the village in the evenings? Or Geraldine? He turns to leave and then has a thought. He returns to the bushy haired youth and his friend. "You know you can use those to find underground aquifers too. Not as cool, but pretty useful. You could make a bit of cash finding well water if you practice in the fields."

"Yeah? Thanks. Grand."

"Yeah," says Bruce, crossing Killenagh road again. A steady stream of costumers is entering the pub. He hopes the gang saved him a seat. With his hand on the door, he looks back at the zombies. He lets a young couple go ahead of him. Across the intersection there's a kerfuffle. Old Desmond is cowering at the centre of a group of youths pointing coat hangers at him.

Bruce looks both ways and sprints across the road. "Clear off, yeah. Do you think that's funny?" he yells at the mocking gang. He pushes his way to the centre of the now silent boys and girls. "Clear off. And take those home with you. This isn't a playground." Bruce is properly mad.

Desmond is crying. He grasps Bruce's sleeve and hangs on, shaking. His other hand clutches his shopping dolly. Bruce slips an arm over the old man's shoulders and pats his arm reassuringly.

"Do you have a hanky?" Bruce asks.

Desmond lets go of Bruce's sleeve and fumbles in his jacket pocket. "I can't seem to get it out."

A woman in her fifties jogs across the road to them. "Hi ya. I saw what was happenin'. Thanks for dashin' o'er so quick, like," she says. "Desmond, how's about a cup o' tea?"

"I want t' go home," says Desmond.

"What *is* the world comin' t' these days? Young people pickin' on an auld man." The woman thrusts out her hand for Bruce to shake. "Ye'll be callin' me Kate. I've seen ye in for yer messages."

"Nice to meet you properly, Kate. I'm Bruce."

"I want t' go home," says Desmond.

"Okay, sorry love. Ye alright then? Ye've had a bad aul dose," says Kate.

"I go alright, but so," says Desmond.

"Okay, love. Best be home." Kate turns to Bruce and gives his arm a squeeze. "Thank ye, Bruce, for clearin' off those young shites."

Desmond, now somewhat settled, grips his shopping dolly tightly and shuffles off without a backward glance. He's going the wrong way.

Bruce raises a hand to Kate in farewell and in a few strides is in front of Desmond's dolly. "Desmond? My name is Bruce. Do you think I could help you home? I think you live up near me."

"Sure, son. If you'll be goin' that way."

"I am." Bruce looks across the road to the pub. People are still filing in. He turns Desmond in the right direction and then matches his pace. He should be able to get back in half-an-hour.

"Have you lived here long?" asks Bruce.

"All me life. Raised me family here. They's all gone now."

"I'm sorry to hear it," says Bruce.

Desmond shakes his head and mumbles. His lips fold in and quiver; his eyes fill with tears again.

"Should we try getting that hanky out?" says Bruce. "Let me help." Bruce reaches a finger into the breast pocket of Desmond's blazer and withdraws the neatly folded hanky.

Desmond takes it from him and gazes up at Bruce, uncertain what to do with it.

"It's for your eyes," says Bruce.

"Oh. Somethin's amiss, is it?" Desmond removes his thick glasses and wipes his eyes, polishes his glasses and places them back on his nose.

"T'at alright, then?" he asks Bruce.

"Good, yes."

"Here's the school, up on t' left. Almost home. When I was a wee lad, the school wasn't so close. The few days we went t' school, like, ye was run off with a bit a bread in yer pocket. And ye'd have it eaten before ye went to the school, like, a couple o' miles t' school. Ooh, we was hungry the rest o' the day," he smiles and blinks up at Bruce.

Bruce laughs with him.

As they reach Village Gate Bruce says goodbye. He watches as Desmond tries the door of Number 8, curses, spins his cart around and heads for Number 12.

HOOKEY

MARY WAITS FOR MARTIN TO step out the patio door before answering the phone. Flower's been their only caller since they arrived, and she would prefer Martin wasn't eavesdropping on all of their conversations.

"Hello."

"Hi doll, it's me. Special treat. We can afford to take a break from the knitting today. I want to show you the other side of the island with a couple of friends. How about it?"

"I'm sorry ye're so far behind. O' course I can come over t' help," says Mary. She can see Martin's shadow lingering on the pavement. He's on the other side of the sliding door, listening. "What time do ye need me t' be there?"

"Is Martin there?"

"Yes," says Mary lightheartedly.

"If you meet us at the corner of Seawright and Central in half an hour does that give you enough time to get ready?"

"Sure, I can do that. I'll get a quick bite t' eat and see ye soon," says Mary.

"Wear shoes with something over the toes."

"Anythin' else?"

"Tie your hair back. See you soon," says Flower before the line goes flat.

Mary hangs up and without raising her voice says, "I'm goin' over to Flower's to give her a hand."

Martin pops his head in the open sliding door. "What's that, dear?"

"I'm goin' to Flower's to help her."

"Be back in time t' make supper, will ye? I'm gettin' tired o' soup or sandwiches for my tea. I need a good hearty meal. It's hard work out here." Martin's round middle has lost some of its girth, evidence he has indeed been working harder than usual. She feels a momentary pang of guilt at not leaving him enough food each day.

"I'll be back by six."

Mary goes to the bathroom, checks herself in the mirror and looks longingly toward her stash of new clothes. There won't be any chance to change into them without Martin seeing.

He's waiting for her just outside the patio door when she emerges from the bathroom. "Come give me a kiss goodbye," he says. "I love ye."

Mary is suspicious as she approaches him. He normally just lifts a hand in farewell and goes back to his gardening.

"I'm only goin' a few hours."

She kisses him on the lips. "I'm grabbin' a cheese sandwich for myself before I go. I'll make an extra for ye and leave it by the door for later."

At 2:00 she's standing on the corner of their street. Two motorbikes appear over the brow of the hill coming from the direction of Flower's place. Mary's heart is suddenly in her throat. Please may this not be Flower and her friends. She cannot get on a motorbike. People die in motorcycle accidents. A vision suddenly plays before her mind's eye — her severed head on the side of the road, a police officer searching for and finding the rest of her body, its limbs scrambled. Bystanders trying to figure out what part of her is what. Martin finding out she was lying.

The bikes stop, but their engines maintain a high-pitched growl that Martin is sure to hear. Flower lifts off her helmet and shakes out light brown waves that catch the sun. "Surprised? The dirt bikes belong to Nick. We're going over to the other side of the island. Another friend has kayaks he's lending us. And then we'll go fossil hunting. I know a cool spot where people find things all the time."

"I'm not sure I should get on. I told Martin I was goin' up to yer house. What if I fall off, or we have an accident?"

The other rider pulls off his helmet. It's Nick.

"Don't be so worried Sugar Tits. I'll look after you. I've been riding since I was twelve. Put this on and climb on the back."

He hands her a heavy white helmet covered in scratches. She checks it for dents.

"Flower, shouldn't I ride with you?" says Mary, giving Flower an urging look.

"Sorry, but you'd be in serious danger on the back of mine. Nick knows what he's doing. You definitely want to be with him."

Mary pulls the helmet on and tucks her hair back. She fiddles with the strap, getting nowhere. Nick leans over to help her as he might a child.

"Climb on. It's okay. Just watch your leg on that exhaust pipe. It's wicked hot."

Mary puts her leg over the seat behind Nick, wary of the pipe. He shows her where to rest her feet. There is nothing to grip. Panic sets in again. She is just about ready to climb off when he revs the engine and pulls away.

"Put your arms around my waist and hold tight," he calls back to her over the noise of the engine. She does as she is told. She holds on for dear life, praying to God to let her live.

Nick is wearing a thin t-shirt. His body is warm beneath her fingers and his muscles elastic and well-defined.

"You're tickling me," he shouts.

She wraps her arms around him again, embarrassed to be caught unconsciously exploring his body. She rests her helmet against his back and watches the view go by with her head turned to the side. The roads are empty. Nick just has to stay in the centre of their lane and nothing bad can happen. Tall firs line either side of the road, their trunks surrounded by thimble and blackberry scrub. Wild daisies and cornflowers sprout from the dry ditches. There are occasional openings in the brush; trail entrances, some of them marked. Mary makes a note to find them again. If there is an again.

Still undamaged, she lifts her head and looks over Nick's shoulder at the road ahead. He is driving slowly, probably for her benefit. The wind sweeping her cheeks and brow is exhilarating. She recollects speeding downhill on her bike, on the edge of losing control. She takes her feet off of the footrests and stretches them out to the side, just a little, the way she used to as a kid, and laughs.

"Fun, huh? I'm glad you're more relaxed," shouts Nick.

She *is* more relaxed. She opens the palms of her hands so that they lie flat against Nick's sides. She can feel him breathing; the sudden intimacy a shock. She's essentially been hugging a near stranger for ten minutes and hasn't had to make an excuse for it, or for enjoying it. She is *supposed* to be hanging on to him — for safety's sake.

They take a right off the main road. She checks behind them. Flower's knees jut out at a relaxed angle and she only has one hand on the handlebar. The other is soaring and diving in the rushing wind. She's wearing her ripped jean shorts and the breeze has opened the top four buttons of her cowboy shirt. She belongs on a record album.

Nick slows the bike to a stop and helps her step off. It's been a short ride but she feels bow-legged and dizzy when he lets go of her hand. He parks the bike as Flower pulls in beside them. While Flower and Nick discuss what to do next, Mary stands awkwardly behind them.

"Hey, let me help you with your helmet," says Flower, interrupting her conversation with Nick. She unsnaps the strap and lifts Mary's helmet. "You were alright. Did you enjoy it?" Flower smooths out the static in Mary's hair for her.

"I did, yeah. What are we doin' next?"

"We were just discussing whether we should kayak or go fossil hunting first. The tide isn't going to be fully out for another two hours. What do you think of kayaking first and then going to Fossil beach after? It means you might be a bit wet while beachcombing."

"I would love to kayak. I've been noticing people out in them since we arrived. Do you think I could do it? I don't have any training?"

"Of course. You just climb in and paddle. They're totally safe," says Flower. "Nick, we're going to paddle first, okay?"

Nick's hair is sticking up. It's endearing. His shirt makes Mary laugh. It's a cartoon of a bulldog on a surfboard being carried across the sand on the shoulders of a pack of worshipful dogs. The faded caption reads *Rude Dog hits the beach*. It's slightly stretched out in spots and hangs a little loosely across his shoulders. Obviously a favourite.

"What are you laughing at, Sugar Tits?" he says, pulling her into an embrace and bear walking her around in circles. When he smiles his two upper front teeth are slightly prominent and worn at an angle. He is easy to like.

Three kayaks sit near the water, courtesy of a friend who pulled out at the last minute. Flower holds Mary's kayak steady while she climbs in. Nick shows her how to paddle and then pushes her off before getting into his own. She wiggles side to side to check the kayak's stability while still in shallow water. It seems fine but she's nervous of making any sudden movements.

Flower leads, hugging the shoreline. Nick paddles beside Mary, pointing out seals as they pop their heads up to look at them, and eagles launching from the brilliant red arbutus and pallid grey oak trees anchored in the cliff's above.

She's on the surface of a giant aquarium. The water is so clear she can see skulpins darting back and forth along the sand-stone bottom past lazing purple starfish, giant sun starfish, black urchins, kelp, and oysters.

"Let's paddle west past Phipps point and get a view of the ferry," says Flower over her shoulder.

Mary didn't bring a hat or sunscreen. Her cheeks and brow are starting to sting but it doesn't diminish the intense joy she feels being out on the water. The paddling is easy. With no fear of running into anything, she can spend her time looking around. She's in competition with Nick to see who can guess where the next curious seal is going to pop up next. So far, she's winning.

Nick brings his kayak close alongside hers and grabs the side. She grabs for the sides too, worried he might accidentally tip her. "Do you think we could meet up in the evening sometime?" he says.

She looks at him, her tongue poised between two possibilities. "I can't, I'm sorry," she finally blurts out. For some reason she omits the, *I'm married*, that usually accompanies that response.

They've passed Phipps point. Without realizing it they've drifted into the centre of the causeway, between Hornby and Denman islands and are now level with Shingle Spit, the Hornby dock. The ferry is just pulling away from Denman, loaded with passengers.

"If we paddle quickly we can get across the ferry's path in time. Shall we?" says Flower, increasing the speed and depth of her strokes before Mary can respond. Nick quickly gains on Flower.

"Um, I don't think I can," Mary calls out, but Flower doesn't hear her. The current is now carrying her past the Hornby ferry dock. She paddles as fast as she can but in an uncoordinated rhythm.

Nick looks back. He stops paddling, hoping she'll catch up. The current is growing stronger, pulling Mary right of her course. Instead of heading for Nick, she's being drawn into the path of the ferry. A rising panic takes hold of her. She stops paddling and pulls her life-vest straps tighter. The ferry charges toward her. Nick's strokes are urgent but precise. She notes the strain in his arms as his kayak torpedoes toward her. The ferry sounds a warning blast.

Nick is five feet from her when he thrusts out his paddle for her to grab. She overreaches. The kayak tips and she's dumped into the cold water, pawing in vain for the outstretched paddle.

"Swim across the current, Mary. I'm coming," says Nick. The ferry sounds a second warning.

She reaches for her kayak, but the wind has taken the empty vessel from her. No matter how hard she swims or Nick paddles the separation grows.

The current begins to swirl her around and with each rotation the white bulk of the ferry looms closer. It's now as big as an ocean liner and she's a minnow.

"Nick, help me. I don't want to die," she cries.

"I'm coming, Mary, just keep your head up."

She imagines what is going to happen to her when she's dragged under the ferry and fed through its massive propellers. She screams and swallows a mouthful of seawater that comes up as a choking vomit.

Nick gives up trying to catch her and waves his paddle back and forth above his head, shouting, "Help! Person in the water. Mayday!"

In the distance Flower is yelling, but the sound is lost amid the chatter and groan of the engines as they are thrown into reverse.

A wave dunks her and she inhales water. She coughs as hard as she can, but can't get it all out, can't take a full breath. She can't yell. She can only wave her arms. She is tired and the relentless drag of the current is weighing her down with a sense of remorseless inevitability.

The roar of the ferry's engines is suddenly close. Three sharp whistle blasts pierce the tumult, while the deep drone of the ship's siren burrows into her ears. It grows louder with each passing second as she is swept forward. She is dunked, silence; back to the surface, commotion. Flower is paddling, trying to intercept her.

Her limbs feel like stone. She closes her eyes, yielding, accepting. To battle is futile. Help will not reach her — she has never known such fatigue.

She turns slowly in the current to face Nick, to say goodbye, then the ferry, its passengers watching her last moments from the crowded deck, then to Flower, then to Nick again. She sees the effort in Nick's face, how he struggles to save her. She goes under again.

In her watery cocoon she hears a new sound, like the high-pitched engine of the motorbike. Surfacing she glimpses a bright orange boat speeding toward her from the far side of the ferry. A man and a woman in vests are calling to her. For the first time she feels hope. She sobs.

The rescue boat maneuvers into her path and cuts its engine. Two sets of strong hands haul her out of the water and deposit her mercifully onto the bottom of the boat. She feels a blanket tuck around her. The engine chatters to life and she is sped to shore, each ripple of water beneath the boat bouncing the hard deck against the back of her head.

"Thank you," she whispers. The word comes out in a slow drawl. She tries again, "Thank you." The woman in the boat is checking her for injuries, rapidly running her hands over each limb, her torso, and her head. The touch is rough and impersonal, but each movement of the woman's hands reinforces to Mary that she is whole. That all is well again.

When they reach Shingle Spit a crowd of people is waiting to help. Her legs don't work and her face is so cold she can't work her lips.

"An ambulance is on the way," her rescuer reassures her.

"I can't go in an ambulance," says Mary with difficulty. "I'm not from here."

"Get her into the Wheelhouse restaurant," someone from the crowd says. "Get her warm."

Nick is suddenly beside her, lifting her off her feet. She swivels to look for Flower. "Nick, I don't want t' go in the ambulance. I'm okay. I'm not hurt."

"You might have hypothermia. Maybe you should go. They'll be here soon."

"Call it off if ye can, Nick. I'm gettin' better already."

She is lowered to a stool in the restaurant's kitchen. The cooks stare at her. Nick unbuckles her life-vest and pulls her shirt over her head. He takes off his own and helps put her arms through its sleeves. She looks down at Rude Dog.

"Can we have a big mug of hot coffee?" he says to the waitress that's just come in to check out the fuss. "And could you please tell the paramedics when they get here that she doesn't want to go to the hospital." Nick takes off Mary's wet socks and shoes and wraps her feet in a dish towel. He is rubbing her all over.

A hot cup is deposited in her hands. She almost drops it and shouts just in time for Nick to grab it. "My fingers aren't working," she says.

"Let me." He places it carefully to her lips and helps her drink. He warms his hands on the mug and places them on her back and chest. He instructs the waitress to call a number he rhymes off to her. "Say we need a ride urgently and let him know where we are. If we're gone by the time Flower gets here, can you please let her know that I left the kayak on the beach and I've taken Mary home."

"Sure, Nick," says the waitress. "I'll keep an eye on the kayak and lock it up if Flower doesn't come. I'll go make the call."

"No. I can't go home," blubbers Mary. "I can't go home like this."

"Okay. Flower's house?" says Nick.

"Yes," says Mary. "Do you know what time it is?"

Nick pokes his head out the swinging door to the kitchen and checks the clock. "5:30."

Tears prick at the corners of her eyes. She is sleepy — and

worried.

"Hey, Sugar T, you're safe. Are you feeling warmer?" says Nick. He gives her a hug and more coffee. "You did great. That was pretty scary."

"I'm not cryin' because o' the accident," sobs Mary. "I'm cryin' because I lied t' Martin and now he'll be furious with me, and I was supposed t' be home by 6:00."

"Wow. Okay. Let's not focus on the fact that you were just rescued from potentially being run over by a ferry, or drifting off to join the merpeople. I'm assuming Martin is your husband?"

"He is. I'm sorry I didn't tell ye I'm . . ."

"What? Married? I had no idea." He slumps, crestfallen. "I'm joking, Sugar Tits. If you remember, I met him on the ferry." He rubs her arms briskly. "Stay with me okay. No nodding off."

"The ambulance is here and no sign yet of Flower," says the waitress.

Two men in blue jackets push a gurney into the kitchen before the waitress can exit. Mary tries to protest, but one look at her condition and they place Mary prone on the stretcher. There is a blood pressure cuff on her arm, and she feels the cold sting of a stethoscope on her chest. Nick is beside her, whispering gentle encouragements. Then she is wheeled out the door.

GOOD VIBRATIONS

THE PUB IS EVERY BIT AS LIVELY as Joan led Bruce to believe. His toe has been tapping since he sat down. The fiddlers are amazing. And he, Cat, Michael, Mags, Claire, Fiona and Eoghan have a table right next to them.

The song ends, everyone hoots and whistles appreciation. In the momentary intermission, the volume of conversation rises.

The senior fiddler, looking comfortable in a tweed jacket despite the heat of the pub, announces conversationally, "Stacks o' Barley." Clearly everyone has been listening while talking, for the room falls silent as the fiddlers touch bows to strings. A button-accordion wheezes to life.

Bruce's heart quickens with the pace of the music. It's not just the music. A rare joy has crept over him. He claps in time to the music, jigs his feet under the table. He is surrounded by people of his father's homeland. If his father had never left Ireland, he might be sitting in the very spot Bruce is now, enjoying the warmth of friendship and community that he himself is.

A young man with a guitar arrives and pulls up a chair next to the fiddlers. He joins in seamlessly as the tweed caller says, "Margaret's Waltz". The mood sobers. The listeners sway shoulder to shoulder.

Bruce looks around and sees his yoga mates in the crowd. They nod to him and raise their hands to Anjali Mudra. He knows now that they are not just mimicking the gesture with which he ends each class. Despite the distracted beginnings, and their occasional impish behaviour, they understand that when they say 'namaste' to one another it is an expression of respect.

The musicians finish, exchanging their instruments for drinks. A young woman in a skirt and knee-high socks arrives with her bodhrán and sits down sideways on the spare chair at Bruce's table.

"Ye don't mind, do ye?" she says over her shoulder. She does a double take. "Ye're new here. Welcome to ye."

"Thanks."

"Sure ye might've noticed those eejits wanderin' the village wi' coat-hangers. Don't go tellin' folks where ye're from that our heads 'r cut a marley. The boys o'er in neighbouring county Wicklow like as not put somethin' in their heads."

"Promise I won't," says Bruce.

Séamus plunks a dark beer down on the table and slides it toward Bruce. "My shout. I haven't seen ye try a Guinness yet. It's somethin' of an obligation in an Irish Pub."

Bruce laughs. "It looks like a meal. I'll taste it for sure, Séamus, but I'm not much of a drinker. Someone else will have to finish it."

"I can do that," says Mags. "Free beer and all, Séamus. You're a generous soul tonight."

Séamus pats Bruce on the shoulder then eases his way through the Thursday regulars toward the fireplace. Eyes follow him expectantly. Without preamble, Séamus casts a spell with one clear high note. He has a beautiful, haunting voice. No one breathes. Before Séamus finishes Bruce's eyes are moist. Mags and Claire both reach across the table to squeezes his hands.

"We've a special friend here tonight," says Séamus, coming back down to earth. "Listen all, I want ye t' welcome Bruce Connors from Canada."

"Dia duit." The pub calls. A couple of people whistle.

"It's a welcome," says Cat, quietly, tapping Bruce on the fingers.

"Play us some flute, Bruce," Joan hollers from behind the bar.

Bruce is used to playing with friends back home. He performs at the local hall on occasion. But he isn't sure as he stands up, what his Irish friends and acquaintances are going to think of his skills. This is clearly a place where talent is as thick as the beer.

He withdraws his pan flute from its satchel and brings it to his lips. The hollow sound rushes like a wind over the gathered heads, brushes the windows with its notes of far away, exotic places. The guitarist picks up Bruce's melody. The young woman strokes her bodhrán lightly. Bruce stops momentarily, overcome with feeling. He smiles appreciatively at them both. The tune, borrowed from the natives of the Andes, skips along the tables almost six-thousand miles from its origin. When he lets the last notes fall, the outpouring of support brings fresh tears to his eyes. He never wants to let go of this moment, these people.

FLIGHT RISK

AS WORRIED AS SHE IS, MARY is grateful for the heat of the blanket wrapped tightly around her body. She closes her eyes to avoid making eye contact with the paramedics hovering over her, taking yet another set of vitals. The ambulance hits a pothole and the gurney bucks like a runaway horse. She looks down at the straps holding her in. She realizes there's no chance she'll fall out, but also no chance to escape.

It's as though they suspect she's a flight risk. And they're right. The first thing she intends to do when she reaches the hospital is make a break for it. It's still light out and the walk to Bruce's is less than forty-five minutes. She'll tell Martin she fell in the water at the beach.

The ambulance turns in and the back doors swing open. Two men roll the gurney out and hustle her through the sliding glass door. A young nurse comes over and shines a light into her eyes, which she objects to. "I'm perfectly fine. I don't actually need t' be here. Everyone is over-reacting."

She remains strapped in, immobile. One of the ambulance attendants wheels her further into the building. After a quick conversation with the nurse and a fleeting glance back at her he is gone. The nurse inserts a thermometer into her mouth and places a warm cap on her head.

"You'll be better soon, Miss? . . . "

"I don't actually want to give ye my name," she mumbles, trying to keep the thermometer in place. "I'm not supposed t' be here, and I don't have any insurance."

"Are you a tourist?" asks the nurse, withdrawing the thermometer and noting her temperature on a chart.

"Yes. And I'm fine. I feel much warmer now."

"I think we'll get you out of these wet clothes." She draws the curtain and unstraps the belts tying Mary to the gurney. "Your temperature is still a little low. I want you to put this gown on and I'll go and fetch more warm blankets."

Mary is alone. She hops down and peaks through the curtain. The nurse's back is turned. She slips through the opening and sidles toward the hallway.

"Oh. You can't go yet," the nurse says. "We need to get you warmed up for your own safety. Don't make me call the doctor, dear."

"I really am fine. I need t' go because I'm late. My husband will worry if I'm not back soon."

"We can call your husband. What's his number?"

"No, thank ye. That isn't necessary."

The nurse leads her back to the gurney, while another helps to peel off Nick's shirt and slip a hospital gown over her head. Mary clasps the t-shirt close, fearful of losing it. She realizes that she doesn't have shoes and socks on.

"Your wet bottoms next. And then hop up and I'll wrap these blankets around you and bring one for your head."

"When can I leave?"

"As soon as the doctor has had a look at you and is satisfied that you're out of danger. Can you tell me what happened?"

"Someone called an ambulance, I'm sorry. I would have warmed up just fine at the restaurant. I just fell in the water. If it wasn't for the current it would have been no different from going for a swim. Right? So, this all seems quite silly. I'm embarrassed to be takin' your time like this."

Mary is embarrassed, and the hospital gown isn't helping. She feels like a fraud, an attention seeker, when attention is the last thing she wants. If they make her tell them her name and they connect her to Bruce's house, they may find his phone number and dial Martin. Even if they don't call, she worries they might send a bill or a record of her visit.

"I'll leave you for a while. Stay put and I'll be back in to take your vitals again in fifteen minutes. The doctor will be in shortly after."

Mary lies flat on her back and wills herself to warm up beneath the blankets before the nurse returns. The tingling in her limbs has stopped and her lips are moving normally now when she speaks. She tries to figure out how she is going to get home and into the bedroom without Martin seeing she's wearing another man's shirt, and her hair and shorts are wet. And her shoes are missing.

She might as well warm up as much as possible before she has to make the painful walk home in the evening air.

The longer she lies here the sleepier she feels. The nurse startles her awake and shimmies a blood pressure cuff up her arm.

"The chill makes you drowsy," says the nurse, gently brushing Mary's hair back under the warm cap. "Your vitals are looking good. Let's pop the thermometer in again."

Mary opens her mouth like a baby bird. The curtain opens again and a smartly polished doctor takes up residence on her other side. She too peers into Mary's face looking for signs of trouble. To avoid being accused of wasting their time, Mary quickly states, "this isn't my idea t' be here. I told them I was fine."

"Nothing to worry about. I'm glad they brought you in. You were showing the early signs of hypothermia and it's always best to play it safe in these cases. Did you hit your head?"

"No."

"Her temperature is back to normal now," says the nurse before ducking back out through the curtain.

"That is good, isn't it? I'll just review your chart and when you feel ready to leave you can get dressed and the front desk will call your ride for you," says the doctor.

Mary sighs. Another hurdle. Is the front desk staff going to insist she can't leave without a chaperone? At least they still don't have her name.

"Mrs. Hughes? There is someone waiting at the front for you," says the nurse, reappearing.

Mary's chest tightens. Her vision vibrates with fresh anxiety. If the doctor is still paying attention to her vitals she's going to be forced back under the warm blankets — perhaps a good thing. It'll give her a place to hide. She can't face Martin. The whole thing is too much to explain. This is what comes of lying.

"Nurse, before you go, how did you know my name?"

"The gentlemen were asking for Mary Hughes. You are the only one admitted, dear."

"Gentlemen?"

"Yes. One asked to come back. I said I would see if you were ready."

The curtain parts again and Nick pops just his head through the opening, a big grin on his face. "They say you're doing better. We can take you home."

"I just have t' get dressed," says Mary. Nick comes in and closes the curtain behind him.

"I'll help her," Nick says to the nurse.

Mary nods to her. A few minutes later Nick is holding Mary's arm across the parking lot and helping her into a truck — Sam, the Farmer's truck. Sam doesn't speak, or even look at her. He has the heat on full. The air in the cabin is close but comforting.

"Well, which will it be?" says Nick. "Home by 7:00, or, dry and into clean clothes at Flower's, and home by, say, 8:30ish?"

"Dry at Flower's, please," says Mary, hoping it's the right decision. Being late from Flower's is less of a sin than home late dripping with sea water and wearing another man's shirt. No way she can pass the Rude Dog t-shirt off as Flower's, no matter how unconventional her friend's wardrobe. The shirt smells strongly of Nick.

"Thanks for lookin' after me," she says.

"I can't help it, Sugar Tits."

"Sam makes a gruff sound and reaches over her head to pull a blanket from the narrow space behind the bench seat. He unfolds it and without a word, and without making eye contact with her, tucks it gently around her body and feet.

PARTY FAVOURS

BRUCE POURS HIMSELF A CUP of tea and sits down at the kitchen table, making room for himself amid the clingfilm-covered platters of food. The ladies all arrived half an hour ago looking very respectable in skirts and blouses. They're giggling in the front room. The gathering is more tea party than bachelorette party. He's relieved.

It might even be more Tupperware party than tea party. He looks up from his book to see the consultant invited by Mags teeter into the kitchen lugging two suitcases and a poster easel.

"Who —? Out!" she snaps, dropping one of the cases and almost tripping over it.

Bruce stands up to help. "I'm B —"

All five-foot-eleven of her, plus three added inches of swaying pink coif, barrel toward him. She clutches his shirt and pushes him through the open patio door.

"Hey, I live here." Bruce steps back into the kitchen, irritated but calm.

"Out. Out. Out!" she barks.

"What's the hurley burley?" demands Cat, coming down the hall. "Sharon. That's Bruce. We said he could stay, so."

"My parties are women only. I made that perfectly clear."

"He lives here and we said he could stay. Mags'll back me up on it, so."

"Humph."

Pink Sharon rights the fallen case and marches from the kitchen with the easel under her arm. She returns a few minutes later to take one of the cases, ignoring Bruce now seated at the table. Before returning to the living room, she pulls out a compact and presses a fake beauty mark more firmly into her cheek. Her eyes dart sideways and Bruce smiles at her. She turns her back and checks her hair in the tiny mirror.

After tugging her scarf straight, she clicks the compact shut and, exaggerating the swing of her hips, glides down the hall. "Okay gals," she calls, "yer journey o' discovery is about t' begin." Bruce wants to laugh at the theatre. He buries his nose in his book.

The front room is quiet. Pink Sharon is speaking. He lifts the plastic from the corner of the lemon tart plate in front of him. He glaces up at the kitchen clock, forgetting it stopped earlier today. He leans back on his chair to look down the hall. The ladies are sitting on the floor in a wide circle. Their skirts are hiked up around their waist and they're looking at their genitals in small mirrors. Bruce's chair drops heavily back onto its front legs.

"What the F —?" He says under his breath. He replaces the plastic wrap on the tarts and picks up his book. He can't see a word. His attention is in the living room. There's momentary nervous laughter, then silence again with only the voice of the consultant urging them on. No wonder the pink dominatrix tried to get rid of him. It's some sort of a . . . masturbation party?

The volume in the other room is rising. Fiona's getting a ribbing. Eyes squeezed shut, he's now eavesdropping with every cochlear fibre he has, hoping, and not, to hear something interesting.

Cat pinches his bottom through the slats in the chair. He snaps his book shut in surprise.

"Gotcha," she says.

Mags, Joan, Claire, Fiona and a bunch of women Bruce doesn't know flow in behind her. They crowd the kitchen sink, washing their hands. That's good, thinks Bruce. He is trying to keep a neutral expression on his face.

"How's it goin' in here?" asks Mags. "Managin' alright?"

"Oh, yeah. All good."

"Pipe down with y'all," says Mags, over the general hubbub. "Let's thank Bruce for lettin' us have our party at Mary's place."

"Thank ye, Bruce," they chorus. He is suddenly surrounded by women stroking his cheek, petting his hair, pulling his ponytail, squeezing his shoulders. A woman loads a plate for him. Drinks are being shaken and poured. Someone opens a bottle of champagne and the cork ricochets off the ceiling. From his seat, Bruce examines the spot for a mark. Pink Sharon is nowhere to be seen.

Mags sits on his lap and kisses his cheek. "Sharon is gettin' ready for Phase 2. We aren't makin' ye uncomfortable, are we?"

Her auburn hair smells of flowers and hairspray and tickles his cheek.

The women are each wearing different perfumes and the scents swirl around Bruce as though he's in a giant mix-master. He can't taste his food. "I'm good. I'm all for experiencing our sexuality — with whomever and however many people we choose."

"Sure, ye can sit in the front room with us. No reason to hide yerself back here." She slides off his lap. "Bruce can sit with us, aye ladies?"

"Aye, why not?" says the woman who loaded his plate.

"Slàinte to Bruce," Cat yells.

He is pulled into the other room and given a place of honour next to Fiona on the couch. Fiona's face is a shade of eggplant. They've made her a ridiculous hat with a huge penis sticking out of it like a unicorn horn. Joan plops it on her head and ties it under her chin.

Pink Sharon taps a green and purple tube of something against her leg. "Let's talk lube, ladies. I'll pass this around, and I want all o' ye t' put a bit on yer fingers and feel the heat and tinglin' sensation as ye rub 'em together. Imagine that between yer legs."

Cat leans over to Mags and whispers, "I can, so. It's called a yeast infection."

Mags is sitting next to Bruce on his other side. She coughs to disguise a laugh.

The consultant is going through her products. "This one's cool and tinglin' — this penis ring'll tickle 'im, and ye — these are cherry flavour edible panties . . ."

"How much are these after bein'?" asks Claire. "Not that I have a man in my life right now, but I need t' know how much t' put by."

"Ye can mark on the card I gave ye which items ye're interested in, and then, after the presentation, we've a private talk in the bedroom upstairs. I can give ye prices then," says Sharon.

"Sorry, we'd really rather know now," says Cat.

"Fine. I'll give ye prices on products as we move forward." She turns and rummages in her case before spinning around with a silky smile and three more toys. She adds them to the procession of things being passed from Bruce's left, counterclockwise.

Fiona hands him the feathered penis ring. He examines it. It's rudimentary. He has friends who could make this for less than two dollars apiece. "How much is this one?" he asks.

Pink Sharon, or Pink Eye, as he's decided to refer to her privately, not liking the glare she's giving him, says, "I'm not givin' prices on the things already circulatin'. And ye're not really part o' this party."

Bruce passes it along. He is starting to enjoy this, despite Pink Eye. He's done a lot of things, but he's never been to a sex toy party.

Fiona shrieks and drops the next item in his lap. He picks it up and laughs. "How much is this one?" he says.

"I'm just about to speak o' those. There are three different models. They range in price from sixty to eighty-five punt. The one you've got there is the six-inch realistic. We've an eight-inch smooth. And then there'll be a six-inch panda on bamboo. The little panda vibrates for added clitoral stimulation. Tis top o' the line, sure now."

Bruce notices for the first time the poster of female genitalia behind Pink Eye. Stuff every woman here should already know. "Sixty Irish pounds for this hunk of rubber?" he says, bringing the penis to his nose. It smells of chemicals. "I can show you how to make something just as good for less than one punt — it's biodegradable and comes in any shape and size you want."

"Get on with ye, Bruce," Mags says, pushing him good-naturedly. She smiles awkwardly at Sharon and says, "I think yer products are grand. It's kind o' ye t' agree t' come tonight."

"I'm serious. Who's up for some veggie sculpting?" says Bruce.

Cat leaps to her feet. "The grocer is open another thirty minutes. Let's do it gals. Who's comin' with me?"

"I'll come," says Joan, downing her drink. "Woopy. Operation dildo!"

"Get a lot of different lengths and girths. Carrots, Parsnips, yams," suggests Bruce.

"Turnips?" says Cat, shrugging into her jacket.

"Ye would," says Claire. "Is that how Michael's built then? Get goin' and be back."

Pink Apoplexy tries to get a word in, aiming to recapture the party. Mags tries to comfort her, sympathetic as only a fellow private party consultant could be. In return, Apoplexy snarls at her. Mags retreats, but in doing so her stiletto *accidentally* comes down on Apo's foot. When she pulls back a hand to slap Mags face, Bruce leaps forward. But Mags is fast. She catches the hand and gives it a sharp twist.

"Sharon, I wouldn't take one o' your expensive dildos now if ye paid me to do it," Mags says. "Bruce is right. His are compostable. Good for the environment. Unlike your rubber shite."

"Well, tough for ye, Mags," says Sharon. "From what I hear, ye haven't been gettin' any. I pegged ye as someone like to get customer o' the month with me." She pulls her hand free and spins her cotton candy head, "Ladies! Ladies! A reminder, fer those of ye not wantin' to use yer dinner t' pleasure yerselves, I'll be up in the bedroom takin orders."

Claire is pouring shots. Fiona is gripping the counter and singing Sheena Easton's *Modern Girl*. Another woman is chasing everyone around the kitchen with a pair of cucumbers brandished like pistols.

Bruce pushes his way through the bouncing, laughing women.

"The bedrooms are off limits to you," he says to Pink Sharon over the noise of the party. No one talks to my friends the way you spoke to Mags. Thanks for coming. Now, pack your things and *you* get out."

FORAGERS

MARY SWINGS THE WICKER basket for mushrooms from one arm to the other. She inhales deeply. The smell of sun-baked grass is sweet and rich, like honey, on the back of her throat. She tries to focus on the uneven path, and the surrounding sentinels of fir, Gary oak and Arbutus, but Nick's broad back ahead of her is distracting.

Nick was especially gentle with her at Flower's house. He helped her find a towel, turned on the shower, then waited outside the bathroom door to make sure she was safe. Afterward, with Flower still collecting the wayward kayak, he helped her go through Flower's drawers for a dry change of clothes. He blow-dried her hair for her because her arms felt too heavy to raise. Then he walked her home. He didn't probe into why she was so worried Martin would find out she went kayaking, however strange it must have seemed to him.

Blessedly, Martin was still in the garden when she returned and didn't even notice she was late.

Nick turns and smiles at her. If it hadn't been for his attentiveness during and after the kayaking scare, she might not have had the nerve to venture out again so soon, despite how much she's been looking forward to this outing. To her chagrin, Sam is the 'other' her beach friends suggested might join the mushroom hunting. He's at the front of the line, rhyming off Latin names and beating the underbrush of salal with his long walking stick. Totally annoying.

Nick holds a branch aside for her. As she passes, he leans close and whispers, "I love your new outfit. Very sexy."

It's hard not to want to encourage him. The blush on her cheeks is not solely the result of his breath against her cheek, nor the resulting wave of energy coursing from her belly to the now erect follicles on her head. She feels more noticed in her new clothes. To avoid Martin's reaction, she changed into her wrap pants and crop top at Flower's house, and they walked together to the rendezvous. Nick wasn't alone among the men to raise his eyebrows and smile when he saw her.

Sam stops and squats at the base of a large fir. "Got some." He holds the salal open to reveal the yellow, funnel-shaped mushrooms sprouting through the moss, their caps slightly nicked and dotted with fir needles. "Pacific Golden Chanterelle, Cantharellus formosus."

He looks up at her, unsmiling. They haven't spoken. When introduced she feigned ignorance, pretending, they hadn't met before. Not at his farm, and not the other night while shivering in his truck.

"Frank, you might as well pluck these and clean them up. We can search the surrounding couple metres for the others connected to them," says Sam.

"Come with me," says Flower, taking her hand and motioning to Jeana and Blue. "Let's search further off the path, around the other firs. Sam and the boys can gather that bunch."

Mary picks up a long stick and swishes salal and fern out of the way, imitating Flower. At the base of an ancient cedar, she sees a splash of red on a patch of green moss. "Is this something?" she calls before she has fully exposed the spot. Spreading the bright green fronds of a fern she sees an ugly crumpled red growth, not what they are looking for at all. "False alarm."

"Let me see," says Flower. "Hey, Mary's found Lobster mushrooms."

"That can't be edible," says Mary. The mushroom is bright red, rough, leathery, twisted, puckered, swollen, dirty and down-right ugly. "Aren't animals meant t' be warned off by red food?"

Sam leans over her shoulder. "Good job." He squats beside her, slices the mushroom free and cuts it in half to reveal a dense pale orange interior. "The distinct shape is the result of a parasitic fungal infection by Hypomyces lactifluorum." He drops the ugly mushroom into Mary's basket along with two Chanterelles from his own basket.

They zigzag through the forest of Helliwell park eventually stopping for a picnic lunch at St. John's Point. Frank, cross-legged in the grass, extends a worn leather wineskin to Mary. She accepts it gladly, takes a long swig of his homemade red wine and dries her lips with the back of her hand.

"This is really good wine. I can't believe ye made it," she says, passing Frank's skin on to Jeana.

"I suspect the wineskin adds flavour. My own version of the oak cask," Frank laughs. "Don't feel you have to sit back here with us, sweetheart. There's a nice view from the bluff. It's just a bit windy over there for my taste."

"Alright then."

Relocating to the edge of the bluff and dangling her legs over the edge, she takes a sandwich from her basket. Nick sits down next to her and then almost immediately excuses himself for a pee.

As soon as Nick is out of sight, Sam makes himself comfortable on a large rock just behind her.

"I want to apologize, Mary." He tosses a pebble over the edge. "And I want to thank you. You were right. My ewe wasn't well and I didn't catch it."

She turns and examines his eyes for sincerity. "I accept yer apology."

"Truce, then?"

"Yes. And I want t' thank ye for the ride."

"Now that we're friends, I hope you don't take offense to what I want to say. You're married, and because of that, there's something you should know about Nick."

"There's nothin' between Nick and I," says Mary, turning away. She takes a big bite of her sandwich.

"Nick's a great guy. It's just that he has a lot of favourites among the women here. He has a very open heart."

"Uhm," mumbles Mary, chewing.

Nick rejoins Mary on the cliff edge and finishes buttoning his ripped jeans. He pulls a strawberry from his backpack and wraps an arm possessively around Mary's waist. "Try these. They're really juicy," he says, bringing one to her lips.

Sam slides off of the rock and onto the grass. "I think I'll join you too, Mary."

He turns to the others sprawled in the field, laughing and sharing a joint. "Hey Frank, how about you bring that wineskin over and share it with we three thirsty travellers."

Sam points to an island about a kilometre off the point. A bevy of small boats are anchored around it. A pair of divers wearing SCUBA tanks are sitting on the edge of one, ready to flip backward into the water.

"You've got to be careful around here, Mary," Sam says. "Did you know we have sharks up to six metres in length swimming right there?"

"What! I've been goin' in the water almost every day!" she exclaims.

"I'm kidding about the danger. They're bluntnose sixgill sharks, Hexanchus griseus. Deep-water dwellers. Too deep for divers usually, but we're fortunate to have a shelf off Flora Islet that they frequent this time of year. They won't hurt you."

He accepts the wineskin from Frank, takes a swig and offers it to Mary. As she tips her head back, she catches a narrow look between Sam and Nick.

"Would you be interested in going snorkeling with me?" asks Sam. "You might catch a glimpse of them if the visibility's good."

"I don't think I want t' go back in the water. I'm kind o' shaken still."

"Can I ask what happened?" says Sam.

"I'm sure she doesn't want to relive it," says Nick.

She doesn't. When she came home, she was so worried about Martin finding out, and so focused on acting normal while she made dinner, that she hardly thought about what might have happened. But that night, in bed, she was haunted by what could have happened had the ferry's rescue boat not pulled her from the water. One moment she was having a glorious, carefree day, and the next, she was fighting for her life, terrified she was going to drown, or be ground up by a propellor and fed to . . . these sharks, or simply carried out to sea by currents and slowly frozen to death.

She smiles from Sam to Nick and chews her sandwich.

"Bring that wineskin back over here will you, Mary?" says Frank. "Those two are hogging you."

Mary jumps up and brushes the grass from her bottom.

"Sorry, but I've been called away," she says to Nick and Sam.

"I'll come too," says Sam.

Mary hands Frank his wineskin and sits down between him and Flower. Flower's eyes are glassy and red-rimmed from the pot she's been smoking. She kisses Mary's cheek and lingers there.

"Did you know your friend is a real eco-warrior? A whistleblower," says Frank.

Mary's blank expression invites him to continue.

"She went to the press when she discovered that the company, Sydney Steel Corporation, that her own father ran, no less, was sitting on evidence that the sludge from its coke mill ovens was contaminating Sydney harbour. It created tar ponds full of nasty chemicals. Oodles of residents were dying of cancer and Sydney Steel Corp knew they were to blame. And then there was what it was also doing to the fish and wildlife."

"Did you really report them, Flower?" says Mary.

"I did. I was in university then. I told you I had an uncle who was a biologist. He got me a summer job doing research, collecting samples from lobster in Sydney harbour. We realized something was terribly wrong, and my own father asked me to ignore it. His argument was that I would put locals out of jobs, with no other industry in Cape Breton to support them. But you can't work if you're sick, so I broke into his office at the mill one night. It didn't take long to find evidence that the company knew about the contamination, and the danger, long before we did our tests. I'm not proud of how I went about it, so I don't usually like to talk about it."

"Never be ashamed. That was so brave of you," says Blue.

"Well . . . it cost me my family. I'm just glad that the government finally listened and dredged the tar ponds. They're actually discussing closing the steel mill once and for all as we speak."

"So that's why ye moved here then?" says Mary.

"It is. And I love it here, Mary, so you can put that sad expression back in your pocket. Honest." Flower pulls her into a rocking hug and ruffles her hair. "I've got a new family."

"That you have, Flower," says Frank. "We are all family here."

BETWEEN FRIENDS

BRUCE NESTLES DEEPER into the cushions, feeling awkward sitting in Mary and Martin's front room with just Mags. She is dressed in a clingy low-cut dress. She smells great, as usual. She looks like a beauty contestant, as usual. Between sips, she idly strokes her wine glass with long fingernails. She isn't his usual type, but he can't deny being affected by her every time he sees her.

"What was yer favourite part o' last night?" she asks.

"I'd have to say when Claire glued dried peas to her carrot dildo and chased Fiona around the kitchen with it." Bruce chuckles and takes a drink of his tea. He sets it down and Mags slides closer on the couch.

"Mine was when Sharon went full banshee and called us all sexual deviants. I think we broke her," says Mags.

Bruce laughs hard with Mags at the memory. It relieves the tension.

"I mean, I feel sorry for her as a consultant myself. I've had some hard sells. But, honestly, I don't think she likes men at all, and she's tryin' t' sell sex t' a bunch o' married, and lookin' to be married women," says Mags, searching his eyes.

"It sure turned out wilder than I imagined it would. Thankfully no harm was done," says Bruce, picking up his mug and sinking deeper into the couch.

"I went home feelin' so restless. Did ye have any trouble sleepin', yerself?"

"I slept well, actually. You guys did a great job cleaning up — even in your drunken state. We could have left it till this morning, but it was nice of you."

"I wasn't in a hurry t' leave," says Mags. "Quite honestly, all those penises — and the way ye looked. Mags stares into her wine glass. "Yer sexuality is so — so, powerful. Ye know? I hoped somethin' would happen. I thought maybe ye felt it too." Mags puts her hand on his leg inches from his groin.

Bruce has about five seconds to decide what to do, before he risks offending her. Mags is beautiful. He cares about her. He leans in before he's even fully considered the options. Her fingers slide between his legs. He takes her mouth. She tastes of cherry lipstick and wine.

She unties the drawstring on his pants and slides her cool fingertips down his belly. He breathes in sharply as she takes hold of his erection. Her earlobe is between his teeth. She groans, low and guttural and her pleasure causes him to rise to her. Their hungry lips find each other again; their tongues dip and soar.

Without untangling their lips, she shimmies her dress up and straddles him as he lifts her onto his lap.

Grasping the nape of her neck, he pulls her closer. Their kisses are fuller, fiercer. She rises to give him her nipple, and he takes it between his teeth.

She teases him with short thrusts against the head of his penis. He arches, wanting to break through the thin shield of her panties.

He lifts her by the buttocks and lies her back on the couch. She is somehow even more beautiful. Her eyes are as hungry as his.

He pulls his shirt over his head. She sighs, gliding her hands over his belly and chest with the finest of touch that fine hairs rise in her wake. He leans forward to kiss her and she tugs his pants playfully over the crest of his buttocks, drawing him closer between her legs.

Reluctantly, he stands to steps out of his pants. His penis sways, like a compass needle searching magnetic north. Straddling her, he takes her mouth gently and deeply. Her fingernails play through his loose hair. His penis nudges the crevice between her thighs.

She struggles to sit up and he helps pull her dress over her head. Pale breasts spring free of the soft fabric and she lies back with her legs spread. His fingers dip beneath her panties.

"I don't have a condom," Bruce murmurs into her ear.

"O' course ye don't. Ye can't get 'em unless yer married," says Mags. "Just be careful, aye?"

Bruce leans forward and kisses her delicious, expectant lips, then pulls back to gaze at her. The air is heavy with the smell of sex.

His hand strokes her soft shoulder and he kisses her forehead. "I can't risk it Mags. I shouldn't have taken it this far. I'm sorry. I'm leaving in just over a week."

"I'm okay with that," says Mags, reaching up to play with the beads dangling from his neck, while urging him on with her hips.

"Won't it be harder for you if we do this and I leave. I probably won't be coming back, and I know it'll be harder for me." He wraps his arms around her, his penis hard between them.

"I'm too roiled up t' stop now. I don't want ye t' stop," Mags says, raising an eyebrow, "and there's plenty we still *can* do." She pushes him onto his back and leaves a line of kisses down his belly, "You first," she says.

"Ladies first," he laughs, directing her onto her knees, spreading her legs and dipping his head.

She gasps at the touch of his tongue. "While I can still speak, Bruce — do me a favour?" He doesn't stop and she groans. "Don't let on t' the others."

"I promise."

BEESERK

MARY, FLOWER AND SAM reach Seawright Rd, having dropped the others off one by one on the walk from Helliwell. Mary's legs and feet are sore, and she realizes she has to walk all the way to Flower's house to change before coming back home. As they near Bruce's house Mary nervously checks for Martin in the front garden. Once past the driveway she exhales with relief.

Screams ricochet off the trees surrounding them.

They stare at each other, listening.

"Where is it coming from?" says Flower, turning in a circle with her hands to her ears.

"That's Martin!" says Mary and she takes off at a run back to the house. Flower and Sam are on her heels. She won't forgive herself if something has happened to him and he's been lying injured all day while she was having fun.

Rounding the side of the house she sees Martin going berserk, waving his arms, hopping from leg to leg, hitting himself and running in circles. His screams are deafening, but she's relieved there's no blood.

Sam runs past her with a heavy canvas tarp dragged from its usual spot on the abandoned outdoor furniture. He throws it over Martin and starts slapping the canvas, whisking Martin helplessly toward them.

"Get inside the main house, quick girls," Sam orders, just before he wrenches opens the side garage door and disappears inside with Martin.

Angry bees are circling Mary and Flower. They make a run for the patio door.

Once inside Mary pats herself down just in case. Satisfied, she runs through the kitchen to let Sam and Martin in through the interior garage door. Martin is covered in nasty golf-ball sized lumps. His eye is swelling shut and his chin and lower lip are twice their normal size.

"We have to get him to the medical clinic before they close," says Sam. "Can I borrow your car?"

"O' course. Will he be okay?" says Mary, appalled at how bad Martin looks.

"Does he have an allergy to bees?" asks Sam.

"No," says Martin, sounding like he was punched in the mouth. His good eye fixes on Mary as she scrambles for the car keys. "Mut the hell are ye marin', Mary?"

Mary feels sucker punched. Sam and Flower ignore the remark. They dash for the car.

Sam halts on the edge of the patio. His jaw moves in slow motion. "Shh — itt!" His eyes absorb the changes to the back garden. "Holy —— fucking —Christ!" His voice quivers with controlled anger. "What — the — fuck? What — the? Jesus!" He lifts his sandaled foot off a dead bird. He looks over at them in disbelief.

Sam throws himself into the driver's seat beside Flower as Mary helps Martin buckle into the back. Sam is cursing under his breath as she buckles herself in. For Mary, the drive to the clinic is a journey of shame.

SKELETONS IN THE BASEMENT

Cat pulls a box from the corner of Martin and Mary's basement and brushes off the dust. "This one, maybe?"

Bruce flips open the cardboard top and shines his flashlight on the contents. "Nope. Old clothes. There are only five boxes left. If the photos and letters are actually here, our odds are really improving," he says with a laugh.

He drags a fresh box along the floor to a spot beneath the swinging overhead bulb. "Hello. What did I tell you? Let's get this up to the kitchen."

After Bruce's visit with Bridget, she rang to tell him she remembered giving a box of old photos and documents to Mary to keep in her basement. She recalled there were photos of Bruce's grandparents mixed in with the photos of Nellie and Mary's mom, Delia. There may even be photos of his dad, she said.

"Thanks for doing this with me," says Bruce. "I was kind of overwhelmed at Bridget's. I think it was emotional for her, too. I hope I didn't wear her out."

"No worries, she's a born storyteller," says Cat. "Sure, it gives her more energy, not less. She's an actual Scheherazade."

"She *is* Scheherazade. I know she didn't tell me everything. So now I need to see her again to get the rest of the tale."

"We're in dress-rehearsals this week. Promise ye'll come and watch."

Bruce drops the box and a musty smell belches from its lid. He organizes the contents into neat piles on the kitchen table. Documents, personal letters, and loose photos.

"Do you mind starting with the documents and letters to see if any have my family's name on them?" Bruce asks.

"Sure," says Cat. "How are ye goin' t' recognize yer da or grandparents in the photos?" She takes a seat at the table and repositions an alligator clip to keep her hair from falling in her eyes.

"I'm hoping they're labelled," says Bruce, flipping the top one over.

"What did ye say the name o' yer da's school was? Fairbridge? Here's a pamphlet on Fairbridge Farm School. But it says Australia."

"That's it." Bruce almost pulls it from Cat's hand in his excitement. "They started the experiment in Australia."

"Experiment, so?"

"Well, do-gooders thought they could help children by sending them away from their families, denying them love and turning a blind eye when they were bullied and abused. Dad had no self-worth when he left the gates of Prince of Wales Farm School. Mom was even worse."

"Ye never talk o' yer mam."

"It's too hard." Bruce lets images of his mom wash through his mind. "She became an alcoholic and committed suicide."

"I'm fair sorry. Thanks for tellin' me, Bruce."

"Not many people know. Dad wanted it kept a secret. Now that he's gone, I'm not sure what I want to do with it. Keeping it bottled up, all of the secrets, all of the missing information about their past and mine, has done more harm than good. And that's why I'm here. I can't solve anything, but I feel like it's time to shed light on all of the dark spaces. It took a stranger at Dad's funeral telling me about their shared past, for me to discover the true horror of what went on at that school.

When she squeezes his hand, he lets her look into his eyes, without hiding anything.

"And yer Da? What was he like?"

"A complicated man. All in all, he did well raising me on his own. Never one to give a hug — or praise, but I knew he cared. In the last couple of years it's been me parenting him. From the time we lost Mom there's been a revolving door of women in his life and eventually he became too much for even them."

"Sorry to hear it Bruce. Was it his health?"

"No, drink and finances. Not good with either."

Cat lets go Bruce's hand and picks up the leaflet. "The pamphlet makes it look like they were bein' sent off t' a posh boardin' school. Yer grandfather must've thought he was doin' somethin' good for his son. Don't ye think?"

"How can any father ship his frightened five-year-old boy halfway round the world? Then never check on him? Never tell him he's missed, or loved?"

Distracted and upset, Bruce flips through the photos. Women and men with guns, farm scenes, sheep, a prize winning at a fair, a little boy with a stick, an old man in a spindly wheelchair, a young girl clutching a toddler's hand, a pretty, fair-haired young woman standing next to a man with a missing leg and, Bruce squints, what looks like part of his face as well.

Bruce is shaking his head, still full of emotion.

"Hey," Cat says. "Look at me, lad." She's smiling. She brings her thumb and the tip of her index finger together on each hand, palms up. "Gyan mudra, right? Releases stress and anger?"

Bruce laughs. "Right." He copies her mudra. The corners of his eyes crinkle. He is so grateful to her for remembering what he taught her, and for catching him starting to spiral. "Fresh eyes and an open heart," he says.

Cat picks up the discarded photos. "Sure so, this one, the old man in the wheelchair with one leg, it's got *James* pencilled on the back. The same man standin' with the young woman is marked *James and Violet*. Aren't these yer grandparents?" She passes the photo to Bruce.

He cradles the photo in his hand. *His* grandparents! It's almost too much to believe. He studies the details of their faces. They seem too different in age to be a couple. James is poorly dressed; he's wearing a misshapen, worn suit with one pant leg pinned up behind. A hand-made cane supports him on one side, his young bride on the other. He's missing an eye. The skin on his face, although blurry in the photo, is puckered and twisted. Next to him, his young bride is petite with long fair hair, erect posture, and a worn but pretty cotton dress and stockings. The toes of her shoes are muddy.

"This is yer da," says Cat, handing Bruce the boy with the stick. "And this. The little girl holdin' his hand is listed as Delia. That's Mary's mam."

Bruce is silent, there is almost too much to take in. He continues to scan the photos and recognizes a short-haired Nellie. In one, she holds an oversized protest sign, a determined arm raised.

"This is gas. Look here, Bruce." Cat points to two men with their arms around each other, each carrying a bottle of spirits. Their mouths are open wide, belting out the verse of a song. "That's yer grandfather. He looks a little older, a little skinnier, but ye can see that, can't ye? Well guess who this younger man is beside 'im. That's old Desmond, that is. Best buds, they look."

"Gee. I never considered that they might have known each other. I should have figured there were other people besides Bridget who might remember my grandparents. Thanks Cat." Bruce hasn't let go of the photo. "Do you think Mary would mind if I take this one?"

"No. Go on, she'd want ye to have it anyway."

MENDING

MARY PLUNKS MARTIN'S SOUP down in front of him. Beans, broth and a cube of potato slosh onto the coffee table.

"Watch it!" he complains.

"The doctor didn't say anythin' about yer legs no longer workin'."

"I'm supposed to rest."

Martin is recovering and can't work in the garden until the risks associated with another bee sting have passed. Not wanting to be alone in his ill-humour, he threw Mary's mushrooms in the bin when they returned from the clinic. She fished them out and washed them off, but didn't dry them sufficiently before bed. By the morning they'd gone mushy.

She hasn't forgiven him. So, they're both in foul moods, and she can't stand to spend another minute inside listening to him complain about their holiday.

Flower let her know quietly, while they were sitting in the clinic's waiting room, that Sam is the one to ask about the bees. Apparently, Martin pulled apart a pile of stacked wood near the back of the property, another improvement with dire consequences, as it was this wanton destruction that unleashed the attack. Sam is due any moment to help settle the bees for them. It was hard to ask, after witnessing his reaction last night.

The doorbell rings just as Mary is putting on her shoes.

"Hi. Thanks for coming," she says opening the door to Sam.

"How are you feeling today?" Sam calls over her head to Martin, lying prone on the living room couch.

"Terrible," Martin retorts.

"By the way, does Bruce know what you've done to his garden?" asks Sam.

Martin doesn't answer.

Mary looks down at her feet. "No. No, he doesn't," she says quietly. She steps outside with Sam and closes the door behind her. "Martin said the bees were in a stack of wood at the back. I'll show you."

"I know the place. I helped Bruce build that habitat for wild bees and other pollinators. Not all bees live in a hive and produce honey."

"I didn't know that," says Mary, following him around back.

"We needed help with fruit tree pollination on the island. Native bees are better at pollination than honeybees. They shake flowers at a certain frequency that releases more pollen. Honeybees want the nectar; native bees want the pollen. Nothing wrong with honeybees though. I keep a few hives."

They carefully walk around the body of yet another dead bird languishing in the dust.

"I don't even want to guess at the chemicals you put on Bruce's garden to cause this," says Sam, shaking his head.

"Sam, please believe me. I had nothin' to do with it," says Mary. "Martin put a pesticide with nico-something in it, on everythin', tryin' t' kill the weeds and clear the ground for replanting the garden."

"Nothing is going to grow in this dry heat. There isn't enough water in Bruce's well, even if your neonicotinoids hadn't poisoned everything in the soil. Worse, that poison will keep on killing for the next six months — at least. Plants, insects, and birds."

"I'm so sorry," says Mary, tears welling in her eyes.

"I want you and Martin to come to a talk I'm helping host at the community hall day after tomorrow, 7:00. Will you come? It's about gardening," says Sam.

They reach the back half of the garden. Mary looks up at the house. Martin watches from a kitchen chair he's dragged over to the window.

"I'll come. I can't speak for Martin."

Sam reaches for her elbow. "There are still plenty of bees and yellowjackets buzzing around. So watch where you step. Or better yet, stay back."

"I want t' help," says Mary.

"There's a good chance of being stung so I'd rather you didn't hang around," says Sam. "I know where Bruce keeps his drill. I'll make a new habitat from the logs Martin pulled apart, and drill holes in new ones to add to the stack. The bees should find the rotting wood and settle within a day or so."

"If I get stung, I deserve it," says Mary.

"You saw Martin's face. You are far too pretty for me to let that to happen to you. I'm fine without the help. Honestly."

"And I won't be able t' forgive myself if I don't do somethin'. Why should it be okay for you t' get stung and not me. You didn't destroy the bee's home. I'm comin' with ye."

"Okay then. You can help me grab the tools and while I stack the wood you can drill holes in new logs. How's that?" He looks her up and down. "You'll need long pants and something to wrap around your face. Did you bring anything like that with you? The pretty outfits I've seen you in aren't going to provide much protection."

"I'll go in and check. Maybe Bruce wouldn't mind if I borrowed a scarf."

Mary enters the house through the garage door. Martin is waiting for her in the kitchen.

"What were ye talkin' t' him about?" He blocks her way as she tries to get past the fridge.

"We were talkin' about repairin' the bee habitat ye tore apart."

"I don't like the way he was gropin' ye."

"Gropin'? He hardly touched me. *I* don't like the way ye're treatin' me right now, Martin. Can ye please move so that I can go and get changed?"

"Changed into something nicer?"

"No."

Mary squeezes past Martin and walks to the bedroom with him on her heels. She feels like she's done something wrong.

Have I done something wrong, she wonders.

"Please stop treatin' me like this. I'm goin' t' change so I don't get stung. I want t' help put right what ye destroyed. Bruce spent a lot o' time buildin' that habitat for the bees and I'm sure he'd like to see they still have one when he returns."

"It was a rottin' stack o' wood. Jesus Christ. And I forbid ye t' go out there. It's for yer own good. I don't want ye gettin' hurt."

"Ye forbid me? Ye don't get t' forbid me. I said I would help and I plan to. It's goin' t' look very strange if I don't return after I said I was just changin'."

Mary pulls open the top drawer and flips through the stack of shorts and pants. Her hands are shaking. She doesn't often defy Martin, not openly.

Neither pair of pants she brought is ideal. One is a pink polyester blend with pleats and pockets. The other, a powder-blue cotton pedal-pusher. She unzips her shorts and tosses them into the corner. Her mood is now even worse than it was when she found her mushrooms decomposing on the kitchen counter. She tugs on the blue pants and marches past Martin to the garage. Bruce's gardening hat with long flaps is hanging from a nail near the door. She slams it on top of her head. She pauses for a moment, gathers herself and heaves a great sigh before rejoining Sam. No reason to infect him with the day's unpleasantness.

Sam is waiting for her by the shed. He already has the wheelbarrow loaded with firewood and some tools. "Ready? Those pants should help. A bit nice for gardening though. I'll have to try not to get you dirty. Somehow I manage to smudge everything with my grubby gloves as I work." He's smiling at her. She hopes Martin can't see them speaking.

As they cross the yard in Martin's sightline, she makes sure to keeps her distance from Sam, and tries not to engage in conversation until hidden by the shrubs.

"There aren't as many bees back here as I thought there'd be," says Sam. "They seem to be settling already. Mind you, we're going to stir them up as we attempt to rebuild, so be ready. As Martin learned, if they do sting, they can sting more than once. But, judging from the number of times he was stung, he likely stepped on a yellowjacket nest or tossed wood on top of one. The yellow jackets are far more aggressive than the native bees. Watch your step and keep your eyes open."

"As long as we don't both end up back at the clinic," says Mary, emitting a nervous laugh. "I probably shouldn't joke."

"Do me a favour and don't tell Martin it's safe to come out," says Sam.

"I think the doctor did a good job puttin' the fear a' death into 'im," says Mary. She glances back over her shoulder and can just make out Martin's face in the kitchen window.

"Can you start on these?" says Sam, lining up logs the length of his forearm. "Are you handy with a drill?"

"Enough, yes."

Three of Bruce's extension cords were needed to reach this far. Mary wrestles the excess cord out of the way. Holding down a log, she deftly plunges the drill bit into the soft wood.

"Make the holes about two inches apart, putting as many in as you can," says Sam. "When you finish a log, toss it over."

They work in companionable silence, Mary drilling and Sam collecting and restacking the scattered wood. He waits for Mary's logs, interspersing them in the woodpile as she finishes them. When they're done a new pile about eight feet long and three feet high sits where the old one was.

"The bees won't lay eggs in a hole open at both ends and the habitat needs to stay dry," says Sam, shaking off an old brown tarp and draping it across the top of the stack. He weighs this down with a final row of wood. "That should do it. And you managed not to get a single sting. You must have a calm energy. I, on the other hand, got stung twice. I must not be so nice."

"Ye were stung? Ye didn't even say anythin'. Do they hurt?"

"I'm fine. I keep bees, remember."

BITTER SWEET

IT TOOK BRUCE A WHILE to figure out the best way to make this meeting work. In the end, Father Fingal was able to arrange for an introduction at the church, so that Desmond would be forewarned that someone wanted to meet him. The gals said that simply knocking on Desmond's door would get him nowhere, as he'd likely be too frightened to open it to a stranger. And of course, the incident with the teens had likely spooked him even more.

Bruce sits in a middle pew and gets comfortable. The arrangement is for 2:00, but Father Fingal warned him that Desmond is congenitally late, not being a good judge of the time needed to walk from home to church. Routinely, his Sunday Mass is interrupted by the noise of Desmond's walker striking the church door, several altar boys holding it open for him, and parishioners leaving their seats as Desmond fights his way to a regular spot in the third pew.

Bruce looks over his shoulder each time the door opens. He brought the photo of Desmond and his grandfather with him. He also has the petition for the Society For Wild Things Area Improvement Project. Desmond was the only resident, besides the missing Martin and Mary, that could not be convinced to sign. Bruce is hoping to find out why.

The church is as quiet as ever; the afternoon Bruce's favourite time to be here. The sun slants through the stain glass windows at a dizzying angle, carpeting everything in colour. The photo, the petition resting on Bruce's lap, his hands, and his knees are painted in a kaleidoscope of colour. It reminds Bruce of street art, images stretched across a myriad of surfaces creating a new whole.

A faint knocking pulls Bruce from his revery. He hears it again and swivels. Once again the church door has stymied Desmond. Bruce rushes over. Sure enough, when he drags the oak door open, Desmond's walker is poised to give it another strike and Desmond is blinking up at him, out of breath, irritation and gratitude etched on his lined face.

"Why'd they have t' go replacin' the door wit' this heavy auld thing. Thank ye, son. You're a saviour. I have an appointment."

Father Fingal has heard the exchange and appears beside Bruce.

"Here on time am I, Father?" asks Desmond.

"Right on time," says Father Fingal. "You've had a brisk walk have ye? Out a breath?"

"No, it's this friggin' new door o' yers. It's no good for people o' my age."

"We haven't got a new door, Desmond. It's the old one — same we've always had. But I'll grant ye, it is heavy," says Father Fingal.

Desmond waves the explanation away like it's an annoying fly.

"I've got t' meet some young lad today, have I?" asks Desmond.

"I'm the one you're meeting, sir," says Bruce. "We actually met the other night when I walked home with you. Do you remember?"

"No. I can't recall. What can I do for ye, lad? Surely ye didn't get me down here for nothin'."

"Would you like to have a cup of tea and a slice of something sweet up at the café on the corner? It'll be my treat. I think you might have known my grandfather. Maybe you'll remember him. James Connors?"

"James Connors, ye say? Connors? I've not heard that name in some time. Do ye think they'll serve cake? I haven't had one o' them for some time either."

"I think they might."

Bruce helps get Desmond turned around and escorts him to the nearby café. They find a booth in line of sight of Desmond's dolly, which doubles as his walker. Bruce remembers the first time they met and the force with which Desmond pinned him to the wall. Desmond's frailty seems at great odds with that encounter.

"Who'd ye say ye wanted t' know about?" says Desmond finally.

He keeps one hand protectively on the dolly he's just dragged back over to the booth, and casts a narrow glance at the ladies seated at table 5, who were clearly ogling it.

The waitress arrives before Bruce can answer. The café interior is pink with a matching flower border running around the top of each wall. A great deal of attention has gone into finding, framing and hanging Victorian paintings of cats. A least ten cat portraits adorn the wall opposite Bruce.

"Would ye like the menu?" asks the waitress, looking from Desmond to Bruce and back with an adoring expression. "This looks like a nice outin' for ye, Desmond, dear."

"I'm havin' cake," intones Desmond. "Chocolate cake," he adds. "I've no idea what the lad is havin'."

Bruce holds up two fingers and smiles. "And tea, please."

"Right. I'll bring a pot, two cups and two slices o' chocolate cake. Milk and sugar with yer tea?"

"You'd better bring some, yes," says Bruce. "Do you take milk and sugar in your tea, Desmond?"

"Hmm? What's that, son?"

Bruce nods to the waitress. She pats Desmond on the shoulder and, flipping the page over on her notepad, leaves to the take the next table's order.

"In answer to your question, Desmond, I'm hoping to find out more about my grandfather. I have a picture of you and him sitting together. His name was James Connors." Bruce takes the photo from his pocket and passes it across to Desmond, who brings it to his nose and then pulls it away until it comes into focus. Desmond's expression flits from mirth to sorrow in an instant.

"Why, that's James Connors and meself. Wherever did ye get this? Well, what I remember 'bout it . . . I was tinkin' 'bout it the other day, just how we used t' go out. We lost himself. Did ye know we lost himself?"

"Yes. He's my grandfather. He died back in 1947."

"Did I ever tell ye what James did for me? He had but the one leg but he did all he could wit' it. I mightn't ha' lived had it not been for James. Many a time I wished I hadn't o'."

Bruce is suddenly hung up on the note of sadness, not sure what to say or ask of his guest.

The waitress returns with their order. Desmond picks up his fork as soon as the plate is in front of him and focusses solely on the chocolate cake. Bruce watches in awe. The cake is half-gone by the time he's poured the tea.

"Would you like milk and sugar in your tea, Desmond?"

"Oh yes. Thank ye, lad." In no time there's nothing but crumbs left on Desmond's plate.

"Would you like mine?" asks Bruce, pointing at his cake. He wonders whether it's been a while since Desmond last ate, or whether he's just a fan of chocolate cake.

"Are you not goin' to eat it?" Desmond reaches across and draws Bruce's plate toward him. Rather than diving into the second piece, he takes a long drink of his tea, looking at Bruce over the rim through thick glasses that magnify his cloudy cataracts. "Back in the auld day . . . me wife and me, she was a beautiful girl, all the people said so. We met at a dance hall. We don't have them now, not like we used to. I asked if I could walk her home. Halfway along we had a snoggle in the ditch, and I told her I was in love. I got her to her mam's place and we had another snoggle under the big chestnut tree in the garden. Then and there I asked her to marry me, and she said yes."

Desmond takes another long sip of tea and sighs. "Had the house together. She kept it oh so neat on the little coin we had. Still live there now. But, lad, there was an auld bitch next door, God forgi' me. Nice neighbours only for the one. The auld bitch liked her shot o' kettle. Suppose we all did. Let me see that photo again, lad."

Desmond's eyes crinkle as he examines the photo. "We got on all right. James and me. Look at us, tinkin' that we were two jammy lads, when the hand o' God was ready to fall upon us. It was rotten, the whole world rotten."

"What happened?" says Bruce.

"It was the auld bitch, leavin' the stove on, she did. Hell was no match for the flames she sent up that night. High enough t' singe the wings o' the angels. James was a comin' home from the pub, worse for drink. He was livin' with us, poor James, after the loss o' his wife and the chil' — unmerciful. Most nights we was out wit' a bottle, but I stayed in with me Maeve, the rare occasion. I was no good, like. And me Maeve a beautiful woman. We were expectin' a wee'n."

Desmond takes a sip of tea and slices off a small corner of the second cake. He takes his time chewing and washes it down with more tea.

"James found me first and pulled me out, wit' just his one leg mind ye. He should ha' taken her first, 'cause when he went back in for her, she'd gotten the burns. Doctor said she couldn't live. He was right." Desmond lifts his glasses and blots his eyes with the flowered paper napkin. Bruce pats the hand still hovering above the cake.

"We were cursed, James and me — but, that's back when God was a small boy. I've lived an age, waitin' for the day I see Maeve again."

Bruce wipes his own eyes and clear his throat. He pours more tea for them both. "My father was James' son. The one he sent away."

Desmond's enormous eyes blink at Bruce. He leans forward and takes another bite of cake. "The light isn't good in here, lad. I wish I could see ye better," says Desmond. "James was riddled with the guilt, same as me. Couldn't shake it till death released 'im. Scarce able to say his son's name. And here ye are. If he could have lived to see it, my Lord God." Desmond takes three more bites in quick succession.

Bruce can see the toll these recollections are taking. He feels guilty that his own search is dredging up painful memories for someone so fragile. It would be best to leave off for today.

"Can I ask you something unrelated, Desmond? I hope I'm not tiring you. Your neighbours are hoping to improve the green space out in front of your house to include more trees, shrubs and wildflowers. Have you seen this paper before? Is there a reason you might not have wanted to sign it?"

"Well, I asked 'em, could I have a chestnut for my dear Maeve. The two young lads couldn't make a promise. And if I ever get a tree, it has to be a chestnut for me Maeve. Did I tell you I asked her to marry me under a chestnut tree? Right out in front o' her mam's place, 'twas."

"That's a beautiful memory," says Bruce. "If I write on this piece of paper that the society will promise to plant a chestnut for you, would you be willing to sign it? It will mean a lot to everyone else if you agree. The two lads that spoke to you are your neighbours, Michael and Séamus. You might know their wives, Cat and Joan?"

"I don't know their names, lad. I just say hi to all the ladies, 'case I give offense. 'Tween you and me, I be thinkin' the men are part of a grove — druids. Worshippin' the sun every evenin' in nothin' but their skivvies. Harmless though, lad. You needn't fear. After the fire, everyone changed in them houses. Pity like, it is. The place don't look the same, sure it don't."

"The ladies are indeed wonderful, aren't they? I'm sure they appreciate what a gentleman you are," says Bruce, and he is rewarded with an enormous eye winking at him affirmatively through the spectacles. "Can I get you more cake? Tea?"

"Should I sign yer paper? A proper tree, mind. I've not enough time to wait for a saplin' to grown into a proper tree."

"A proper tree. I'll do my best," says Bruce, fishing in his pocket for a pen and writing next to Desmond's signature block that he is promised a chestnut tree — as big a one as they can find.

The only hurdle left now is to figure out how to get the last remaining signature in time for the one-week deadline.

PEN TO PAPER

THE PETITION IS NEAR complete, with just the signatures from his hosts at Number 8 to get. Bruce stops at city hall on his way home. The receptionist smiles as he approaches her desk.

"Ye're keepin' well? Gettin' on?" she says.

"We are almost there," he says.

"I've heard the buzz in the village. What can I do fer ye?"

"There's a footnote at the bottom of the petition referring to an appendix. Do you know where I can find it? It's not in the original documents."

She opens her file cabinet. Her fingers skip across the folders. "Ah, I have it here, lad. Appendix A. It's just a list of definitions."

"May I have a copy?"

"O' course. I'm sorry I missed it the first time." The phone rings and she leaves him the copy, still warm from the Xerox.

Bruce scans the small print. And there it is. He motions the receptionist over when she hangs up the phone.

"Questions?"

"Do you read this the same way I do? Definition of resident says, person or persons domiciled at the listed address at the time of signing. Is there anything in this paragraph to suggest the signatory has to be the property owner?"

She takes the paper and studies the paragraph. "No. Accordin' t' this, any changes to public property use must be approved by all adult residents o' the affected properties, and resident accordin' t' this, is the person currently livin' at the address. Does that help?"

"It helps a great deal. May I have a pen?"

Bruce's pen hovers over the empty space next to Number 8. Technically he can sign, but still he hesitates. He doesn't want to usurp the rights of his generous hosts. But, if he doesn't, the council will surely fixate on the missing signature and deny the petition.

His pen hovers as he tries to anticipate the consequences, then he quickly scribbles his name. He hopes it's not a leap to believe that Martin and Mary would be in sync with their neighbours. The enthusiasm for the new plan has been unanimous — thanks to the promise of a chestnut tree — and, he believes, the strength of the proposal. It's right for the environment, and it will enhance their community.

"Here you go. Petition complete," says Bruce, sliding the forms across the counter. "Would you please do me a favour and highlight this paragraph in the appendix before you staple it to the forms?"

"O' course. Congratulations. It looks like this will make a lot o' people happy. Except perhaps one. We all know *his* name."

Bruce's smile dims. "You mean Martin from Number 8? I hoped the others were exaggerating Martin's potential opposition to the idea. May I borrow your phone and a phone book?"

"Sure. What number are ye lookin' for?" She plunks a thick phone book down on the counter. "The listin's are by county. We're near the front."

Bruce searches the numbers then dials the pub. "Séamus? It's Bruce. We're good. I hope. Your rules say my signature is valid. I hope that wasn't too presumptuous of me. I'm just a guest in your community."

"Bruce, ye've done us all a huge favour. Mary would certainly have signed. Martin, well, that was goin' to be a fight for sure, but he shouldn't be allowed t' hold up progress for the rest o' us. Ye've saved us a huge effort tryin' t' convince him. We'll deal with the fallout, don't ye worry — he'll come 'round eventually."

"I hope so," says Bruce.

"Too bad ye don't drink. We all wants t' buy ye a round."

PARADISE LOST

MARY ACCEPTS A PROGRAM from the young woman at the door and takes a seat on an orange plastic chair. The hall is more than two-thirds full. A young man on stage is blowing and tapping into the microphone. He centres the slide projector's light on a pull-down screen behind him and kicks a few cords out of the way. Sam steps onto the stage as the lights dim overhead. He takes the mic and nods to the young assistant.

"Welcome everyone. Tonight's talk is sponsored by Gemma at Woodwind Nursery and snacks afterward are generously provided by Pizza Galore." Sam pauses for applause. "Tonight we'll be talking about environmentally conscious gardening. It's an approach that energizes living soil by building up organics, encourages the spread of native species, and ultimately supports the animals and insects with whom we share this planet."

The audience applauds and hoots so enthusiastically that a giggle escapes Mary's lips.

Sam introduces the first speaker. The darkened room is suddenly bathed in colour as the first slide, a split image of a traditional garden on the left, and a wild garden on the right flashes on screen. Mary does a double take. The wild garden is Bruce's. *Was* Bruce's. She leans forward as her stomach drops. The significance of Martin's destruction slithers through her gut, leaving her cold. She shifts uncomfortably and leans on her elbows. The next slides are close-ups of what the presenter lauds as life-supporting species in the local ecosystem: yarrow, woolly sunflower, ocean spray, knapweed, pacific willow, phlox, and red columbine. All of which, Mary realizes, were the limp and lifeless corpses she helped toss in the back of a rented truck. She hopes Sam can't see her in the crowd.

More slides go up. The speaker rhymes off species she's never heard of, but which nevertheless appear to resonate with the audience, judging by the many nodding heads. Next, he turns to their characteristics, revealing a depth of knowledge she realizes is truly intimate. Bees see purple best. Ladybugs eat aphids. Centipedes hunt soil dwelling mites, baby snails and slugs. Birds depend heavily on caterpillars for food, seeds not providing enough energy for migration. Foxglove is ideal for butterflies and long-tongued bumble bees. Birds need snug evergreen growth to survive the winter. Marigolds should be planted near tomatoes. Chives and garlic around roses. It's like an instruction manual for the earth.

She feels a warm hand on the centre of her back and sits up.

"If the lines between your brows get any deeper you'll hurt yourself," whispers Sam into her left ear. He's perched on the edge of a seat behind her. He moves his hand from her back to her shoulder and gives it a squeeze. "I didn't invite you here to make you feel bad."

She twists in her seat and can barely look him in the eye.

"Martin didn't come?" he asks.

She shakes her head.

The woman next to Mary shushes them. Mary turns back around and gives the speaker her full attention. Sam keeps his hand on her shoulder and after a few minutes she reaches up and gives it a grateful squeeze.

When the last speaker finishes, Sam leaves to go back on stage for closing remarks. The lights come on and the fluorescence seems especially cool and stark after the joyful greenery of the presentations. Mary mingles with the other attendees grabbing a slice of pizza, then wanders with her paper plate to survey the displays. On a table devoted to wild gardening a book catches her eye. She runs her finger over the glossy covers. Bruce's name jumps out at her.

"Jesus." Her throat tightens. "Could it get any worse? He's a published author on gardening, and we've destroyed his garden." She heads to the bathroom.

The reflection in the mirror stares at her expectantly. "What can ye do? Ye have a week. What the feck can ye do to make this right?" The reflection waits for an answer. "I don't know!" She shoves her plate and the remains of her pizza in the garbage. "I know one thing, though — I've had it up to ninety with Martin!"

She splashes cold water on her cheeks and drinks from the tap. She needs to leave. But she doesn't want to go home.

Just as she crosses the threshold of the double front doors, Sam reaches for her hand and pulls her aside. The night wraps them in a cloak. Crickets and tree frogs drown out the chatter from within.

"You weren't going to say goodbye?" says Sam. "Flower just arrived. Did she find you?"

Mary takes a step backward and looks through the open doors. She can only see a portion of the auditorium. She half-heartedly scans for Flower.

"I really don't want to talk to anyone right now." She slides back into the shadows. "Sorry, Sam. Tell her for me I'll see her tomorrow." Tears spill from her eyes.

"Hey, hey," says Sam spinning her toward him, his hands on her shoulders. He bends to look into her downturned face as one would a child. "*You* didn't do it," he says giving her a gentle shake.

"We've totally betrayed Bruce's trust. What a shite thing t' do, pardon my language, and I just keep imaginin' how he's goin' t' feel when he sees it. Somethin' like how ye did — but worse. So much worse," says Mary. The tears keep rolling down her cheeks. "I can't think o' anythin' that'll make up for it."

He leans forward and kisses her forehead. "Shh. It's okay."

She pulls back, surprised, stiffening under the weight of his hands on her shoulders.

"Sorry," he says. "That was wrong. I should respect that you're happily married." He slowly lifts his hands.

"I'm . . . married."

His soft bangs swing forward, covering one eye. She supresses the urge to brush them back. He's still talking, "but maybe I'll see you on the beach again before you leave, and this time maybe you'll let me rub sunscreen on your ass, or we can take a swim, together." He grins. "I felt something for you the first time we met. I'm sorry.

Jesus. This isn't right for me to be still going on. You're married."

"At your farm? The first time we met at your farm?"

"No. Little Tribune."

The memory surfaces for her, but it's completely different. His face is now in it, his smile, his caring eyes. She steps past him and stops, her hand caught in his.

"I'm leaving in a week, Sam. And I am married. I can't think about *this* right now. There are so many bigger problems for me to sort out. I need to go. I'm sorry."

FORGIVENESS

B RUCE GOT LUCKY and found a guide book on native Irish plants in the tourist rack of the village store. Pocketing the careworn book, he leaves Number 8 and walks the narrow path through the fields to the graveyard. The sun, just up, sparkles with the light of a thousand diamonds in the long dewy grass. Its rays have yet to touch the frosted headstones shimmering in the cool morning air.

He searches the perimeter of the church wall hoping to find forbs such as sheep sorrel, lady's bedstraw, garlic mustard, Irish eyebright, and wild thyme.

Using a small spade borrowed from Martin's shed, he cuts a wide square around a clump of bird's foot trefoil. Just as he lifts the flower into a plastic bag, he feels a tap on his shoulder.

"Father! You startled me," says Bruce pressing a dirty fist to his chest. "You don't mind, do you? I thought I'd gather a few starter plants for the neighbourhood wilding project over on Village Gate. Have you heard of our little project?"

"I have. Exciting." Father Fingal rocks back and forth on his heels. "I was just poppin' my head out the back door when I saw ye. I thought I'd come over and see how ye're makin' out with yer grandparents and such. Was the talk with Desmond helpful?"

"It was. It revealed a side to my grandfather I'd never have known otherwise. Desmond said that James saved him from a fire and tried to save his pregnant wife. I found photos of my grandfather in a box at Mary's. He didn't look like a very well man with just one leg, one eye and suit that had grown three sizes too big. The rescue must have been incredibly difficult."

"Well, you can be proud o' that."

"Yes." Bruce stirs soil into the hole left by his excavations and then tamps it down firmly with his boot. "I'm wondering if we might talk, Father."

"Of course. Let's have a seat by my back door."

Bruce picks up his bag of transplants and follows Father Fingal to a small, sun-dappled patio. On a weathered table, a mug half-full of coffee sits forgotten next to a plate sticky with jam. Father Fingal dries off the bench with an old rag before offering Bruce a seat.

"Don't mind my mess," says Father Fingal. "What would ye like t' talk about?"

Bruce tries to compose his thoughts, which have become tangled in the last few weeks.

"I came here, primarily, wanting to find out more about my family . . . maybe find family. But I suppose I was also hoping to put some demons to rest, for myself and for my father. I'd do the same for my mother, if I had any idea where she was from."

"Did ye find out what ye needed? About yer father's side?"

"Yes and no. Learning more about my grandfather and his disability, for instance, and the circumstances of my grandmother's passing have humanized them for me, I suppose. My grandfather is no longer the heartless father I presumed when you and I found that headstone. But, I know in my heart, Dad would have been better off here, no matter the circumstance, than where he was sent."

"Why do ye say that, son? Life has been very hard here for some over the years. Can ye be certain o' that?"

"I can. I haven't talked about it much, Father. But, a close friend of my dad's, from his time at Fairbridge, spoke to me at the funeral. I always knew something was wrong with Dad. That he carried a heavy weight. I thought perhaps it was knowing my mother had been molested at the school and that he hadn't been able to stop her from taking her own life. But it was his own trauma, not just hers. The monsters at that place, they preyed on girls and boys. If they hadn't sent him away . . . anything here would have been better than what happened to him. That fact, the helplessness of his existence, has left me feeling profoundly angry. It's an anger that seems so deep I don't know how or if I'll ever get rid of it."

"His pain is gone now, son. He's at peace with God."

"I called him a terrible father more than once. I was so frustrated that I could never meet his expectations. It wasn't until I was older that I realized he hadn't had an example to follow as a parent, no one to model his own parenting on. I suppose he pushed me because he felt so inadequate himself. They probably all did, coming out of that place. Then finding out what he had endured, not just the bullying, but terrible abuse, I feel even more guilty for how I lashed out. It seems I only added to his pain. And there's no way of making that up to him." Bruce looks up into the enormous canopy of the tree above them, hoping to keep his eyes from tearing up.

"Yer father loved ye, Bruce. The fact that ye're here shows that ye loved him in return. Of that there is no doubt. Ye must find it in yerself to forgive others — but also to forgive yerself."

"I make it a habit to see the good in others, to forgive and to maintain an open heart," says Bruce. "Yet, where this is concerned, I've not been able to forgive what happened to him and my mom. No matter how much I meditate or try to surround myself with positive energy, I still can't rid myself of it."

"No one expects ye to forgive the people who abused yer parents. We should call out evil for the evil that it is. Those abusers will face our mighty Lord and receive fit punishment. But, as for yerself, and yer relationship with yer parents, there isn't a teenager in this parish that doesn't rail against their mam or pap most the week. The adult ye have become must now forgive the young man ye were. Just as yer father would have done. Just as all parents do."

"I wish I could apologize to him in person."

"Life without regrets is a life not lived. We all know regret. Tell me, do ye think yer grandfather would've regretted sendin' his son away if he knew what became of him?"

"Yes, of course. How could he not? And when I think about it, Desmond said as much. He told me James couldn't even say my dad's name."

"Aye, that sounds like regret. At its core, regret is a plea for forgiveness, isn't it? Askin' for forgiveness is an act of goodness, and the wonderful thing is, ye have the power to grant that forgiveness to yerself, and others. God forgives as well, when ye ask him."

"I haven't been to a Catholic church since I was a young boy. I have a different spiritualism now, Father. It would be so easy if God could lighten this burden. I would so much like that to work."

"You have confessed and ye're forgiven, son."

"Thank you, Father. And thank you for listening. These things are hard to share, and I sometimes feel I don't have the right to. My parents tried so hard to keep them secret."

"Part o' what troubles ye, Bruce, is that ye want to reverse what happened to them. Ye want to save them. It was never yer job to save them, son."

Bruce takes a sudden deep gulp for air and begins to sob. Father Fingal stands and leans over to lay a hand on his back. Bruce cries uncontrollably until he finally catches his breath.

"Yes. They were my parents, yet, when I think of them now they are always those little children. Yes," says Bruce.

"Ye're right to talk about it. There can be no healing until we speak the truth. Secrets fester."

"I'll be alright now, Father. I suppose I've taken up quite a bit of your time." Bruce wipes his face dry with the sleeve of his shirt. He stands and holds Father Fingal's hand in both of his. "You've helped so much. I will always remember this." He waits for Father Fingal to disappear inside with the dirty dishes before heading for home.

SABOTEUR

MARY LISTENS, WAITING for Martin to start the shower. She opens the sliding patio door and, as soon as the water starts, she strides across the dusty yard in a pair of Martin's boots. His shears are arranged by size on the workbench. She grabs a hammer off the wall, takes the biggest shears, and carries both around to the back side of the shed where a thick web of ivy has nearly obscured a large rock. She quickly slides the shears into the ivy and balances them on a flat spot. Lifting her arm, she targets the hinge and brings the hammer down with all the force she can muster. Pain shoots through her as metal hits metal and skids off the rock. She tests the shears. They're unharmed. Unlike her shoulder.

There isn't much time. As soon as Martin is dressed he'll come looking for her.

She tries twisting the shears out of shape but again produces no discernable effect. She looks around in desperation. Poking out of the ivy skirting the rear of the shed are a handful of rusty iron stakes about a quarter inch in diameter. She opens the shears and clamps down on one as hard as she can. The shears pivot sharply, twisting the blades. This time when she tests them, they won't close. Bowlegged, their tips cross. She repeats the process on every set of shears Martin has before carefully returning them to the bench.

Watching the house, she gathers Bruce's shovels and rakes from the bar of hooks next to the shed door and manhandles them out to the head of the driveway. Flower, her accomplice, is waiting.

"I'll be back with the wheelbarrow. Thanks for doin' this," says Mary, giving Flower a quick kiss on the cheek.

Mary runs back to the house and listens under the bathroom window. Martin is out of the shower. The electric razor hums and she hears him singing *The Wild Rover* in accompaniment. She dashes for the shed once more and loads the chainsaw and Bruce's electric hedger into the wheelbarrow. She races back to Flower.

"I'll keep these until Bruce is back, hey?" asks Flower.

"Yes, please. And sorry it'll be awkward walkin' up yer hill with 'em," says Mary.

"I'll leave them at Sam's farm," says Flower. "Now go. I'll see you tomorrow."

She's back in the kitchen before Martin emerges from the bathroom, safe from discovery, for now. She pours two cups of coffee and replaces the pot. Her hand has the slightest tremor.

The doctor told Martin to avoid any risk of stings for at least five days from the time he was attacked. Sam told Martin the bees needed a week. So, thanks to the bees, she and Martin are walking to the Natural History Centre today. If she's creative, she can keep him away from the house until supper.

As for tomorrow, she has no idea what she'll do.

POTLUCK

BRUCE CLAPS AND WHISTLES as the cast take a hasty bow, simultaneously removing wigs and turbans and unfastening sheer skirts and bright satin harem pants.

"Remove *all* of yer costumes. No exception. Everythin' back on their hangers," shouts Geraldine. "Only one more rehearsal tomorrow. And you're all still too sloppy. Not one of ye is waitin' for yer cues — ye don't just speak when ye feel like it. And Paul, please, the flute was pitchy start o' act four. Let's not burst ear drums. That might be fine down the pub but our audience won't be so full o' drink."

"Course they will, Paul," chides Padraig. "Geraldine, I don't know why I stayed. Ye haven't taken a single suggestion o' mine. And my costume is still not showy enough. I'm supposed t' be a rich Sultan. I should shine. The audience won't know me from a merchant."

Eoghan interrupts, "Ye haven't listened t' my suggestions either. I should be makin' love to Mags in the openin' scene," he says. "Maybe I should be on top o' her. We're lovers. We should be shiftin', at least."

"Keep your hands off o' Maggie," says Callum. "Show her respect."

"It's for the good o' the play. The audience needs to understand why the Sultan chops her head off," says Eoghan. "You agree, don't ye Mags?"

"Stick t' the script, Eoghan, or I tell Fiona ye're a lech," says Mags.

"I'm famished, and it's been fair hard deliverin' my lines while lookin' at that spread o' food," says Cat. Her costume lies in a heap centre stage. "Help me down, Bruce. I'm too tired t' go round t' the stairs. And that," she says, indicating the two young men now standing toe to toe "could go on a while. Callum asked Claire to print a personal ad in the paper a while back. He's only nineteen, and his *desperately seeking* was a perfect description o' Mags. Needless to say, Callum was ragin' when he didn't get Eogan's role as Ali Baba."

Bruce lowers Cat to the ground and ruffles her already messy blond hair. "Thanks for inviting me to the party. This spread looks great. You guys look great," says Bruce.

"Ye're honorary cast. Ye've been here enough," says Cat. "Grab a plate."

Mags lines up behind Bruce at the buffet. He turns and winks at her. "You did alright, hey? And great job on Bridget's makeup. She doesn't look a day over forty. Better than promised."

Mags elbows him playfully in the ribs and lifts an eyebrow. "Openin' night I'll have her down t' twenty-five, ye'll see. Seriously — I've got tape."

"Who made the food?" asks Bruce.

"We all brought somethin'," says Claire. "I'm veggies. Cat's ambrosia salad. Bridget made the pineapple and carrot bundt. So on and so on. It's usually the same every time."

Bridget shuffles up beside him and pats his back. "Nice to see ye, love. We didn't finish our visit. Will ye come by on the weekend, once the show is all done? We can talk some more. Ye still have six more days, that so?"

"I will for sure. And here, Bridget, you can have my plate. Tell me what you'd like and I'll bring it over to ye."

"Normally I'd argue, lad, but it's been a long day," Bridget says, pointing at the Ambrosia salad. "A spoonful o' that, t' start."

"Help," squeaks Paul. "Help," he calls more urgently. "My front teeth. Help. Help me find the — the pieces." He is holding his plate in one hand and covering his mouth with the other. His eyes sweep back and forth along the floor. "No one move. Don't step on them."

"I see 'em, Paul," calls Eoghan. He pinches two small triangles of tooth off the floor and drops them into Paul's waiting hand. "How'd it happen?"

"It was the carrot," says Paul as he spits something into his hand. "It had this stuck to it." He shows everyone a shriveled pea floating in a dollop of spit.

Bruce looks from Mags to Cat to Claire. He looks down at the veggie platter, his imagination reassembling the julienned carrot sticks into a full-size, pea-studded penis.

Cat spits her carrot onto her plate and wipes her tongue with her napkin. "You didn't," she says to Claire. "Did you . . . use it first?" Cat holds up a carrot stick to the light.

"No! I just didn't want to waste it. Honest. I'm single, I have money put aside, and I wanted the real deal, the Panda model." Claire's face is white. "I guess I missed a pea."

Bruce laughs and puts his arm around Claire. "I suppose if you plan on using one every day, that would certainly be a lot of carrots. So, in a way, your Panda could be responsible for feeding millions, Claire." He squeezes her shoulder and lifts the veggies off of Bridget's plate.

Paul is attempting his repertoire but only managing sharp whistles and short blasts of air. "Shite," he lisps, His tongue probing the sharp contours of his incisors. He brings the instrument to his mouth again; discord.

"I'm fair sorry, Paul," says Claire.

"We're ruined. We can't do the play without the music," says Geraldine throwing the loose pages of her script onto the floor. "Somebody get me a shot o' kettle."

"That's bad," says Cat to Bruce, raising her eyebrows. "Geraldine's practically president o' the temperance lodge."

"What do we do?" asks Mags.

Joan grabs Paul's whistle out of his hand. "Fer God's sake, stop that racket so we can think. It's not gettin' any better the more ye nurse it."

"Ye're goin' t' think I put Claire up t' this," says Cat to Bruce. "I was that determined t' get ye into the play. Joan, give 'im the whistle. See if he can play it."

Bruce cleans off the end of the whistle and puts it to his lips. It's not much different from the one he left at home. He plays a quick tune — a passable attempt, though not as good as fully dentate Paul.

"Ye've been here enough, Bruce. Can ye remember which songs go with which scenes?" says Joan.

"I think so. I'll need to practice. Can I get a copy of the music and the script," says Bruce.

"Stall the ball, ladies," says Geraldine, waving her hands. "I'm cancellin' the whole show. We're not havin' this degenerate twitterin' away wit no clue as to what he's about. I'm the director. I'm the one the whole village will blame. And I won't be made the fool on account o' him." She waggles a finger at Bruce, her jowls following suit. "My decision is final."

Geraldine plunks down at the head of the table to finish off her heaping plate of ambrosia and pineapple bundt. "Poor Father Fingal," she laments between forkfuls, "he'll be that sad for me, he will. How I suffered for weeks with ye. And all fer nothin'."

"So ye'll accept, Bruce dear?" says Bridget.

"I accept," says Bruce. "I'll be here first thing."

BEACH DAY

M ARY GROANS. She was enjoying a sleep-in.
"Wake up!" shrieks Martin. "Call the police. We've been burgled." He is shuttling back and forth between the bedroom and the sliding patio door.

Mary throws back the covers and swings her legs out of bed. She didn't consider that Martin would want to call the police. Do they have police on the island?

"I'm comin'," she says, rubbing her temples vigorously. "I just have t' pee and then I'll call."

When she picks up the receiver, she makes sure Martin is outside. She dials Flower. "Hi. He's seen the shed. He wants me t' call the police. Are there any here? Is there any chance we can delay them? We leave in six days."

"I thought this might happen. The constable is a good friend of mine. He lunches in the market near my shop every day. Last night, I called him and explained the situation, just in case Martin called. Still, try to stall as long as possible."

"Ye're amazin', Flower. Thank ye. Geez. I have t' go. He's comin'."

Martin's hair is standing on end, he hasn't shaved and his eyes are like saucers. "Was that them?"

"Yes. They have t' get someone special here by ferry. It could be a few days." The lie slides smoothly off her tongue.

"They destroyed my shears. What a feck'n dodgy shite-hole ye brought us to. Those shears were expensive. And they'll be hard t' replace."

"The police said t' make a record o' what was stolen or damaged and they'll take it all down officially when they come."

"Well, Bruce's stuff isn't worth much. Old shovels, old wheelbarrow. He's hardly the kind o' guy to look after things. What I want t' know is, how I am goin' t' get compensation fer my stuff? Do ye think a guy like Bruce has insurance?"

"I'm not sure. Let's not sit around and stew about it, though. We could have a beach day. We can't do anythin' else and it'll take yer mind off of it. The museum was nice yesterday, wasn't it?"

"It was alright, for a tiny place like this," says Martin, scratching his scalp and looking out the back door. "They took the tools but not the patio furniture. Maybe they'll be back tonight."

"I'm sure they're smart enough to suspect the police will be watchin' our place from now on," says Mary. "Let's have a big breakfast and go t' the beach."

"Fine. Do we have sausage?" Martin pounds his forehead rhythmically with his fist. "I just can't get over the loss o' my shears. They're irreparable. I can't figure out why someone would destroy 'em. It's so . . . random. But, ye know, Mary, it feels personal. Now why? Haven't I kept t' myself, Mary?"

"Ye have. And it wasn't just yer stuff taken."

"I suppose," says Martin.

"Go shower and find yer suit and I'll put somethin' together." Mary kisses his cheek and smooths his hair. She feels guilty about how upset he is, even though her cause is just.

Three hours later, they are finally on the beach at Tribune Bay, though not the section Mary is used to. Lying side by side on their towels, they are surrounded by tourists with beach umbrellas, portable boom boxes and crying children. Mary is struck by what a different experience it is. A Frisbee-tossing teenager keeps kicking sand on her, thanks to his partner's lousy aim. It's getting on her nerves.

Martin is enjoying himself, if the positive comments peppering his relentless whining are any indication.

"Why haven't ye suggested we come here sooner?" he says. "These are all normal people, normal families."

"I invited ye t' the beach several times. Ye never wanted t' come."

"Well, ye didn't sell it properly."

Mary closes her eyes and flips onto her stomach. It occurs to her that she's going to get tan-lines from her bathing suit, and says a moment of thanks that Martin never cottoned on to her seamless tan.

"I'm goin' t' pummel the gobshite who ruined my shears. Problem is, it could be any one of the unshaved, unwashed and half-clothed clowns running around this god-forsaken island."

"Ye know, Martin, I'm tired of ye running down the people I've made friends with here. They are really cool, considerate, wonderful people."

"Cool." Martin smirks. "Like that flakey friend of yers. What kind o' a name is Flower. Can ye imagine the type of parents she had."

"That's it Martin. I'd rather spend the rest o' my life with people like Flower than sit here with ye." She stands and gathers her things, shoving them into her beach bag. She shakes her towel out with such vehemence that Martin is peppered with sand. She marches straight down the beach until she reaches the path leading through the trees to Little Tribune Bay. As she leaves the blaring music and harsh laughter behind her stride lengthens and her shoulders begin to release their grip on her earlobes.

She spies Blue lying in the lee of a bleached log, book draped across her midriff. Nick is standing above her with the sun to his back, casting shade for Blue as they talk.

The sound of Nick's belly laugh puts her heart further at ease. He looks up and sees her. Saying goodbye to Blue, he lopes over to gives her a hug.

"I hoped I'd be seeing you again. You're leaving soon, hey?" He's leaning on a long stick, smiling, not in a rush for her reply.

"I am. It's nice to get a chance t' say goodbye, just in case. I wish I could stay right now, but I'm just cuttin' through on my way t' Flower's. I've had a lot of beach time already today." Mary points over her shoulder to larger Tribune Bay.

"Promise to come tomorrow then. I've missed you." He leans forward and gives her a kiss on the cheek.

Just as he pulls away her heart plummets.

"Hey ye! Get away from my wife!" Martin is charging toward them, leaping the beached logs, fists ready.

"Run," says Mary.

"No way," says Nick.

Martin swings. Nick ducks. Martin swings. Nick side steps. Martin ploughs forward, arms wrapping Nick's waist, both topple.

Martin hesitates briefly as he registers he's grappling with a naked man. Nick flips him and slips his arm quickly round Martin's neck. Caught in a sleeper hold, Martin's eyelids flutter shut.

"Let him go, Nick," Mary pleads.

Frank pulls Nick off.

"Sorry Mary," says Nick, dusting the sand from his body. "He'll be fine in a moment."

MIDNIGHT CALL

BRUCE FLIPS ONTO his back, suddenly awake. It's full dark, with the exception of the streetlight casting hollow shadows on the bedroom wall. There it is again. The phone. His legs are still half asleep as he stumbles down the stairs and rushes into the kitchen.

"Hello." There's a momentary clicking in the phone and then silence. Bruce looks at the receiver and then replaces it to his ear. Have they hung up?

"Hello, Bruce? This is Martin. We agreed that we'd be comin' home on Monday, the first, but we've had a change o' plans. We'll be leavin' here Friday mornin' on the first ferry. That puts us home early hours Saturday mornin', or as late as the afternoon. I would appreciate it if ye're out by Friday night."

"Hi Martin. It's middle of the night here." He glances at the kitchen clock forgetting it stopped yesterday afternoon. He draws a hand down his face. "Or rather, it's very early Thursday morning. I'm helping in the play Friday night. Do you think it would be alright if I left Saturday morning? I could sleep on the couch Friday night if you think you'll be arriving overnight."

"No. I'm not okay wit that. Bein' in the play is none o' our problem. Mary and I need our house back."

"Is everything okay?" asks Bruce.

"No. But that's none o' yer business."

The line goes dead.

KEEP AWAY

MARTIN DEPRESSES THE PLUNGER on the wall-mount and ends the call, offering the phone's handpiece to Mary. She is so frustrated from the game of keep away she and Martin have been waging throughout the call that she wants to knock him on the head with it.

"That was really unfair t' Bruce," she says.

"What? It's our house."

"We made a promise. We're disruptin' his time. And I'm not ready t' leave," Mary says, hugging the handpiece protectively to her chest.

"When ye're done with that, I need it t' call the airline," says Martin.

The steady tone from the earpiece is insistent, pressuring her to act. "Ye can't call the airline yet. When I said I'm not ready t' leave, I meant I am not leavin'. If ye go home early, ye're goin' on yer own."

Martin scoffs, "I'm sure Bruce will be happy t' come home and find ye camped out in his bed. Or maybe that's what ye want. The guy on the beach wasn't enough for ye. How does it happen that ye were kissin' a naked man minutes after leavin' me? Did ye two have a prior arrangement?"

"No! It's not like that. If ye had taken the time t' look ye would have seen that everyone on the beach was naked. And it was a kiss on the cheek. Why would I keep lyin' t' ye about it?"

"A bunch o' social deviants. I can't wait t' get off this fricken island. What happened t' the nice Catholic girl I married? Ye'll be in the confessional for months. Poor Father Fingal will be stretched t' come up with enough penance. Ye're a bloody, sinnin', God damn whore."

"I did nothin' wrong," says Mary, slamming the phone back on its cradle and storming out of the kitchen.

"Ye were shiftin' with a naked man!"

Martin follows her into the bedroom. She sidles toward the bedroom door and retreats to the open space of the living room. "He's a friend. He was sayin' goodbye."

"Ye're defendin' him? Tell me the truth. Have there been other times when ye've seen him naked?"

Mary hesitates. Martin's face is cherry red. "Yes. In fact, I've seen all o' my friends naked. There's nothin' wrong with it."

"The lads? And not just the gobshite on the beach? And were *ye* naked with all o' them?"

"I don't want to talk about this," says Mary, moving closer to the easy chair. "Ye're actin' the brute."

"How many have ye slept with?" Martin's voice is calm now, chummy. "Ye can tell me. I won't get mad."

"None o' them," she shouts.

"Liar!" he hisses, lunging, grabbing hold of her arms and forcing her back against the window so hard it rattles. His face is inches from hers, his rage is a heat, searing her. She looks at him blankly, focused now only on calming him, worried what could happen, playing dead in his grip, hoping he'll move on. He shakes her so that her head drums against the glass and then let's go, pushing away from her.

She takes cover behind the couch and crouches down. She can see his reflection in the glass. "Now I wish I had," she mumbles under her breath. Louder she says, "I'm sleepin' on the couch until ye're gone. I'm not comin' with ye. In fact, I don't know if I ever want t' come home."

"Well, ye can't divorce me so I guess ye have no choice. And what skills do ye have if ye could?"

The remark stings. Of course he's right. She's been housekeeping for him since they were married. Profound exhaustion weighs her down. She glimpses the life in store for her back home and feels with dread its promise of limits, loneliness and loss. This, her magical, free-spirited time, has been nothing more than a brief reprieve. When she eventually steps on that plane she will be dressed in her polo shirt and cotton peddle-pushers once again. She will wake up in her house on Village Gate, make Martin's breakfast and clean his house. Not even her friends back home are likely to accept, or understand, the self she has become while here.

She hesitantly stands up.

"I'm going to bed."

She inches around him to grabs the quilt and a pillow from the bedroom. When she returns, he is on the phone with the airline.

A PRETTY COUNTRY

BRUCE COULDN'T GO back to sleep. According to his watch it was four in the morning when Martin wrang off.

He called the airline. He made a cake with what remained of his baking ingredients, cleaned the house, washed the linens and took out the trash.

His bags, minus the clothes he needs today and tomorrow are packed and waiting downstairs. He is overwhelmed with a feeling that he has come so far and somehow squandered the time he could have used to discover more about his father and grandfather. It felt like he had more time. He *did* have more time. Now he has thirty-six hours, if he doesn't count the day of the play.

It's 8:00 a.m.. He dials Bridget.

"I hope it's not too early," Bruce says, detecting a bit of hoarseness in Bridget's voice.

"Not at all, dear. I'm up at half-five, regular as clockwork, whether I want to or not."

"I got a call from Martin and Mary last night. Sounds like they're coming home early and need their house back by Friday night. I've rebooked my plane ticket and now leave Ballycanew Saturday morning. Do you think I could see you again before I go?"

"Let's do one better than that. Come over here today. Bring all yer stuff. Ye'll stay wit me until ye leave. In exchange, if ye don't mind, maybe ye can help me with a few things around the farm and cottage. It's not often I get the services of an able young man."

"Are you sure?"

"O' course. It'll be like havin' family. Can ye be here around

11:00? That gives me time to get a list o' fix-its drawn up."

"I sure can. Thank you, Bridget."

Bruce replaces the receiver. He looks around the kitchen, at the hallway with its horrible wallpaper and clashing colours. He'll miss it here. He's made a lot of good memories.

He picks up the phone and calls Cat. He gets a number for Mags, Joan and Claire. He draws up a list of yoga poses for Séamus and pencil drawings of each, simple routines to follow, a few challenging poses, in the hopes that Séamus will carry on the group after he leaves. They are twenty-strong now. And so far, none of the non-member residents has complained about their uniforms.

It's 10:50 when he finishes on the phone. He borrows one of Mary's notecards, writes a message and stuffs it in an envelope. He opens the front door, sets his bag on the walk, looks down the street, and leaves the cake on the front stoop with the note clearly visible, FOR DESMOND written on the front.

Cat swings her car out of the driveway and pops her trunk. He takes a last look at Number 8 Village Gate.

"Who's the package for?" say Cat.

"Desmond. I've actually grown quite fond of him. We had tea the other day. I let him keep the photo of him and my grandfather. It seemed to mean a lot."

"That was good of ye. I suppose ye should've rang Mary t' see if she'd let ye keep some o' the other photos for yerself. It's too late now, sure, ye've left the key in the house."

"You're right. I was so surprised at having to leave early, I've left a few things unfinished."

"So, ye got on with the 'auld codger?" Cat swings the car onto the main road and Bruce grips the dash as he sees a truck coming toward them full speed on the narrow lane. He lets out his breath only when the truck is safely past and in the rear-view mirror.

"I did. Did you know he lost his pregnant wife in a fire? My grandfather saved Desmond. He managed to pull his wife out, too, but wasn't in time to save her."

"Bruce, he lost his wife *and* their five-year-old daughter in that fire. He didn't mention his little girl?"

"Jesus, no."

"There were a bunch o' run-down, ancient row houses on Village Gate before the ones there now. They all burned t' the ground. That's how it is he still thinks he lives in Number 8. He's a confused old bugger."

"He's a dear, frightened, old man, Cat. It breaks my heart how his life was touched by tragedy like that. I know you care for him yourself."

"Alright, I do. Though he doesn't know me from Eve. Did ye say yer granda' was the one to pull 'em from the fire? Ye're sure?"

"Yes. According to Desmond, he was living with them after my father was shipped away."

"I don't know if I should say this, 'cause it might not ha' been your granda', but the man that pulled Desmond from the fire that night died goin' back into the house for the little girl. Mary's said sometimes she thinks the house is haunted, or at least the ground it sits on."

Bruce looks out the window in silence. The countryside is so beautiful, so peaceful. It's hard to fathom the bounty of misery it's witnessed.

SLIP SLIDING AWAY

MARY PULLS HER SUITCASE out from under the bed. The shower is running. She arranges her clothes on the coverlet in neat piles. She has one pile for those she knows Martin prefers her in — lace blouses, knee length pleated shorts, a pair of pale-pink dress pants. These will all go to the charity shop. Another pile is for clothes she might wear if she's desperate: polo shirts, cardigans and narrow thigh-length cotton skirts. The last pile is all the clothes she loves — her new clothes. Some of these she tucks into an overnight bag. The remainder, and the contents of the desperate pile she stuffs into the case along with her spare shoes and jewellery. She locks it and stows it back under the bed.

Steam is billowing from the bathroom into the narrow hallway between the bedroom and living room. She tiptoes along the hallway until she can see Martin shampooing his hair. When he turns into the shower stream to wash his face, she darts in to grab her makeup bag and toothbrush. These she slides into the small overnight bag slung across her shoulder.

She takes the key to the front door and writes a hasty note. One word. Goodbye.

Flower knows she's coming.

YIELDING

THE TRANQUILITY OF SAM'S lower field is at odds with the chaos in Mary's head. The grass is a golden yellow and the sky beyond a cornflower blue. The grazing sheep shy as she approaches and then one by one return to pulling grass while keeping a wary eye on her. She sits cross-legged at a comfortable distance and watches them.

The pastoral scene recalls her life in Ireland. She hasn't been to her grandmother's farm for some time. She misses cheesemaking. *If she could stay here* — maybe Sam would be kind enough to partner with her and she could sell cheese locally. Martin is wrong. She does have skills. She hails from three generations of cheesemakers.

She gets to her feet and heads for the gate. Sam is just coming in with the dogs. Even if she wanted to, and she doesn't, she couldn't avoid him. She dries her eyes.

They don't speak until Sam is in front of her and taking her hands. "I heard," he says.

"There was nothin' between Nick and I but friendship. Martin just assumed."

"You're going to Flowers?"

"Yes. For the night. The Filberg festival starts tomorrow. She said I could come with her and help sell the hats and socks we've made. We're takin' the earliest ferry."

"Did she mention I'm driving," says Sam. His hands are still holding hers, his fingers softly stroking her knuckles.

"No."

"She has too much to carry alone, obviously. I always help out."

"Were ye and she a couple?" Mary asks.

"No. Just good friends," Sam says, a grin spreading across his face. "She's always been clear she isn't looking for a serious relationship."

She's surprised by her relief. "Ah, good then."

"Why is that *good then*?" he says, still smiling and examining her face.

Mary feels warm all over. She can tell she's blushing. She rotates her hands in his and grasps his wrists. He inches his hands up her forearms to her elbows and pulls her closer.

"What are your plans?" he says.

"Long-term? I don't know. Short-term, I'm not goin' with Martin. I'll stay until Bruce gets home so that I can apologize in person — even though that won't be enough. I still have no idea how t' repay him."

"I've got a few ideas. Will you come stay with me here tomorrow night? Flower usually stays in Comox for the whole festival."

"I don't know." Mary fights the urge to fall against Sam's chest, to ask him to hold her. "I'm married. In fact, I have no way o' bein' unmarried." She loosens her fingers still holding Sam's forearms. He doesn't let go of her elbows.

"Come back with me tomorrow regardless. You don't have to decide right away whether to stay the night. I won't pressure you. I *really* like you. In fact, I wish you could stay on Hornby permanently."

"I'll give ye my answer tomorrow. Okay?"

"I'm just happy that wasn't a no," he says. "I'm going to kiss you. I'm sorry if that makes me a bad guy."

Mary doesn't pull back as Sam's lips take hers. She feels like she's whirling on a dancefloor. He's dipping her, leading her, reading her body and taking her where she wants to go next in this glorious moment of time. He is both powerful and gentle. He yields to her and she presses closer, sliding her fingers behind his neck.

He lifts her onto his hips.

The dog's barking brings her back to herself. She smiles shyly as they pull-apart and he slides her back onto her feet.

"That was . . . incredible. Thank you," she says. She's never been kissed like that before, ever, and she would gladly lean in to do it again. With one touch he erased every thought of Martin and the present calamity she's in.

"I hope you won't resent me later for crossing a line."

"No. And ye haven't. I stepped across that line o' my own free will."

WORK FER YER SUPPER

CAT SWINGS THE CAR OFF the main road through the narrow opening in the high stone wall, a wall made higher by years of untended ivy and brambles. Bridget is at the top of the drive, shotgun in one hand, a dead rabbit swinging by its feet in the other. She lifts the animal above her head and smiles like she's won the Irish Lotto.

"Remember t' pick the pellets out first," Cat says to Bruce. He looks at her blankly. "Ye're havin' rabbit stew for dinner." She squeezes his leg and gets out briefly to wave to Bridget.

Bruce unfolds himself from the passenger side and shakes out his legs. He pulls his case from the trunk and kisses Cat's cheek through the driver side window. "Thanks for the lift." He waves, then follows Bridget to the door.

Bridget holds the rabbit out, expecting him to grab it while she opens the latch. He hastily switches his case to the other hand and takes the limp creature. The rabbit's soft feet are still warm in his grasp. He lifts it and studies the furry face and shiny blue eyes.

Already out of her boots and coat, Bridget is padding toward the kitchen. "Come in, son. I've got a list o' things I'd love the help with, but perhaps ye can get the rabbit ready first and I'll set it in the pot for our supper. Drop yer case down, now, and take that rabbit through to the back. Ye'll find the knife, block and hammer all ready for ye."

"I should tell you," says Bruce, examining the rabbit, "I'm a vegetarian."

"Well, I'm not. And this is a special recipe. You'll just have t' pick around what ye don't want."

Bruce looks down at his shoes, muddy from the dooryard, and backs out the front door and around the side of the cottage. What the hell is he supposed to do with this? He's not a hunter. If he finds a dead rabbit in the garden he's more likely to give it a memorial than a skinning. She's killed this for their supper though, and to bury it would be worse than eating it — than Bridget eating it.

He sets the rabbit down on a butcher block that's mounted to a small wooden table outside the kitchen door. It shows evidence of heavy use. He tests the sharpness of the knife with his thumb. Eager to get this over with he lines the knife up with the rabbit's neck and turns away. His whole-body quivers with revulsion as he presses down through the soft fur and feels the crunch of bones in the creature's neck. The knife comes to rest against the forgiving wood and he reluctantly peeks. The head is severed. Blood seeps along the old slash marks on the butcher block. He gags and dry heaves into the wild rose.

Bridget pokes her head out the back door. "Are ye about done? What's this?"

"More honesty, I have no idea what I'm doing. I just wanted to be helpful," says Bruce.

"Help me down the step." Bridget takes up the knife and in five minutes has skinned, gutted and smashed the rabbit's bones to bits with a massive mallet. "Don't feel bad, lad. I've got a whole list o' things for ye t' do that I've been keepin' on the long finger."

"As long as they don't involve disembowelling animals then I'm your man."

After setting the rabbit to stew, Bridget leads Bruce across the yard to a low stone building with a new door. A heady odor of sheep's cheese hits his cribriform plate as she opens the door. Even as the overhead fluorescent tube sputters, the room gleams with stainless steel sterility. Massive round vats, long countertops, overhead nozzles, dangling hoses, and a shiny white linoleum floor stand in sharp contrast to the buildings aging stone exterior.

"I'm puttin' on a new cheese once the play is done. I wish ye could stay to help with that. But in the meantime, the job o' sterilizin' the cheese room is gettin' to be too much for these old bones."

"It already looks so clean."

"No. It needs a fresh wash, or we risk contamination."

"Do you need to make cheese?" Bruce asks.

"Aye, I depend on the income," she says sharply. "We always have. Just lookin' after the sheep isn't goin' to make anyone rich."

"Can you hire help?"

"There'd be not a penny left for me if I did."

Bridget supervises his scrubbing, soaking, mopping and rinsing, and then when they're done they remove their rubber suits and back out of the room.

"Are ye okay with heights?" Bridget asks sizing him up.

"Sure, if you have a good ladder."

The good ladder turns out to be a withered, wooden twelve-rung collector's item.

"Be careful of the slates up there. The broken aerial is just over the peak," says Bridget, watching him climb the slippery roof with her ancient leather satchel of tools slung over his back. "Once ye've done that, I've got a new hinge for the shutter on the guest bed window ye might as well fix, now we've got the ladder out."

By the time supper is over, Bruce is exhausted. Filled with fresh rolls, supplemented with potatoes and carrots separated from the rabbit stew, he's ready to fall asleep in the easy chair. He had an early morning, followed by a busy afternoon, followed by a long rehearsal, then a heavy pruning of the brush overtaking Bridget's front gate. He hopes his aching fingers can still play the flute tomorrow. Just as he drifts off, Bridget jolts him awake by dropping a stack of sheets and blankets on the arm of his chair.

"This is for yer room. Top o' the stairs and t' the left. Mary's old room."

INTERNAL BRUISING

Flower holds Mary at arms-length and searches her face. "You're glowing. I thought you'd be arriving at my door an absolute mess." She gives Mary a quick hug and then examines her face more closely. "You sounded so . . . broken on the phone," says Flower. "Come here, honey."

Mary drops her head to Flower's shoulder and the tears start to flow.

"Do you want to tell me more about it?" says Flower, guiding her down the hall.

"I think I've really messed everythin' up. I don't know why I'm lettin' Martin get t' me so much. I never used to. I'd just brush off our fights, knowin' I would eventually forgive him and things would go back t' normal."

"That's no way to live. Let me make you a cup of tea."

"Ye might be Irish yerself, Flower. Ye've always got a cup o' tea for me when I need it."

"Mom always said a cup of tea can cure all ills. My tea *literally* can. It'll do you some good. How about something calming?"

"I'm sorry to be such a burden the day before the festival," says Mary.

Flower pushes a pile of hats aside on the couch to make room for Mary. Knit wear and half-full cardboard boxes are scattered on the floor.

"I'll help. Just tell me what to do."

"I've got time to listen first," says Flower, hovering over her.

"I'd feel better if we talk while getting' ye ready," says Mary.

"Okay. Hats in this one, socks in this one, scarves in this one," says Flower, moving the boxes closer to Mary. "Did that bastard kick you out?"

"I left him. We've nothin' good t' say t' each other before he leaves tomorrow. I couldn't stand to be around him another minute. I used to be able to carry on with my day while things simmered between us. But, I just couldn't this mornin'."

"I heard about Nick and the beach. You would tell me if Martin hurt you, right? You wouldn't keep that a secret?"

"He didn't. Not really."

"What do you mean, not really?"

"He pushed me." She rushes to add, "I'm okay though. Just a few small bruises."

"Jesus, Mary. There are no small bruises."

"What I'm feelin' is worse than that, or — not worse, different than that, I guess. It's somethin' I've been mullin' over for years, and now he's turned a dial and I can't stand to feel it another day. It's as though every mornin' I'm expected to rise true to the mould he's cast me in. Almost all my friends work, but Martin thinks it's shameful for a married woman t' earn money. He thinks it's the '70's and the Marriage Bar is still a thing. So I stay home, go where he wants, make what he wants for tea, wear what he wants me to wear, and only see the friends he approves of. I'm not doin' that stuff for him ever again. He doesn't deserve it."

"Let me see your bruises? Did you fall when he pushed you?"

"No. He grabbed my arms and pushed me against the window."

Flower rolls up Mary's sleeves, and sees the bruises, then runs her fingers through Mary's hair. There's a spot on the back of Mary's head that makes her wince despite her effort to play it down.

"Has this happened before?" asks Flower, stroking Mary's hand gently.

"No. Honestly. And as I say, I'm not here because I was afraid he was goin' to hurt me again this mornin'. It's that he suddenly seems like a different person. He looked so evil when he grabbed me, and in that moment all o' my years o' unhappiness came into sharp focus. I feel like throwin' up at the thought o' goin' back t' my life with him."

"If you could change your life with him and convince him to give you more freedom, like getting a job, would you want to stay with him? Is it him, or the life you have with him?" asks Flower.

"It's — it's about so many things I can't sort them all out." Mary folds the top down on a full box of hats. "I want t' grow wild into what I was meant to be — and he keeps cuttin' me back like I'm one o' his damn topiaries penned up in our back garden."

"If you don't love him and are that unhappy, will you ask for a divorce?" asks Flower. "Can you get half of your house so that you have the money to start over? Do you have any savings of your own?"

"I'm wasting yer time, Flower. We should be gettin' ready for tomorrow."

"We have time. Have you thought about what you want to do? Is it safe for you to go back to him while you figure this all out? If he's done this to you this time, next time something makes him mad it could be a lot worse."

Mary shakes her head. "I *am* truly wastin' yer time. I can't get a divorce. There's nothin' real I can do t' change my situation. And Martin knows it. I'm trapped with him. Everythin' I'm sayin' about not wantin' to live with him is just wishful thinkin'. But wishes are all I have. It makes me feel hopeful imaginin' there's a way out. That there's some other life for me."

"Nothing is impossible, Mary."

"Tell that to the Church and the Irish government."

"What?"

"Not only is there no divorce in Ireland, but Martin can force me t' return t' the house if I try to live away from him."

"What! That is outrageous!" puffs Flower. She wraps her arms around Mary and slowly rocks her back and forth.

Mary melts into the embrace. Flower smells of herbs, lanolin and coconut shampoo.

"I wish I could stay here forever," says Mary. "Do ye think the Canadian government would eventually come lookin' for me if I did?" She tries to laugh.

"Well, how long can you actually stay? My bed's big enough."

Mary straightens her back and looks Flower in the eye, "Are ye offerin' seriously? Could that really happen? As I was crossin' Sam's farm on the way here, I got such a strong feelin' that I didn't want to leave. Would ye honestly let me stay here?" says Mary.

"Definitely. Listen, this will be packed and at the front door in half an hour. We'll go for a walk, have a nice dinner and then crawl into bed early. Tomorrow, the Filberg festival will be so much fun it'll take your mind off Martin. Then, once he's gone, you'll have more room to plan what comes next."

"Okay," says Mary. Except that she can't stop thinking about Martin and how many feelings and emotions are tied up in their life together. She has a duty to stay with him — eventually care for him when they're old. If she reneges on that promise she'll be ostracized by the Church, her community, maybe even her friends. She'll have no money and nowhere to live. She'll be leaving behind her comfortable home, with Cat and the rest of her friends just a hop away. And, if she does this, it's quite possible she'll have no friends to hop by to. On the other hand, if she stays on Hornby, she'll be free in a way she couldn't be back home. And what they say won't hurt if she's not there to hear it.

Her stomach is in knots, partly because she just kissed Sam, and liked it. More than liked it. The kiss was a revelation. A complication but a revelation.

GUILTY CONSCIENCE

BRUCE FINISHES SPREADING the quilt on Mary's childhood bed and takes a thoughtful look around the room. It's papered with tiny pink flowers on a pale green background. A teddy bear and a doll sit on the end of a shelf that also supports three hurley trophies, a few jewelled trinket boxes and a framed magazine cut-out of a teen heartthrob and his tastefully nude female co-singer. There is evidence of her more mature life too. Books on philosophy and animal husbandry, as well as romance novels. There is more of Mary in this tiny attic room than there is in all of Number 8 Village Gate. He flicks off the light and heads back downstairs.

Bridget has set a cup of tea for him next to his chair. He lifts the cup to take a drink but has to stifle a yawn first.

She's already sipping hers, smiling. Her tiny frame is engulfed by the deep upholstery of her own chair; barely a ripple reveals the presence of her legs beneath a lap blanket.

"This time tomorrow we'll be soakin' in the limelight," says Bridget, eyes shining in the glow of the tabletop lamp. The rest of the room is steeped in shadow. "There won't be too many more leadin' roles for me, I'm afraid."

"Nonsense. You're bound to win an award for this performance. Next season you'll be wanted on every stage from here clear to Dublin."

Bridget's tone flattens, "It's time that I told ye more about yer father."

"That reminds me. I didn't tell you, I found the pictures of him and my grandparents in Mary's basement," says Bruce. "Violet was so much younger than my grandfather, and very pretty. Was that . . . normal? The age difference? I noticed too that my grandfather was missing a leg, and perhaps . . . disfigured?"

"Yer grandparents were in love, Bruce. Violet fell in love with James at a very young age." Bridget takes a long sip of her tea. "Back then, during the civil war, we targeted rail lines. I was with Nellie the night o' yer grandfather's accident. I was young, and for me, things became real that night, more so than the night we were taken from our beds, more even than the night our brother was blown up. The explosives went off too soon, ye see. Yer grandfather lost his leg and was badly burned. I had t' put my hand in the shattered stump o' his leg. I'll never forget that feelin', desperately searchin' for the artery, watchin' his very life blood flow out o' him. It was my neck scarf that controlled the bleedin' in the end."

Bridget downs the rest of her tea and holds the cup out for Bruce to refill. She swallows a quick dose and continues. "The Free State set upon us and we hid yer grandfather at the house of another member. Violet was this man's daughter, just turned thirteen. She nursed yer grandfather back t' health. Afterward, they wrote t' each other fer years. When she turned eighteen, she up and left home and they were married. She didn't care that he was crippled and had no money. She was a hard enough worker for both o' them."

"How old were you when the explosion happened?" says Bruce.

"Seventeen. Let me finish, lad. The day Violet died, we all grieved somethin' awful. A very sweet brave woman she was. Died on the kitchen table givin' birth. And what was yer grandfather t' do with the babe? There he was, standin' in the kitchen, a new babe in his arms, bawlin' his eye out, the smell o' blood still thick in the air. Nellie offered to help. Not a second thought."

"It sounds like you were there."

"I was. Nellie and I had been called in t' aid with the birth. Nellie and he went back, ye see, to the years o' trouble together. We only came t' help with the delivery. When we left, we left with James and a new babe in tow. Well, it wasn' long before they fell in love and were married, James and Nellie. He supported her activism. She continued work down the factory, while he helped wi' bits o' the farm work. What he could, mind. Most o' it fell t' me, the farm work and lookin' after the children, Delia and Ambrose, yer father."

"So you knew my father well," says Bruce.

"He was such a cheery little darlin'. Which made it all the harder when everythin' fell apart."

Bridget drops her teacup into its saucer. "I need more tea."

Bruce takes her cup and splashes milk into it. He removes the cozy from the pot and wraps his palm around its belly. Satisfied, he pours Bridget a strong cup. He tops his up and replaces the cozy.

Her cup balanced in her lap, Bridget looks him hard in the eyes. "We'd been strugglin' for years, ever since '32 when de Valera made it illegal for married women to work in factories. If we didn't have the cheese . . . I don't know what. I did my best. I wasn't married, and never would be after that law passed. I knew by then the importance of a woman's ability to earn a wage. Nellie never gave up on what was right, and what was due t' every woman in this country. She kept fightin', even though Cumann na mBan had been outlawed around the same time. In '35 she was struck on the head, dead, while marchin' for a woman's right t' contraception. Some man, opposin' the march, threw a rock. Don't think he was aimin' for her. Any woman would have satisfied him. But he threw it t' kill, of that there's no doubt."

"That's how she died," whispers Bruce.

"Aye, that is how, indeed. Yer grandfather couldn't work and couldn't look after the children. I couldn't support everyone on the meager income from the cheese. We heard o' the Farm School, and through an old Cumann na mBan friend o' Nellie's, from before The Trouble and The Great War, I managed to get yer father to Wales on a fishin' boat. She passed 'im off as British and we were that glad when the school agreed t' take 'im. The brochure promised so much more than we could give. It was me that sent 'im away. I'm so sorry, son. I hope ye can forgive me."

"Couldn't one of you have written to him, given him some sign that he was loved?" asks Bruce, tears in his eyes.

"Yer grandfather fell apart. He had nothin' left. I'm afraid the drink took 'im and held 'im till his death. I should've written. I see that. I should've."

They sit in silence for a while, one of them remembering old ground, the other exploring new terrain.

"Thank you for telling me all of this," says Bruce. "I don't know what to feel. Relief to have found out, but sadness too, thinking of the love and life, even in poverty, that he could have had here."

"We thought we were givin' him the best life we could. We were fooled."

"I saw the brochures."

"Ambrose and Delia were like my own children. I'm a grandmother to Mary. If you want, and if ye can forgive me, I'd like it if ye would think o' me as family too," says Bridget.

Bruce leans forward in his chair and takes Bridget's soft hand. Her skin is like tissue paper. "I'd like that. I don't have family. So, I would *very much* like that." Bruce sighs with a kind of relief. "And of course I forgive you. How could I not?"

They stay up late, Bridget begging company because she can't sleep the night before a performance. They talk of the past, and of the present and of Bruce's life back home in British Columbia.

Sometime well after midnight, Bridget shakes him awake and he climbs the stairs to drop into bed. Bridget is with him. She tucks him in and kisses his forehead goodnight.

HEARTFIRE AND DAMNATION

MARY IS AWAKE BEFORE the alarm. In the dark, Flower's naked breasts press against her own through the thin cotton of Mary's pajamas. One of her arms is draped across Flower's waist, the other under her neck. Their bare legs are entwined. They must have pulled together in sleep.

A damp musky scent rises like heat from the thin space between them. With every exhalation, Flower's breath lifts a strand of Mary's hair and tickles her ear. Pleasure and shame are a caffeine, making her jittery, keeping her awake.

As the predawn light tiptoes softly through the door Mary wonders what Flower will think if she opens her eyes and catches her staring, enjoying their embrace. She closes her eyes and focuses instead on the sensations humming through her from every point of contact between them. Flower. Nick. Sam. What is happening to her? Why does she suddenly feel attracted to everyone? Everyone but Martin. Is something wrong with her? Or right?

The alarm startles Mary, rousing her from her thoughts as though from sleep. Before she can move, Flower stretches and squeezes her closer. Instead of pulling away in horror, Flower softly kisses her lips and strokes her hair. "Everything is going to be just fine today. You'll see."

Mary's mind is a step behind, still experiencing the kiss as Flower rhymes off their schedule. She manages a nod. If she was brave she'd stop Flower from speaking and return her kiss. But she's not. Uncertain whether Flower's kiss was one of friendship, or more than that, she contents herself with Flower's generous smile and soothing touch for as long as the moment can last. Which isn't long enough.

"We better get up," says Flower, kicking the remainder of the covers off. "Sam will be here in less than an hour." She rolls to the edge of the bed and flicks on the small bedside lamp. The glow from the pink shade warms the sheets, where moments before there'd shared a warm embrace. Flower throws her arms above her head and stretches the length of the bed. She yawns broadly and turns on her side, dangling one leg off the bed, readying to get up. "Excuse me. Still tired."

Mary's eyes explore the contours of Flower's naked body. She so badly wants to hold her again — before it's too late — to run her fingers through Flower's rumpled hair, to slide a hand down her side and over her smooth hip. Before she can stop herself, she reaches across the bed and gently places the flat of her hand against Flower's back.

Flower turns to her with a smile. "Look at us. We'd better get a move on . . ." The words evaporate in the unmistakable heat of Mary's expression.

Mary takes a quick breath and leans toward Flower, worried she could destroy everything between them if she's judged this moment incorrectly.

Their lips gently brush. Mary hesitates, and then, knowing the look in Flower's eyes as her own, she takes Flower's mouth fully. Flower bites Mary's lip causing her to moan, not just with pleasure but with a release of all the confused yearning she's felt for Flower from the beginning. She threads her fingers into Flower's beautiful hair, gathers it and tugs. She plants a chain of kisses under Flower's chin, down her neck and around each areola. Flower's eyes glow with a look deeper than any kiss.

Rolling on top of Mary, Flower presses her thigh between Mary's legs, separating them, and Mary's hips rise to meet her. Mary has no idea what will come next, what she should do, these feelings so familiar, yet so different, their touches so secret.

Suddenly Flower pulls apart. "Oh my, we've got to go," she says, "I enjoyed that." She gives Mary a quick kiss on the lips. "Do you want to shower first or me?"

"Ye can go first," says Mary, rolling off the bed and to her feet.

The schism in their lovemaking throws her off balance. Their kisses play back in her head. Each touch was electrified, and taboo, in a way that takes her breath away. Yet — as she listens to the shower start in the next room, she wonders if Flower's offer to live with her was as a friend or as a girlfriend. Did the kiss mean as much to Flower as it did to her? Despite Flower's eagerness Mary feels more confused about their relationship than ever. Maybe Flower has done this before, maybe often, and it doesn't mean what she thinks it means. And what, Mary wonders, does *she* want it to mean?

And then there's Sam. Ever since her kiss with Sam, she hasn't been able to get him out of her head. Surely that means something. There is no confusion where Sam is concerned. But is there a future with either of them?

Flower shuts off the shower. Mary straightens the bedcover and finds her clothes. Glancing at the clock, she sees they really do have to hurry.

At 5:30 Sam's truck rattles across the ramp of the Hornby ferry. Mary is wedged between him and Flower on the bench seat, her heart tugged in both directions. She looks up at Sam and feels warmth spread through her in response to his smile. She looks at Flower, and down at their clasped hands which bounce up and down on Flower's bare thigh in time with her tapping toe.

"Are ye excited?" Mary asks Flower, a shy smile playing on her lips at the memory of their kiss.

"Nervous and excited," says Flower. "There is always so much preparation and I guess I'm hoping everyone likes what we made."

"You're going to sell the whole lot," says Sam, his warm hazel eyes bright in the early light.

Blue knocks on the window of the truck bed. Sam slides it open.

"You guys warm enough back there?" he asks. Blue and Nick are huddled under a blanket between the boxes.

"Plenty," says Blue.

The ferry pulls smoothly away from the dock. Off the port-side, the rising sun tips a ribbon of pink taffy into the sea.

"Did you know, Mary, that Martin was going to be on this ferry?" Blue says.

"What? No." Mary's stomach lurches; her hand in Flower's

begins to tremble. She lets go and twists in her seat. She spots Martin sitting in their blue Toyota four cars behind and one lane over. His hands are planted firmly on the steering wheel. Mary turns back around and slides down the seat out of sight.

"You okay?" asks Sam.

"It looks pretty silly, me hidin', doesn't it?" says Mary, looking up at him.

"You do whatever you need to do. We aren't going to let him give you any trouble."

"Oh my — what about Nick? What if he sees Nick in the back?" says Mary poking her head up briefly to see if Martin is still in the car.

"Nick can look after himself," says Sam.

The ferry soon bumps the Denman dock and lowers its ramp. Blessedly their lane is off-loaded first which puts Sam's truck at least ten cars ahead of Martin's on the road to the ferry between Denman and Vancouver Island.

Mary's leg bounces impatiently during the short ride between terminals. Because of the way the boat is loaded, Martin is now only two cars behind them, sitting in the car, staring out the side window. She stays low in her seat.

Blue raps three times on the glass above her head. Sam turns to look. "He's coming," he says flatly.

Mary wants to crawl under the seat. Her heart is beating so wildly she can't think or see straight. Martin shouts at Nick. Then she hears her name. Flower squeezes her hand harder.

"I'll have t' get out," Mary says. She feels like an automaton. Her liquid legs practically pour out of the truck. "Stop yerself, Martin," she says coming round the back of the truck.

"Did ye sleep with him last night? And now ye're sneakin' off?" shouts Martin, jabbing his finger at her.

"O' course not," says Mary calmly. She can feel Sam and Flower behind her.

Martin grabs her roughly by the upper arm. "Ye're comin' with me. Yer suitcase is in the car and yer ticket is booked." He pulls the ticket from his jacket pocket and waves it at her.

"Let go!" She pulls away and he squeezes her arm tighter.

Sam moves between them. "Let go."

Martin releases her but stands his ground. "Get in the car, Mary."

"Ye had no right to rebook my ticket or take my case. I'm not leavin'."

"Well, how are ye goin' t' get home then? Ye don't have any money and I have yer passport," says Martin smugly.

"What if I hadn't been on this ferry?" says Mary.

"Ye heard me tell Bruce we were leavin' on this sailin'. I guess I knew ye'd wake-up and realize ye had no choice. If ye don't come with me now — ye have no way home. I don't really give a shite either way."

Mary is floored. She has no passport. He has changed her ticket and she has no way of changing it back. She looks to Flower for direction.

"I don't know what you should do," says Flower, helplessly. "There's room for you here, you know that." She turns to Martin and snaps, "You are a bloody asshole."

Mary's legs give out. She slides down the side of Sam's truck until she feels the cold metal of the ferry deck against her bum. She drops her head in her elbows. She can't think fast enough. The ferry is nearing the terminal. He's won, again. She reaches her arms up to Sam and he pulls her to her feet. His eyes are sunken with anxiety; she can't look at him.

She throws herself into Flower's arms. "I have t' go with him. I love ye. I'll write. Good luck this weekend. Thank ye for everythin', I'll never forget ye." Sam gives her a brief hug, followed by a long hug by Nick and Blue together.

The crew make an announcement. They've arrived. She gets in the Corolla and slams the door. Ahead of her, Sam's truck starts up. In a second her new life in this magical place has ended. She cries all the way to the airport.

THE SHOW MUST GO ON

THERE IS A GREAT DEAL of excitement and shuffling of chairs front of house as the lights dim and Bruce is given his cue. He brings the flute to his lips and releases the first notes. A few hands clap but are quickly hushed as the heavy velvet curtain lurches across the stage to reveal the Sultan's opulent bedroom. Behind the shear drapery of the bed, Mags reclines in Eoghan's embrace. The Sultan's wife and her lover.

Bruce serenades the audience with a sultry Persian melody. Mags moans and pets Eoghan as rehearsed. The petting becomes increasingly animated and Bruce picks up his pace. He doesn't remember this in rehearsal. From the corner of his eye he can see Eoghan trying to kiss Mags on the lips. Before Eoghan can achieve his mark, she's saved by Padraig, the Sultan, cutting off her head. The curtain jerks closed.

Bridget is on next. She swings her hips and attempts a little belly dance crossing the stage. She's ditched Geraldine's sister-in-law's walker, but it's clear the audience doesn't share her confidence; a collective sigh of relief is released as the Sultan finally lowers her to her cushion.

Eoghan, now as Ali Baba, is back on stage. His costume is askew, his turban backwards and he's walking with a pronounced and unscripted limp, courtesy, Bruce guesses, of Mags. Bruce flips to the sheet music for the cave of wonders. He's added cymbals to the original version and applies them liberally as Ali Baba discovers the treasure. The audience seems to really be enjoying it. Fiona, in the middle row, enraptured by Eoghan's performance, claps after he delivers each set of lines.

Bruce's yoga students, scattered throughout the crowd, send him encouraging signals each time he puts the reed to his lips. As a stand-in at short notice, he's made a few mistakes, but hopefully no one noticed.

Before long it's Cat's big chance to perform her sword dance for Ali Baba, his wife and the leader of the thieves. From his position stage right, standing below the actors, he can see the rest of the cast waiting in the wings stage left. So far they've carried the show off without a hitch. Only two acts to go. Callum, perfectly cast as leader of the thieves, is projecting his anger and cunning so well that the audience is on the edge of their seats.

Bridget is still narrating from her cushion. Padraig is at her feet continually altering his facial expression between surprise, wonder and disgust in a manner that has nothing to do with the storyline. Bruce spots a row of young boys near the front that appear be betting on what expression the Sultan will adopt next.

Cat and the girls are wheeling around Callum the thief, their scarves and harem pants flowing and billowing as they move. It's almost time for Cat to stab Callum. The spotlight shifts, leaving Ali Baba and his wife in the shadows. Bruce can see Mags fidgeting. Eoghan, as Ali Baba, suddenly lunges at her and kisses her awkwardly on the lips in another unscripted moment the village is likely never to forget. Eoghan, still holding Mags, pulls back and smiles at the crowd, improvising, "Oh wife, what a happy —"

He never gets to finish. Mags wrenches herself free and slaps him so hard his turban flies off.

Before Eoghan can react, Callum throws off his cape and jumps him. They roll, and Mags has to scuttle out of their way.

Bridget, the pro, ad libs the story, "The thief attacks Ali Baba, intent on killing him. His poor wife looks on, wondering if that kiss will be her last."

Callum pins Eoghan to the stage and pummels him. Eoghan's struggling long legs connect with his discarded turban and send it spinning into the audience; they're impressed. It all looks so real.

Bruce continues to play and adds a little tambourine. Given the donnybrook on stage, he wonders if he should use a trumpet and play the theme from Hockey Night in Canada instead.

In an effort to save the show, Cat, Claire and Joan resume their dance and circle the wrestling pair at a safe distance. Cat picks up her sword.

It's unclear whether the audience has caught the departure from the storyline, until Fiona rises from her seat and shrieks, "Let go o' him, Callum. You'll kill 'im."

"I'm doin' this for both o' us, Fiona," grunts Callum.

Eoghan rallies at the sound of Fiona's voice. He gains the upper hand and with a lucky punch knocks Callum out cold. Cat quickly stabs the sword into him, and motions to the young stagehand to close the curtains.

The audience is stunned, silent, with the exception of Fiona. She shoves people out of her way, intent on rushing the stage. Bruce lifts the flute to play, but the curtain cracks open and Padraig's face appears through the hole. In a high tenor he asks, "Is there a doctor in the house?" The curtain snaps shut and Padraig reappears in front of Bruce, below the hem of the curtain. "Keep goin', lad. Make up a tune. Stall."

Bruce riffs, replays music from act one, and then watching the curtain jerk this way and that with no sign of it opening he adds some of his music from the Andes. The audience is still seated, although mightily confused about what is and isn't part of the play.

At last, the curtain jerks open and Ali Baba and Morgiana the slave girl are centre stage. Eoghan's costume has been put to rights, minus his turban and the addition of a bandage to his nose. Cat plasters a smile on her scarlet face as Ali Baba pledges his gratitude to her for saving him from the thief. Callum is spread-eagled against to the backdrop, a doctor bent over him. It would almost make sense, if the doctor were in costume.

There are two more scenes, but Bridget wisely gives the abridged version. The play is over.

The cast rush on stage to take a bow and the hall erupts with loud cheers and deafening applause. Cat beckons to Bruce and he leaps up, takes her hand and they all bow again. Callum comes to as the curtain closes.

"That was mad as a box a frogs!" says Claire. "For feic sake,

Eoghan!"

"Yeah, ye little shite," says Mags. "Keep yer gob off o' me. Fiona doesn't deserve ye. Ye near ruined the show."

"What? It was actin'," says Eoghan.

"Thanks t' Bridget for pullin' us through. Ye're a real professional," says Cat, raising Bridget's arm.

"It was nothin' at all," says Bridget demurely. "Though we did well enough tonight, aye, despite the young brigade."

"You were great," says Bruce, kissing Bridget's cheek. "You all were. God, I'm going to miss you."

"Brilliant job ye did, playin' it on the fly, Bruce. Everybody loved ye and we sure don't want ye gone come mornin'. I miss our Mary, but this place won't be the same without ye," says Cat.

"You've a heart o' corn, Bruce," says Joan. "C'mon over t' the pub, all o' ye. Let's celebrate with a real hooley. I feel so good I might even let Geraldine join, that old wagon. Though she hardly deserves it.

SECURITY

MARY CHECKS HER WATCH and thumbs through her passport one more time. She wipes tears from her cheeks and idly moves her suitcase from one side of her to the other, just to have something to do. The plane will be boarding soon.

It was nice of the couple landing in Comox to offer her a ride to the Filberg. They overheard her asking for a bus — and apparently there isn't one.

The couple dropped her at the entrance, but she couldn't get into the festival, not having the entrance fee. Once she found Sam's parked truck she climbed into the bed and made a cushion of the blanket. She has no other options now, than to wait.

She left Martin as soon as she had her passport in hand and had spoken to the check-in agent about switching her flight back to the original date. Martin made an odious scene, yelling at the agent that she had no right to change the ticket without his permission. The agent threatened to call security and he stopped hollering only long enough for it to be explained that Mary had every right to change her own ticket.

He disagreed.

Security arrived and he was forced to pipe down and take a seat.

Mary grinned with admiration at the way the gate agent handled the situation, and at the speed of her typing. In no time Mary had a new ticket in hand. The woman inspired exactly the kind of gumption and professionalism Mary knew she wanted to cultivate in herself.

She looks up as a commercial turboprop climbs overhead from

Comox airport and banks toward the mainland. Martin could be looking down at her right now —at her lounging in the back of Sam's truck. She sticks her tongue out at him.

She eventually nods off and is woken later in the day by the sound of engines. People are leaving the festival. Cars are pulling away from the parking along the tall hedge that surrounds the park. Soon Sam's truck is one of only a handful.

Sam emerges from a gate and walks toward the truck carrying some of Flower's empty boxes. He doesn't see her until he throws the boxes into the truck bed.

"Hello," she says, smiling broadly.

He vaults the side of the truck and pulls her into a tight embrace, both of them on their knees.

"It's so good to see you. I've been worrying about you all day," Sam says.

"I don't know what I'm doing. I just know I couldn't go with him. Does your offer still stand for tonight?"

"It sure does. And don't worry. As much as I want to, I won't try anything."

"Thanks Sam. I need a friend, a shoulder to cry on and a clear head. Plus, ye said ye might know how I can fix Bruce's garden."

"Hop in the front." He jumps down and unlocks her door. "Not fix his garden, necessarily, but start the process, yes," says Sam.

Mary's tension eases as they near the Buckley Bay ferry terminal; the spectre of darkness and fear that has shadowed her for the last two days dissolves.

Sam stretches his arm over the back of the bench seat and plays with her hair.

"Are ye really not goin' t' try anythin'?" she asks.

"Nothing. This," he looks at her hair entwined in his fingers, "is platonic love making."

She laughs. "Tell me about yer ideas for the garden."

"I have a friend with a horse stable and I'm sure he can give us a load or two of manure. I think I can spare some from the sheep, as well. Spreading it on the dead soil will replace the organics and give everything we plant a better chance to survive. You won't be here in the fall when it's safe to replant, but I've got lots of native perennials, and so does everyone else on the island. In fact, the perennials may have been Bruce's originally, as he's been a prolific sharer over the years. Plus, tomorrow morning, if you're up to it, you and I can go collecting wild seed to replant his meadow."

"I'd like that. Can we put the manure down before he gets home? I want t' do as much as possible t' help."

"I'll make some calls. Why don't you squeeze over next to me. I'll give you platonic hugs the rest of the way back."

Mary unbuckles her seat belt and slides close to him. He helps refasten her. She never wants this sense of well-being to end.

The sun is low on the horizon, sparking off the rippling waters of the straight as they make the first crossing. "Do you want to get out and look over the edge of the boat?" Sam asks.

"Can we stay just like this?" she says, looking up at him and sweeping his long bang out of his eye.

HOMECOMING

BRUCE OPENS THE FRONT DOOR to the fresh scent of Pine-sol. The kitchen is immaculate and vacuum tracks form parallel lanes running from one end of the living room to the other. He flips off his sandals and sets his case on a kitchen chair. Tipping the handle of the kitchen faucet away from him he swings a glass under the cold stream.

Water overflows, cool and fresh, on his wrist and fingers — through the kitchen window Sam and a slender woman with strawberry blond hair are raking manure across the great Sahara that used to be his garden. He stretches forward and raps on the glass. Sam looks up, frowns, and nudges the woman who noticeably deflates at whatever Sam says to her. She looks familiar.

Standing on his back patio, he's dumbstruck. Restrained emotion spurts from his amygdalae hampering all thought.

Mary is crying and through hiccups tries to explain what's happened.

He wonders aloud, "Aren't you supposed to be in Ireland?"

Sam is apologizing for not stopping Martin sooner.

Bruce is trying to figure out how the homeostatic ecosystem he took years to establish could have been destroyed by one man in under a month. It would have taken considerable sustained effort.

"Maybe we should go in and sit down," says Sam, putting an arm over his shoulder. He allows himself to be led back to the living room.

Sam places a glass of water in front of him on the coffee table and he automatically takes a drink.

Mary, still crying, is more intelligible, which is a good sign. He must be calming down himself.

"I wanted t' stay and make it right, Bruce. The manure was Sam's idea. Just tell me what else I can do and I'll do it. We've collected wildflower and grass seeds." Mary pulls a bag from her back pocket and places it on the table between them. "As for the perennials, Sam called yer friends and they're goin' t' bring over transplants from the ones ye once gave them. I feel so ashamed, Bruce. I saw yer book. I know what this meant t' ye." Mary halts. "I'm babblin'. Go ahead and yell at me." Mary gropes for Sam's hand. "Please, will ye say somethin', Bruce?"

"She's not the one to blame," says Sam. "She's been tearing herself up about it, so if you can go easy on her . . ."

Bruce looks at Mary properly for the first time. "You don't look like your pictures. Or rather, you don't look like the pictures of you around your house. You look more like you do in the ones Bridget keeps about."

"Ye met my granny, Bridget?"

"I did. It's a long story. I'm just a little too tired, and shocked, to talk about it right now."

"Again, I'm so sorry," says Mary. "Can I make ye a cup o' tea for yer nerves?"

"Where are you staying? Is Martin here? You *were* expecting me back, right?" says Bruce. He massages his temples then combs his fingers through his hair, expelling a long breath through his teeth. "Listen. I really need to sleep. I can stay at Sam's if you weren't ready to leave." He looks to Sam for confirmation.

"Mary's been staying with me since Martin left. So all is good. We'll let you get some rest," says Sam.

"Can we come back tomorrow t' rake the rest o' the manure?" asks Mary.

"Oh yeah. The manure. Is that your manure, Sam? Don't you need it?"

"I can part with it. Desperate circumstances and all."

"Mary, this isn't how I thought our first meeting would go," says Bruce. "I'm so glad you're still here though. I was going to call you once you were back in Ireland. Come over in the morning, but not to work on the garden."

"It would make me feel better t' work on it." Through the oversized living room window, Mary looks at the pile of unspread manure.

That," he waves at the garden, "is not your fault." He lifts her limp fingers and wiggles them encouragingly until she looks at him. "We're alright, you and me. I promise you. There's nothing to forgive. And I have so much to talk to you about."

FAMILY ADVICE

MARY STUDIES BRUCE INTENTLY. His appearance and his sense of ease remind her of both Sam and Nick. He has Nick's sensuality, without his flirtiness, and Sam's calm demeanor. He must have come as a shock to Ballycanew, what with his long hair, drawstring pants and open kaftan. She hopes they treated him better than Martin treated her friends here.

"How's your tea," he asks.

"It's good. I've really gotten used t' herbal teas. How was yer time in Ballycanew? Did ye find what ye were lookin' for?"

"I found what I needed and more. I won't forget the experience. Especially your friends. Cat brought a welcoming committee first day."

"Cat. I miss her. Who else did ye meet?"

"Mags, Claire and Joan first. By the time I left, I felt like I knew the whole village."

"Ye don't know how happy that makes me t' hear it," says Mary. "I'm goin' t' miss Flower and Sam especially when I leave. If I leave. I'm not sure I have anythin' t' go home to though," says Mary, suddenly breaking down. "Ye're goin' to think I'm a crybaby. Last night and now this mornin'. I'm not an unhappy person, honest."

Bruce hands her a Kleenex. "Your chakras are narrowing. I can see that. Before you go I can give you a Reiki treatment if you want," says Bruce.

"Thanks, but I think I just need t' figure this out."

"How did it happen that your husband is in Ireland, and you're still here in my living room? Does it have any connection to you staying at Sam's?"

"Sam's a gentleman. He's been lettin' me stay in his guest room while Flower's at the Filberg Festival. I needed time t' think. Yet, time doesn't seem t' be helpin'. I'm still so confused. And scared. Leavin' Martin at the airport felt great — until I realized I don't have any money, or a plan."

"You're welcome to stay with me if you need, just in case," says Bruce.

"That is more than kind o' ye, Bruce. Because right now, I don't know if I'm comin' or goin'. Flower said I could stay with her but she doesn't even know I'm still here. The last she knew I was flyin' home with Martin."

"I suppose Sam has already tried to reach her?"

"Yes. He doesn't know which friends she's stayin' with so doesn't have a number."

"That's usual. She gets fully immersed once the festival starts and we won't see or hear from her until it's done."

"Flower and I've become really close," says Mary. "I think I can say that." Mary has a sudden and clear vision of Flower, and their kiss; also, a flash of realization that what they have will never go beyond a kiss, infatuation and deep friendship.

"It may seem odd," Mary continues, "but I think Flower, and Hornby at large, opened me up and what sprang out can't be pressed back in. What if I go back home t' Ballycanew and my friends can't accept me? Plus, there'll be a genuine garboil if I leave Martin. I'm not sure I can face it. Fear of ex-communication from my friends worries me more than ex-communication by the Church, and that worries me a lot.

"Surely that won't happen."

"It might. Ye don't know about me and Martin, o' course, so it's hard t' explain, but I can't abide livin' with him anymore. I don't love him. It'll eat at me everyday t' wake up and see him there beside me. When and if I go back, there'll be consequences, guaranteed."

"Your friends are pretty cool, and they love you. I think you'll be pleasantly surprised by how happy they are that you're looking out for what you need. I can't imagine any of them abandoning you if you choose to follow your heart."

"Ye think? Ye think there's still a home for me in Ballycanew?"

"I'm sure there is," says Bruce, getting up with her cup and taking it to the kitchen to refill.

"Even if that's true, and I'm not just bein' a coward, I genuinely love the life I've been livin' here, and the friends I've made. I wonder, do I have to go back? It isn't unheard of for people t' move from home t' somewhere new and far away. My mother did. Not that I don't curse her soul for it. Forgive me, for sayin' so."

"That reminds me," says Bruce, "as you know, I met Bridget, your grandmother. It was fate that I stayed in your house. It turns out that Nellie, Bridget's sister, was my grandfather's second wife. Bridget and Nellie raised my father until he was sent away. So, you and Bridget are the closest thing I have to family." Bruce pauses to let Mary absorb this. "We're stepcousins, if you'll have me. And I love Bridget to pieces. I wish I could've stayed to help her more."

"Is she not doin' well? Did somethin' happen?"

"No, no. It's just that I get the sense the farm and cottage are getting to be a lot for her. She admitted she was having problems with the cheesemaking."

"She did?" Mary looks anew at Bruce. "She must really trust ye. She doesn't admit weakness t' anyone."

"Such a strong lady. She seems to live life on her own terms."

"She does, that. And now I appreciate why she never married. To be a married woman in Ireland is t' give up yer freedom, and the Church and State will see that ye never get it back."

"How is that?" says Bruce handing her a fresh cup of blackberry tea.

"Divorce isn't possible in Ireland. If I return and don't want t' live with Martin, he can force me back home."

"That's archaic. Do you seriously mean the most you can hope for is that you leave him and aren't marched back by the police? If so, I can understand your reluctance to return. If you are set on leaving him, that is."

"I didn't appreciate how little say I had over my own life until I came here. Meetin' Flower, especially, helped me see that the way I was livin' isn't how I need t' spend the rest o' my life. My granny Nellie spent *her* whole life standin' up for a woman's right to work, vote and control her own body. What have I done? Obey Martin, that's what. Didn't argue when he forbade me to work; saw only the friends he approved of; spent the whole of our marriage servin' him. For what? Where did it get me? I don't want t' go back t' putterin' around the house waitin' for the clock to tell me it's time to make his breakfast, tea and supper."

"I don't blame you," says Bruce.

"I can't imagine though, knowin' him, that he's goin' t' let me leave. That's why I feel I need t' run and never go back."

"Are you thinking seriously about staying on Hornby then? I'm not sure what the rules are. I can look into it if you need me to."

"I don't know — yet. This all happened so suddenly."

"What was it that happened? If you don't mind me asking?"

"He saw Nick kiss me goodbye at Little Tribune. He thought somethin' was goin' on."

"Was there?" says Bruce.

"No," says Mary emphatically.

"It wouldn't be the first time someone fell for Nick's charm."

"Sam warned me before anythin' could happen. It was good of 'im," says Mary, colouring.

"Sam is a great guy," says Bruce. "What will you do if you stay?"

"I know how t' make sheep's cheese. Sam has sheep. I wondered maybe . . ." Mary turns away so Bruce can't see her face.

"Is staying here about more than getting away from your life with Martin?" asks Bruce.

She's not sure how much of her desire to stay is about Martin, how much about herself, how much about Sam, and until a few moments ago, how much about Flower. She knows how she feels about Martin; it's her feeling for Sam that has her out of kilter.

"I don't know," she says, leaning forward and toying with her mug. "I've piled this much on ye, I might as well burden ye with it all." She sets her mug on the coffee table. "I kissed Sam. I really care for him, and I think he cares for me. That part makes this so much worse t' sort out."

"That certainly does complicate things. How long until you need to decide?"

"My flight is booked to leave in two days."

"Is Sam aware that he's part of your equation?"

"I don't know. He said he wishes I could stay," says Mary.

"May I leave you with a thought? If you decide to go back, I think Bridget could really use your help, and she's kept your bedroom. It could be good for you both. Who better than a woman like Bridget to champion your independence?"

"That's a thought. I guess. I'm goin' to need a new place to live whatever I decide t' do. Now, here I am so wrapped up in myself, I should have said t' ye right away, I'd be lucky to call ye cousin. Forgive me for not sayin' it straight off."

Bruce stands and pulls her into a snug embrace. Tears gather at the corners of her eyes. She's had so little warmth these last few years, she can hardly handle the strong dose.

LIE OF THE LAND

BRUCE DIALS CAT'S NUMBER. It's 9:00 pm in Ireland. He debated for an hour after Mary left whether he should call.

Michael picks up, "Nice t' hear from ya, lad. How was the flight?"

"It was good. Long though. I'll probably be in bed by four this afternoon," says Bruce, laughing. "How's everything there?"

"Well — Martin's got a right puss on his face. He's not makin' friends since he got back. But I'll let Cat tell ye 'bout that. Good hearin' yer voice, boy'o."

"Yours too."

"Hello?"

"Hey Cat, it's me. I guess I couldn't go two days without Ballycanew gossip. How's Bridget recovering from all the excitement?"

"Bridget's sad ye've left, actually. She's that fond o' ye. Don't know why. And I guess we're all sufferin' our share o' after-show blues. Is she the reason ye called?"

"Partly," says Bruce.

"Ye don't fool me, Bruce Connors. Ye could've called Bridget directly. This is about our Mary ye're holdin' hostage there. Martin is fit to rip the sidin' clear o' the house, he's that mad. Snapped my head off when I went over t' welcome them home," says Cat.

"I'll have to leave it to Mary to tell you why she isn't home early," says Bruce.

"Well, fair play to her if she finally stood up t' the shite. Ye know, she's a degree in maths and never got t' use it. There's more than a few marbles in that pretty head; she should be the school principal, not him."

"I didn't know. How did Mary's mom afford to send her to university? I got the feeling from Bridget that they were always scraping by."

"I see Bridget left some o' the story untold. Did she not tell ye about Delia?"

"Not much," says Bruce.

"Back in the day, Mothers in this country were always bein' left behind. It was like a funeral when their children left, usually for America, never to be seen again. Mary's mam was one of 'em. Ran off with a man in '64 when Mary was just eight. Hardly a word after — never sent money for support. And Mary never knew her father, so that's him out o' the picture. If she hadn't won a scholarship, ye're right, she couldn't have gone. All's the more shame Martin kept her from workin'," says Cat.

"I might as well fess up. I'm calling to find out what Martin has been saying about her. She's worried about how she'll be received if she comes back."

"Martin's makin' out that she was playin' offside. He's not gettin' sympathy; bad enough when he stormed into the middle o' Séamus's yoga circle and called all his friends fairies, but when he began raggin' on about ye not lookin' after his garden, and the changes to the green, I thought the lads o' the SFWT were goin' to jump 'im. Besides, everyone loves Mary," says Cat. "I don't speak ill for fear o' bringin' on damnation, but for years I've silently wished for God t' intervene and free Mary from her marriage. God forgive me."

"That support will really mean a lot to her. She's won friends here too."

"Tell her I love her. Sure now, I do. And that she can dial me collect anytime."

"I think it would be better if she didn't know we spoke. But I'll suggest she calls you, now that I know more. I'd better ring off. Miss you all. Bye to Michael."

FOOTSIES

MARY ACCEPTS A PLATE of chickpea curry and tabouli salad from Sam and lifts the edge of the blanket for him. He settles on the couch, facing her, with his feet on either side of hers beneath the blanket. Beyond the glow of a candle on the coffee table, the large living room is in shadow. On the carpet beside them, Sam's dog sighs and lowers her head.

"That was nice today, workin' with yer sheep. It's been a long time for me — ten years," says Mary.

"We probably could have done something more exciting."

"No. I loved it." Mary takes a couple of bites of her dinner and smiles at Sam. "How is it that Flower's yarn is so soft? There's nothin' uncommon about yer breed, that I can tell."

"That's because Flower's yarn has as little Joni, Mitchel and a touch of Garfunkel in it."

"Ye're kiddin'?" says Mary. "So the dogs aren't touched with mange after all.

"No. And I can assume her secret is safe with you." He raises his brow and narrows his eyes at her across the humps of their knees. "How many sheep did you have, by the way?"

"Grannie Bridget has ninety-five at the moment, if ye can believe it. She has a shepherdess now, but there was a time that she and I did everythin'."

"I can't imagine. I have enough work with twenty," says Sam. "Especially around lambing season."

"Did you mean what ye said about wantin' me t' stay? Would ye be sick o' me after a month? Sure, we barely know each other yet, like. Ye don't know my bad habits," says Mary.

He runs his hand up and down her calf. "I care about you, a lot. You probably need me to see into the future right now, but it's hard for me, knowing you're basing such a big decision on it. Do you understand?"

"Sort of. I feel like I'm reachin' out for somethin' solid t' hold onto and it's all just will-o'-the-wisps. I'm sorry. It's unfair and unrealistic o' me t' want t' know with certainty what this is between us. The way my heart has opened t' ye, I feel like I've known ye for years."

"I can tell you that I'll miss you terribly if you go. And if you stay you'll make me a very happy man. But, you said to me today that Martin always dictated your decisions. I want you to make this decision based on what you want, and what you want to *do* with your life," say Sam. He leans forward. "C'mere." He takes the curve of her cheek in his palm and draws her to him. His kiss lingers.

When they sit back, Mary's fork dangles from her fingers, she has too many butterflies to be hungry. The candlelight plays over his angular features, sparkles in his vibrant eyes. His brows follow a perfect thick arc, disappearing on one side beneath his unruly bang. His skin is golden, marked by faint crow's feet and smile lines. He's smiling now, in the way he does when he teases her.

"God this is hard," she says, popping a forkful of tabouli in her mouth.

"Well, you don't have to decide tonight. Finish up, we'll do the washing, check the sheep, and if you're lucky, I'll teach you a new card game before bed."

"I'm goin' as fast as I can. This is delicious." Under the covers, she slides her legs up onto his lap.

FAIRY LAND

After midnight, lying in the guest bed alone, watching the leaves rustle on the arbutus outside, she makes her decision. She pads softly down the hallway; midnight air dances on her naked skin. Sam's door is open and he sits up when she enters, pulling back the covers.

"Have I told you how beautiful you are?" he says, drawing her tight to his body and wrapping the blanket snug around them. They lie like this awhile, as though sleeping, but far from sleep.

Mary raises her chin and touches her lips to his, as lightly as a butterfly alighting on a petal. Outside, tree frogs sing. She listens, wanting to remember every moment of this first time with him. She shivers at the touch of his fingertips stroking her back from nape to tailbone. His lips brush across hers and she opens to him. Their tongues entwine.

Crickets join the chorus of tree frogs as the sylvan shadows of ancient firs rimmed in moon-frost sweep the carpet and bedroom wall. Sam is facing her, his contours dark against the pale sheen of his pillow. His eyes are fathomless, committing her to memory as she is him. Everything about him is novel to her: his thick hair heavy against her fingers as she strokes it, his muscular body, lean and smooth. Her fingers gently brush the line of hair on his belly then follow the muscular inner curve of his hip. He stills and falls slowly onto his back, watching her play with him.

"You're a fairy in the moonlight. My Irish fairy," he says.

He pulls her on top of him and she rests her head against his chest, listening to the quick rhythm of his heart. His hips move beneath her and she straddles him so that she can see his face. He glides his palms over her hips and circles her breasts as she guides him inside her. She rises and falls, a slow caress, coming forward to let him take her nipple in his mouth, and then giving him her mouth in return. He smells of lanolin and fir and dry, dusty fields. They are scents she knows, that she'll find again, that she'll remember him by.

WILDLING

THEY CRUNCH DOWN THE drive together. Mary holding Sam's hand; Bruce a few paces ahead, trying to give them their last few moments of privacy.

"Have you got everything?" asks Bruce.

"I think so. I wish I could've said goodbye t' Flower properly. Tell her I'll miss her. And that she has changed my life. In the best way. Tell her I'll write."

"I will," say Sam and Bruce together.

Bruce lifts her case into the trunk of his car while Sam holds the passenger door open for Mary. Their eyes are red. Bruce takes his time arranging the bag. Sam, unshaven, hair on-end, leans into the car for a final kiss.

"I'll miss ye most of all," Mary says, jumping back out of the car to wrap her arms around Sam.

"We'll write. And call me, once you have some pennies saved." Sam kisses her again. "Maybe someday I'll come see you in Ireland, if you'll have me."

"We'd better go. We can't miss the ferry," says Bruce.

"I know. I know," says Sam. "Mary, I'll say it one more time, I absolutely hate your decision — but I respect it, and how hard it was to make. You're going to do great on your own."

"I hope so."

Bruce backs out of the drive. Sam and Mary wave to each other until the house is out of sight.

"He's right. You are going to be fine. And if you ever get tired of Bridget, we're still here for you," says Bruce.

"Thanks, cousin. But I fear that once I get on that plane everythin' here will slip so far away I'll never be able to find it again." The tears she's been fighting begin to fall. She pulls a tissue from her bag and blows her nose hard. "How will I ever be able t' afford a plane ticket on my own. I don't want t' go. I don't want these friendships t' end. I don't want t' lose hold of how I've felt since I arrived here."

"You won't lose hold of it. You're a very strong person and you've got good friends back home. I have every faith that you'll find happiness, now that you know what you're looking for." He pats her knee and turns to give her a reassuring smile. "Is your plan to make cheese with Bridget?"

"It is." She wipes her eyes with the back of her hand and takes a restoring breath. "But that isn't enough anymore. And it's not a full-time job. I think I'll enroll in evenin' classes and get my accountancy. Maybe start with bookkeepin' t' earn the tuition," she says, sitting up straighter.

"Who's picking you up at the airport in Dublin?"

"Cat. Sam let me use his phone t' call her and Bridget yesterday," says Mary, twisting in her seat as they pass the Co-op and market. "Bridget was excited when I asked if I could move back home. Ye were right."

"You'll be doing her a great favour, too. Remember to give her the letter I wrote. I want her to have a few pictures of Dad," says Bruce.

"I will. Is yer garden goin' to be okay?" says Mary, taking her eyes off of the trees to look at him.

"I'm sure it will. Last week of August, when the rains usually come, I'll sow the seeds you collected. I plan to use this as a teaching opportunity. I can offer classes on how to turn a sterile landscape into an attractive, wild, species rich habitat. I might even get another wilding book out of it. This time, with before and after illustrations."

They pull into the ferry line-up. "Can we get out and watch the ferry dock?" asks Mary.

"Of course."

"I can't believe I'm leavin' all this behind." Mary steps out of the car. A breeze catches her skirt and it billows up behind her. Bruce traps it just in time.

"You just about had a Marilyn Monroe moment there," he laughs.

"It might have been a bit more scandalous than that," laughs Mary in return. "I've left all my, what Flower calls, 'granny pants' behind, along with a lot of other things that no longer suit."

"You are a *true* wildling now, Mary. Don't let anyone else clip you again.

Acknowledgements

The author's profound appreciation to . . .

The rest of my four-quarter family, talented writers all, for the support that can be found nowhere else. Thank you for listening to and discussing fresh ideas, and for your help editing and sorting technical issues. It is because of you that my life is blessed and maintains its continual sense of purpose.

My first readers, Stacey Lively and Robyn Flesher.

Kate Furnivall for her continued encouragement.

My long-lost friend Josée, and all the people that formed my experience coming to the Island in the '80's.

Jeff, for having been ready, like me, to drop everything, especially clothes, to plunge into newly discovered waters.

Edward K., whom I've never met, for helping me with original business and place names on Hornby in the 80's.

My mother-in-law, Monique, for revealing family secrets.

Author's Note

While this is a work of fiction, it's one that's personal to me. In my teens I had the good fortune to know, for a short-time, a kind woman — all five-feet-nothing of her quick to come to the defence of a young girl, no matter the cost to herself. She, and the man that fathered her first born, were two of the original children shipped from Britain to the Fairbridge Prince of Wales Farm School, located on Vancouver Island, British Columbia.

The Fairbridge Society sent a total of 329 children to the Prince of Wales Farm School between 1935 and 1948. Its stated intention was to take children from British slums and provide them with a healthier rural environment, while enhancing the Empire's white stock abroad. A *Child Migration Programmes Investigation Report* into child sexual abuse noted that as early as the late 1930s cases of abuse were being reported and continued to be reported until the school closed in 1951. Although the report focuses on the deeds committed by three men in positions of power, there were more.

Duties Master CM-F219 admitted in 1938 to sexual misconduct with boys. To preserve the school's good reputation with high-ranking officials in the province, the incidents were hushed up by the principal, Harry Logan.

A second man, Duties Master Rogers, originally dismissed from the school for suspected sexual abuses, was rehired by principal Logan with the excuse that abuse of this kind need "be viewed in its true light as something which may occur in work of the kind which we are doing at Fairbridge." By 1943 Rogers could no longer be protected and was convicted and imprisoned for immoral relations with young boys. He was also suspected of similar behavior toward older girls.

A third Duties Master, CM-F217, was known to be "fooling with girls".

In 1944, Isobel Harvey, Superintendent of Child Welfare for BC, investigated the school, interviewing the children and staff. She noted that the children were unkept, ignorant of hygiene and had no sense of personal worth. Cottage mothers viewed the children as inferior and failed to foster a feeling of home. Harvey also mentions several additional cases of staff sexual misconduct not noted in the Child Migration Report. She warns that the children harmed by Duties Master Rogers may harm other children. Some of these may be those called "sex perverts" and "sodomites" by the disgruntled cottage mother who gave evidence to the report. The high illegitimate pregnancy rate among the girls at the school, 33% between 1938 and 1944, was partly a result of relations between the students and partly the adults caring for them.

Principal Logan was finally dismissed in 1945, but a culture had firmly taken root. By 1949 the previous sex problems had not entirely disappeared and irreparable damage had been done to many of the children. The school lost its funding, and a decision was made to close and board out the remaining children.

Pictures of the time show children with happy, smiling faces, their arms draped carelessly around one another. There were doubtless happy times and strong friendships formed, but the instinct to defend a young teenager that so moved that gracious lady I earlier mentioned, was without question a product of her experience in this troubled unloving environment.

I've mentioned my appreciation to my mother-in-law, Monique, in the acknowledgments. Recently, she, with my father-in-law's permission, shared details of his family history that had never been spoken of. I hope not to upset other family members by allowing our fictitious Violet Pillow (my grandmother-in-law's real name) to share the real Violet Pillow's fate upon a kitchen table. Nellie Vera Larkin's history is closely based on my grandfather-in-law's second wife (third wife really, but that's just confusing) — the woman that raised my father-in-law, his baby sister, two half-brothers and her own son.

The choice to set our story in Ballycanew is partly due to its proximity to Ballymoney, where my father-in-law and his siblings were cared for by their deceased mother's sister until their grieving father could find someone to help him.

As for Hornby . . . Hornby is Hornby and its magic still exists today.

I hope you enjoyed the novel and that it provided you with food for thought.

Holly

Manufactured by Amazon.ca
Acheson, AB